I0638706

CHARTER TO REDEMPTION

Charter to Redemption
Published by Wombat Books
PO Box 1519, Capalaba Qld 4157
www.wombatbooks.com.au
www.evenbeforepublishing.com

Copyright DJ Blackmore. 2014

Cover Design by Kremena, Elance.

National Library of Australia Cataloguing-in-Publication entry
Author: Blackmore, D. J., author.
Title: Charter to redemption / D..J. Blackmore.
ISBN: 9781921632884 (paperback)
Subjects: Redemption--Fiction.
Dewey Number: A823.4

All rights reserved. No part of this publication may be reproduced, stored in, or introduced into a retrieval system, or transmitted, in any form, or by any means (electronic, mechanical, photocopying, recording or otherwise) without the prior written permission of the publisher.

CHARTER TO REDEMPTION

D. J. BLACKMORE

To Lachlan, Alec, Cordelia and Mariah.
For Sarahanne's listening ear,
and to those who came before.

ONE

The ship ploughed a furrow through the waves as Emma sought fresher air on deck. Still the taint of unwashed humanity lingered though the wind blew the canvas sails like bellows and swept the breeze over the deck. Yet what Emma encountered as she stepped into the light churned her stomach more than the stench.

Tied by the wrists to the mast, a prisoner's back bled scarlet in the morning sun. Bright drops dotted the lash master's cravat. Still, the convict didn't sway as the scourger lashed his back, even though his shirt hung in tatters upon the wide frame of his shoulders.

When the punishment was over, there was weariness in the man's slow movements, but his step didn't falter despite the fetters that bound his ankles. He held his shoulders high and his eyes burned with defiance.

He met her look with his own, and she sensed he cared not for her thoughts of mercy. The blue intensity of his stare struck her as hard as the brilliance of the sea.

Somehow Emma felt as if he blamed her for his punishment. Her sense of guilt was unaccountable, but it remained. She fought the desire to turn away.

'Good morning, miss,' the convict said. His greeting was a rebuke, nothing more.

'No words of yours for the lady,' the soldier snapped. 'Keep

1

your eyes averted.' But the prisoner didn't listen. His gaze remained fixed, unswerving.

'What?' he whispered, his eyes chill and his contempt colder still. 'No good morrow for the likes of me?'

Emma stared back, words stuck somewhere in her throat, the smile she had mustered swept away.

'Cat got your tongue?' He smiled without humour.

'It certainly didn't take yours, sir,' Emma said, as much to herself as to the man who stood above her. If he felt her retort's sting he didn't show it. If anything his smile widened, but she suspected it was only due to malice.

Dimly she heard the soldier's irritated threats then the dull thud of the truncheon as it glanced off the convict's back. And then, she did what she feared she might, and fainted.

When she revived, the captain helped her to her feet.

'I beg your pardon,' Emma whispered. She stood unsteadily, her sea legs having forsaken her along with her dignity. He offered his arm solicitously and led her in the direction of her cabin. Emma glanced self-consciously behind her. The deck had cleared. Relief washed over her.

'No need to apologise, Miss Colchester,' the captain said. 'It's the heat. It gets worse than this though, that's for sure. Still, you'll get used to it soon enough. Have to, eh?'

'Yes, indeed.' No one had thought to warn her about the weather.

'Still, that villain didn't help matters any. There's no room for insolence on this vessel. They've got to learn how to function in society, miss, and if they don't get pulled up on small misdemeanours, then they won't be of any use in the colony.'

Emma supposed that in some ways he was correct and wondered whether the captain's opinion was common to the colony.

'Tell me Captain, what offence did the prisoner commit to receive a flogging?'

'Who can say? But they're all the same. Don't turn your back. That's the best bet. I'm only sorry that a lady such as you has to put up with the likes of belligerent convicts. Still, there are more felons than free settlers, and the brig would have been docked in Sydney Cove a sight longer if she didn't have a cargo of convicts to fill the hull.'

'Now,' the captain said, 'allow me to have you brought some refreshment. That and a rest for an hour or so before we enter the harbour will do you a world of good.'

'I would appreciate that. But I am curious, Captain, as to what I should expect when I arrive. Is Newcastle as black as it's painted?'

The captain's eyes were downcast as he smiled. 'No Miss, I can assure you it's far darker.' A chuckle escaped his barrel chest. Emma smiled in return.

'I only hope this wind doesn't get any worse, else it'll have us dashed against the shoals. Macquarie's Pier will keep the harbour as calm as bath water when the break-wall's finished, but there's many a good vessel that's come aground in high wind. Still, I've been through in worse than this. I reckon we'll get through, no worries.' He gave the wind clouds a threatening glare as they headed below. 'I certainly hope so, Captain.' Emma had every intention of marrying Gideon Quinn. Unforgiving weather and a threatening convict aside, *that* was her objective. She had come too far for failure.

As he left her in the privacy of her cabin, she gazed at the miniature around her neck, which had cracked. It threatened to peel, and this time she removed it before she washed her sun-parched skin. She treasured the likeness of her intended, thrilled at the thought that soon they would meet.

Plymouth was long gone, and with it village life and all she had known. Her mother, widowed, and with three other daughters still unspoken for, had not wanted Emma to leave, but the financial help that Officer Gideon Quinn would provide when he and Emma wed would be a Godsend to the family.

3

Emma's thoughts wandered to the moment she had given her consent to marry him. Their written courtship had lasted many months. Her uncle's wife had brought the officer to her attention as a genuine, long-standing friend, an assurance that vouched for his character within the colony. How different her Gideon would undoubtedly be in comparison with the convict she had spoken to above deck. Emma's head swam again when she thought of the man's belligerence. At least she wouldn't have to suffer his presence at any garden parties. Yet she had hoped to comfort individuals such as he with the Bible. Would they all be such hard nuts to crack?

After taking a rest – which refreshed her only a little – Emma peered out at the sea from the small cabin window. She braced when the vessel dipped and reeled, and realised that her lack of balance had nothing to do with the dizzy spell she experienced up on deck. The ship was being tossed like a cork.

An immense rocky island came into view, dwarfing the boat as it bobbed and pitched on the waves. A wave of sickly unease rose within her.

Emma heard hammering behind her. Then the door swung wide open and slammed against the wall. 'Cap'n said you'd better get back up on deck, miss,' the cabin boy said 'Thinks it might be harder to enter the harbour than he first thought.'

'And the convicts?' Emma wondered.

'They are to be unchained I believe, miss.'

'Can you swim?'

'No, miss. I can't say as I was ever taught.' His grim smile pulled a little tighter in his brown face. Emma had been taught to swim, but she wondered if she would remember how.

Moments later, she clambered to the upper deck as the brig creaked and groaned beneath her. The vessel leant at a riotous angle, pushed towards the shoals. Emma knew there was no point in remaining with the ship, yet she hung on for dear life, terror held in check by the thread of a prayer. She met the eyes of the convict she'd encountered only that morning. His gaze locked onto her before he turned away.

In this unguarded moment of fear, Emma didn't stop to think of impropriety as she watched him strip to the waist. Distantly she registered the broad, muscled strength of his arms and shoulders, marred only by the lash marks that crossed his back in livid stripes. He removed the blood-soiled shirt and threw it down on the deck, and without another backward glance, he dived into the churning waters.

She had no time to make the decision to jump overboard. As the ship again lurched to the side, she was thrown into the sea. As a cold wave rose to claim her, she heard her own surprised intake of breath before the water filled her throat and she plunged down into the wash.

After what seemed an age, Emma surfaced and fought for air. Then, with no other alternative, she tried to swim for the shore. Brine streamed from her nose as she coughed. Resolve soon gave way to desperation, for these waters were nothing like the millpond where she had learnt to swim. The waves hit her time and again as the saltwater threatened to fill her lungs.

She glanced behind her at the fast sinking ship. Men clawed at it like terrified children at their mothers' skirts.

The power of the words of the twenty-third psalm helped her hold the panic at bay. She mouthed the phrases that had grown with her from childhood. If this was to be the day she died, she was determined to fear no evil.

Ahead of her swam the convict who had made a bid for freedom. Just as she had done, he turned to look behind him. Then he saw her. For what seemed like long moments he considered her, and then he began to swim back to where she struggled.

The possibility of experiencing a death other than drowning

flashed in Emma's mind. Then a wave washed over her and she gagged on the water before it dragged her below. Then she felt large hands haul her to the surface, and as she was pulled up and out, Emma choked on a breath of salty air. She coughed and barked as water splashed her face again.

'Remove your skirts,' he said curtly.

Emma stared 'I beg your pardon?'

'Do it or drown, milady, for if you remain in that dress, you're sure to.'

'I can't,' she rasped. Even as she said it, Emma knew that it was ludicrous. Anyone tossed into the broiling harbour should have concerns other than propriety.

'Put your arms around my shoulders and I'll un—'

'As a gentleman, you would understand that I –'

A wave slapped him full in the face. He shook off the blow and growled, 'Gentility? Now?'

He began to loosen her garments as another wave took her below. 'Grab hold of me, or we'll both die.'

In spite of herself, she found herself pushing him away even as she went under time and again.

'You may keep your clothing, but you will drown in your good manners! My life matters more than that!' he barked.

Emma stared hard at him for a moment then did as he said. Between them they fumbled with the hooks and buttons. He left nothing save the thin decorum of her chemise and a pair of hook and eye boots.

'Now lie back against me,' he commanded, 'and kick like fury.'

Emma obeyed. Every wave that passed washed over her mouth and nose. She tried to hold her breath at each approach, only to inhale the inevitable spray and wheeze until the next wave dumped itself upon her. Her legs cramped excruciatingly as she sent up a silent prayer.

Still he towed her doggedly through the waves.

The waves threw them roughly onto the shore. Emma gasped as shells grazed her thighs. She rolled off the convict and laboured to breathe. Salt burned her eyes as she intermittently coughed up seawater and gulped on fresh air.

She saw the convict sit up and turn to his side to hack up some water, and she saw that his back ran red afresh, raw from the lash and the shore's debris.

'You're bleeding.' Emma said, breathless as she wiped her streaming eyes.

'Aye, but I'm alive.' He told her roughly, just as greedy for air as she was.

Emma glanced at him. She had expected that his reason for rescuing her was anything other than noble, but she had been wrong. 'I must thank you,' Emma said, 'for your goodness in what you did.'

She touched his shoulder to convince him of how gracious he had been, but he flinched as though he had been hit. Emma realised she had acted without thought.

'I did what many others would have,' he said, 'so save your soft words and your delicate hands for him.' The convict pointed to the miniature around her neck. 'You're only wasting your time on the damned.'

'No man is truly damned,' she told him. He snorted at this, and rose with a stumble to haul someone to the burning sand of the shore. The convict rolled the body over, and she heard him curse.

Emma turned at the sound of running feet. She glanced back at her rescuer. 'What do they call you?'

'Nothing you'd like to hear repeated.' He turned away to stare out to sea.

'Your Christian name?' Emma found the bravery to smile. He said nothing in response and her smile faltered and fell. This man did not want her hand of friendship any more than he would accept her thanks. As though he anticipated the approaching soldiers' intent, he turned and waited until they reached him. They grabbed either arm and began to escort him away. He stood head and shoulders above both men, far broader than either of the two, and yet he let them lead him away like an animal, when he surely could have barrelled them down to the edge of the churning sea.

'I want to talk to you about that man!' She called. Her chemise and petticoats whipped wetly around her legs as she stumbled after them.

'Never mind, miss,' one called over his shoulder to her. 'He'll be taken care of.' Emma stood dumbly, hair plastered to her neck like seaweed. The convict looked back and met her gaze for just an instant.

'He saved my life!' She said, but they didn't stop. She remembered then that she was almost naked and clutched at her body in an attempt to cover herself.

Emma watched them walk away over the dunes. The convict did not lift his head to hers again.

TWO

Emma turned her head in surprise at the elderly officer's solicitous hands upon her shoulders. She hadn't realised he had been standing there.

'Wrap this around yourself, my dear,' he said, as he held out a heavy woollen blanket. Emma smiled her thanks self-consciously. 'How did you come you to be in such a state of undress?' he asked.

'The convict. He told me that I'd drown if I didn't remove my clothes.' It sounded stupid to her ears now.

'Did he indeed?' The officer sounded dubious. He fingered his moustache thoughtfully, until his eyes fell on the miniature around her neck. He smiled.

'Yes, he did.' Emma pulled the mantle around her more tightly and covered the locket with a closed hand. The wind tugged at the shawl and her petticoats, which clung to her body. A small party hurried up the beach. She recognised her uncle with his family in tow. It had been almost two years since they had decided to make their home in New South Wales, and they waved frantically as they rushed to join her. The hems of the ladies' gowns and the ribbons of their bonnets fluttered like the wings of birds.

'Emma dear,' her aunt cried. 'Thank goodness you are in one piece! This could have been so unfortunate. We are indeed blessed.'

9

The woman embraced her then only released her to chafe her damp, sandy hands with her own warm dry ones. 'I cannot believe our good fortune. What a wonderful Christmas we will be able to share together.' The woman looked to the elderly officer and offered him a self-satisfied smile.

'Indeed, wife, we will,' her Uncle George said as he clasped both his daughters —Euphemie and Phoebe— around the shoulders in hearty agreement.

'And what an unconventional, though thoroughly romantic way for you and Gideon to have met,' her aunt said.

'I took no notice, Aunt Adelaide,' Emma admitted ruefully, with a glance back along the stretch of yellow sand to where the two young soldiers had departed with the prisoner just minutes before.

'No, no dear,' Aunt Adelaide laughed merrily. 'Let us explain ourselves. This is Gideon. Gideon Quinn, please let allow us acquaint you with your betrothed, Miss Emma Colchester, our dear niece.'

Emma turned as the grey-haired officer swept her a low, old-fashioned bow.

'My dear Miss Colchester, at last we meet.'

'You are mocking me.' Emma was exhausted but she managed to chuckle at the joke. The party exchanged glances.

'There must be some mistake,' Emma whispered. She glanced at the likeness that hung around her neck then looked up at the officer before her. Then she realised why the painting was so cracked and the image had begun to peel.

The young man in the locket stared up in sudden ridicule. The face that had seemed to look back so lovingly had been left behind with the hands of time. Only no one had thought to tell her.

'That was painted some years past.' The officer smiled. The others beamed happily. 'We can have as long a courtship as you wish, Emma dear,' she heard Gideon say. She glanced at him without reply. What could she say? No matter how long the courtship dragged, one thing she knew: her betrothed would always be as old as her grandfather, whereas Emma had only just seen her eighteenth birthday.

The ribboned miniature that she had hung round her neck for so many months now pulled like a weight. She suddenly felt the urge to throw it into the sea, but knew that it would make no difference. 'You must come and stay for supper this evening, Officer Quinn,' Aunt Adelaide said. 'Just a quiet, private affair, Emma dear, nothing too taxing.'

'Perhaps tomorrow would be better,' Uncle George said. 'After all, Emma has survived a tiring ordeal. She is lucky to have swum the distance.'

'Of course dear, you are right.' Emma thought her aunt seemed disappointed. For her own part, she was in shock, and it had nothing to do with the sea and the waves and the dark-haired Irish convict. She looked down the beach.

He was long gone.

Gideon Quinn smiled down at Emma with undisguised anticipation. *He* was not disappointed in the long-awaited meeting, she could tell, nor was he surprised. He had known exactly what to expect, for she had certainly been frank. If only he had been the same.

'We all of us have forgotten our manners, to be sure. How selfish we have been, hardly thinking of your needs, Emma dear. Perhaps we can look forward to your company tomorrow evening, Officer Quinn?'

'Madam, I can think of nothing better than spending a night with you all.'

'Celebration is warranted, that is certain,' her aunt said, 'and on more than one account. Emma dear, one day you must teach my girls how to swim. You appear fragile as porcelain, but I know you must have the constitution of an ox.'

'Then I must rejoice in my good fortune also,' Gideon agreed, 'for a hale and hearty wife is a blessing to any man.'

'Come, Emma,' the eldest cousin, Euphemie, said. 'I believe Mama has forgotten you stand in next to nothing.'

'And your Herculean effort aside,' her uncle said kindly as he rejoined them, 'you do need to rest. I will take my leave of you all. I must see what can be done for any others who have made it ashore.' As a doctor, Emma knew her uncle could not always choose his hours, but must be available at a call, at times such as this.

'Until tomorrow evening, ladies.' Gideon bowed and followed him.

As she walked with her aunt and cousins away from the foreshore, Emma stared at a chain gang as it moved slowly along. Most went without shirts, and those who had them were hardly better off, for their threadbare trousers seemed held together by willpower and nothing more.

'I had forgotten that all I am standing in is a blanket and shift,' Emma admitted. 'Although considering what most people are wearing, I suppose I'm well dressed.' She looked down at her boots, now waterlogged and covered in white sand, and wondered how badly they would shrink.

'Oh,' Phoebe breathed, as she looked down at herself in dismay.

'Not you, you ninny, she means the convicts,' Euphemie said.

Phoebe blushed while her dark curls bobbed to shield the pinkness of her face. 'Oh, I *am* a silly. You mean the prisoners. They aren't counted.'

'They are still worthy of adequate food, clean clothes and respect, surely? These men look half starved.' Emma said. Her aunt turned round to her niece.

'They may be human beings, my dear, but they long since gave up morals for depravity and live in perpetual sin of their own making. No one made them who they are save themselves. Newcastle is for second offenders, my dear, and they are all of them an ill-begotten lot. They journeyed the road to damnation of their own free will and can blame no one but themselves for their destination.'

'Best ignore them, cousin,' Phoebe said, 'else you may start having nightmares about them as I do.'

Once more Emma glanced over at the prisoners, curious, though she knew she shouldn't be, and it was then that she saw him—the convict who had saved her life.

She watched him and a few bedraggled men listen as the commanding officer clarified the rules of the Newcastle colony —the rations, the regulations, the reprisals. He saw her then, she knew. His eyes still blazed as if fuelled by a furnace, and in spite of her resolve to dismiss curiosity, she met his gaze and held it.

'Of all the rudeness,' Euphemie said, then turned away with an arrogant pull on her skirts.

'Come, girls,' Aunt Adelaide advised. 'Keep walking or you may suffer called out insults all the way home.'

'The soldiers will have them flogged if they dare,' Euphemie assured her mother. With a quick glance at her sister, Phoebe explained to Emma that unless the commandant ordered corporal punishment, no felon was given the *cat*. 'As the doctor, Papa has to oversee every flogging,' Phoebe informed her.

The commanding officer looked their way and nodded a polite greeting. Emma held back a smirk when Phoebe, Euphemie and their mother tittered and fluttered their hands like birds' wings the moment the man's back was turned. Emma quickly scanned the convict. Blood had darkened and crusted on his back. Flies crawled on the dried scarlet streaks. No shirt graced his back now to keep the swarm at bay.

'What are you staring at, convict?' A constable sneered at him offensively.

'Doesn't hurt to look, does it, mate?' a man behind the dark-haired convict said. The injured man glanced back at the old prisoner fettered close by. A partly toothless grin lit up humorous eyes in a mahogany face.

'Don't think a lady like her would look twice at the likes of you,' Emma heard the soldier say with confidence. 'Why, a lady like that wouldn't allow scum like you to touch the hem of her gown.'

She had done more than that. She had allowed him to divest her of all modesty until all that had remained was her petticoat. But the convict did not say a word about it, though she thought many would. She knew, as he had said, it was either that or be drowned. He looked up at the overseer.

'By the way, the name's Freeman,' she heard him say. The soldier laughed in his face.

'Not yet you aren't,' he assured him. 'Not for a long time.'

THREE

If only all had been as Emma had been promised. If only her betrothed had spoken the truth. Now all her plans of a wondrous marriage and her desire to help the needy faded when it dawned on her that her own plight was in some ways just as desperate as theirs. For what young woman, she asked herself, would not be dismayed at the prospect of a union with a man old enough to be her grandfather?

Yet Aunt Adelaide didn't seem to have stopped to consider why her niece was reluctant to sort through fabrics and lace in preparation for the upcoming parsonage supper. Emma hadn't been interested to look through Phoebe's many castoffs to see if any could be altered to fit her either, and so Phoebe, directly after breakfast, had occupied herself with the task. Emma's disinterest in the supper seemed a mystery to her aunt.

Still, Emma was glad that her uncle's daughters were of the fairer sex. 'I would be grateful for anything that you are able to spare, since all my belongings are doubtless at the bottom of the harbour.'

'Perhaps tomorrow we can see what we can procure with new gowns in mind.' Her aunt had been generous enough to make the offer, and Emma was glad of it for the sake of decorum. For now, Emma resolved to search in case her portmanteau was washed up on the shore.

'Why, Emma dear, where on earth can you be going?' Aunt Adelaide called after her worriedly as she set out.

Emma halted.

Her aunt pressed one hand to her capacious bosom in alarm. 'You don't know who's around.'

Emma stifled a sigh as the older woman hurried up the path to the white-fenced gate and whispered conspiratorially. 'We never leave the house alone. And if we need to use the *outhouse* we try to go accompanied. Just in case … you know?'

Emma nodded her understanding although she wasn't at all sure if she *did* know. But she was confident about one thing: she could see to her *necessary* arrangements without being chaperoned, surely!

Another thing was certain, and that was the necessity of time alone. She was sure that the women in her uncle's household could not fail to see the despair that had clouded her brow ever since she met Gideon Quinn, yet so far as she could tell they seemed oblivious to all save the wonders of the new-found love they believed would begin for the two of them

Emma walked along the cliffs scanning the water for any sign of her trunk. She lifted her gown to step over the native grasses and coastal trees abundant with bees. The wind from the preceding day had dropped and the heat had abated, and but for the dilemma at hand, Emma almost found herself in buoyant spirits. Almost, until she recollected the previous evening spent with the venerable Gideon Quinn.

The time she had been left alone with him he had been very circumspect. His behaviour, she admitted, could have been called perfectly gentlemanly. Only he was no gentleman, for he had deceived her all the while their courtship had continued, and no man of decency would ever do that.

Her opinion now seemed to make little difference. When she

accepted him by letter, even before she had left the dock, her troth had been binding, and she prayed for the strength to love the man, for just then she had none.

Emma felt cheated, at a loss to know how to remedy her situation. Her mind drifted back to the night before.

'I have plighted my troth unswervingly to you, Emma dear, and have no intention of giving you up.' His lips had cut a thin line of impatience.

She had gently disengaged her hand from his. *'The parson has told me that he will be more than willing to carry out the service of a formally witnessed betrothal on Sunday. You have been separated from your home and family, have been almost drowned in the port, so your reticence is understandable . . . but it will soon change.'*

It had been obvious how much Gideon looked forward to retirement in the near future, so much so that he had appeared oblivious to her reserve as he told her about the sandstone home that was being built for their life together.

For the rest of their lives they would cling as husband and wife like the ivy to the oak, a hard thought which brought Emma back to the present. As she looked ahead of her out at the expanse of sea, she only wished that she could fly free.

She surveyed her surroundings then, sure that she must have lost her way, when she heard male voices ahead. When she hiked down a track in the cliff-face Emma beheld a man bathing in a rock-hewn swimming bath.

'Hello there!' he waved expansively.

'Oh, I do apologise,' she blushed before she spun away, her cheeks scarlet even though the man's shoulders alone were revealed. The men nearby snickered in ribald fashion.

'What can I do for you miss?' a soldier asked.

Emma's cheeks flushed brighter still. 'I wondered if I might see the commandant.'

The soldier grinned. 'Large as life, miss.' He pointed. 'The commandant would be more than pleased to speak with you, I'm sure, only you had better stay here while I go and fetch him from his morning tub.'

'Oh, of course.' Emma nodded as she spun away once more and shielded her eyes. She sat down on a sandstone ledge and upbraided herself for her impetuous action.

Moments later, the commanding officer rounded the corner and bid her good morning.

'Commandant Morisset?'

'Major Morisset, commandant of Newcastle, and sometime magistrate,' the man said good-humouredly. How may I assist?'

His smile was quirky and friendly, she thought, and he would have been a handsome man except for the scar that marred his face. His eyes winked darkly, and his tousled black hair dripped onto his hastily buttoned coat.

'I arrived on the brig that foundered the other day,' Emma began.

'Indeed, your arrival created something of a disturbance, to say the least, but now that I see what a fair passenger was on board, I must admit that I am glad you were one of the lucky ones.'

He cut short, as though he had given the compliment before thinking, but when she smiled, he appeared pleased he had spoken his mind.

'None more so than me; that is certain, Commandant.'

'Please forgive my folly in speaking of the discomfort you doubtless suffered in the ordeal. I mean no disrespect.'

'And nor am I in any way offended,' Emma assured him as she dipped her head. He looked at her with appreciation and an enchanted gleam, until he seemed to realise something.

'Are you Miss Emma Colchester by any chance?'

'I am, yes.'

'Then you are to wed Gideon Quinn.' It was a statement, not a question.

'You are well informed.' Emma knew no joy lighted her features. He looked sympathetic.

'Still, that's not the reason I'm here,' she said. 'I've come to ask your mercy on a prisoner who was on the same ship.'

'Oh?'

'He saved my life. I would have drowned along with all the others, I can assure you, if it wasn't for him.'

'What's his name?'

'He never told me.' Emma bit her lip.

'That makes things more difficult.' He gave a comical frown.

'I suppose it does.' She felt slightly foolish and fervently wished that she had thought twice about her intrusion. The commandant offered a look of reassurance.

'Even so, I'll be sure to ask around,' he said. 'Not many made the shore to safety.'

She hoped he would. But the distracted look in his eye as he watched her walk away, made her wonder.

*

As Emma made her way back down the cliff's face, she passed the infirmary. She wondered if she might be better employed wrapping bandages for others rather than sewing seams for herself. She indulged the opportunity to consider the role she hoped to take on in Newcastle. Perhaps it would help her to forget about Gideon Quinn for a short time.

The weatherboard building looked respectable enough. A verandah made the most of both the shade and the sea breeze, and Emma had been told it was built to bed sixty convicts if needed.

But when she entered the door, the hospital shocked her. Most of the patients who were bedridden lay naked, and the sheets that covered their bodies were yellowed and patched. The sun that shone in through the unglazed windows illuminated the sand blown in from the sea.

The smell of night-soil also lingered nearby. Left in an open-air garbage area near the hospital, its unsanitary smell wafted through every available crack and crevice. The foetid odour was enough to make the toughest constitution sickly. Surely there was a better area to deposit it?

Emma stood in the open doorway and smiled when her uncle, the surgeon, beckoned her to where he sat in an alcove reading a letter. Sunlight reflected off his spectacles as he looked up.

'Well, yes, there is always something to be done, that's certain,' he agreed when Emma told him of her wish to assist. 'Still, it is mostly the women convicts who work here. I don't think it's appropriate that you should work side by side with them.' He pushed his glasses farther back onto the bridge of his nose. 'Some might see it as unseemly.'

Emma drooped. Surely she could do something for someone to take her mind away from the miserable thought of becoming Mrs Quinn? 'Yet now that I am here, today at least …'

Her uncle softened as he pushed his glasses flat against his face with a nod. He closed the door and led her into the whitewashed ward. A breeze wafted up from the sea and touched the tendrils of hair at Emma's neck.

'Where shall I begin then? Peeling vegetables or bathing wounds?'

'I'm not sure what will be easiest to find, clean linen or sound potatoes.' He said with a smile. 'Most of the ailments we see could be avoided with nutritious food and better sanitation, but unfortunately, we can only do as much as we are able.

'The Limeburners are served vegetables twice a week where they work on the peninsula, but the convicts here have a monotonous diet. Bread and salt beef can only do so much for the body. We endeavour to make up gruel of some sort when we can. There haven't been any complaints yet, although the recipe usually leaves something to be desired. A hospital garden would be a boon in the colony, although there is a government garden, and the commandant sees that a basket of fish or vegetables is brought either here or to the gaol upon occasion.'

'So seafood is plentiful?'

'Sometimes yes, sometimes no, although I am told the natives spear crabs, fish and waterfowl in the swamps with long spears with no effort whatsoever.'

Emma imagined the taste of fresh fish and swallowed. She knew the convicts were not the only ones who subsisted on mutton, salt pork or beef. Her diet during the voyage had consisted of much the same, although her short stay in Sydney had seen her eating much better.

'Don't feel inclined to sympathise with that convict over there by the window, Emma dear. He has had a ligature just below his knee for who knows how long and will be lucky not to lose his leg.'

Emma looked at him askance and her uncle sought to explain. 'He tied it there himself.'

'Why on earth would he do that?' Emma was aghast. From where she stood she could see that the calf was red and swollen.

'To get off the chain,' he said and shrugged. Emma didn't know what the *chain* was. She raised her eyebrows and tilted her head.

'The chain-gang. The chains go from the ankles and are secured at the waist. He is able to lay straight now though, I suppose, so maybe he thought it would be worth it.' Emma frowned, determined to temper her compassion as her uncle continued. 'In fact, don't go near him. The old fellow at the other end of the ward needs care for those ulcers on his ankles, and he appears harmless enough. If you could begin by washing them, that would be helpful. I only hope your aunt doesn't skin me for allowing you to help,' he mumbled as he walked away.

Emma took a basin and began to soak some cloth in warm water. The old prisoner's ankles were scarred and bruised. He too, had worn chains. The fetters had rubbed the skin raw in places.

'Have you no stockings and shoes?' she asked.

'Sold them.'

'You sold your own shoes?'

'Only way to get enough grub to eat.'

'You eat grubs because you go hungry?' asked Emma.

He chortled and wiped his eyes with a grimy hand. 'Nah, we save them for the natives. Still, we don't get enough to feed a sparrow. I could get used to shacking up here. Can stretch out for the first time in weeks, *and* I get to talk to a lovely lady like you, so it's not all bad.'

Emma smiled.

'It's not flattery, miss, only truth. You get to enjoy things that would have passed you by without thought when you live on the thin edge of the wedge.

'Now that big handsome brute that had his eye on you the other day,' he grinned, with a wag of his finger, 'he'd understand my meaning.'

Emma looked at him sharply. 'Very black hair and blue eyes?'

The old man laughed so much he began to wheeze.

'Black as a raven's wings, my dear, but as to the colour of his eyes, I can't rightly say because I never got that close.' He gave her a knowing smile and winked.

'He *told* you?' Emma's face grew warm.

The convict frowned.

'He didn't tell me anything, but I do have eyes in my head, and I know he had his peepers fixed firmly on you.'

'What is his name?'

'Don't know that either,' he said, then smiled as if he was pleased with himself. 'Hold on, I recall him saying Freemason, or Freeman or something. Still, his name means naught. He's a government man, and unless he's handed a miracle, its life on Penury Street until his time's up.'

'A government man?'

'Yeah, waiting on his majesty's pleasure, like the rest of us. A convict, in other words.'

'Oh.' Emma nodded and began to wash the man's wounds, and as she did she told her patient what the brawny, dark-haired convict had done to save her in the harbour.

'No one would have cared, miss, even if they believed him. But that bloke aside, tell me, why is it that you would willingly leave old England for this hell on earth?'

Emma smiled wearily. 'I received a proposal of marriage, and what I thought would be a life of purpose. Village life seemed very dull before I left.'

The old convict thought on that and shook his head without understanding. 'Must have been a pretty good offer.'

'It seemed so at the time.' Emma knew her smile held no more warmth than the wintery sunshine back home.

The man stated that nothing would induce him to willingly leave the mother country, which he knew he probably would never see again.

'Your sweetheart, is it anyone I know?'

'One of the officers.'

'I probably know him.'

Emma looked up from her task. 'Gideon Quinn,' she said quietly.

He stared in surprise. 'That old –?' But the man stopped short.

'Pardon me for asking, miss, but are you in love with him?'

Emma smiled at the audacious question. She'd already learned there were no social niceties in this place of retribution. 'That doesn't matter. I plighted my troth. I gave it in writing, and when all's said and done, it's a long way home.'

'You can say that again.'

Emma glanced at the prisoner. The old man looked sagely back. 'You may as well be in shackles like the rest of us.'

*

That night, Emma dreamed that she was by the sea once more. She hung in mid-air and clung to the edge of the cliff with all her might, but when the tumultuous wave came to claim her, she wasn't strong enough to save herself.

She fell farther than she had ever done in her life. The shoals below her rose and foamed, strewn with seaweed, and as she plummeted to what she knew was her death, the wind snatched her last intake of air.

Emma awoke with a gasp, her cheeks awash with tears. She lay in the dawn light, her body weak with relief, but she thought for a moment that the house was rocking like a storm-tossed ship. She dressed hurriedly before she stumbled outside and drank in the still air of morning.

The harbour was calm. The evening before the wind had whipped the bay into turmoil. It had given way now to serenity.

In the distance smoke curled from an unseen campfire. Her thoughts turned to the natives as a white plume made a lazy spiral between the trees. Emma peered into the distance in curiosity and suddenly grew hungry. She could only smell the salt beef that bubbled somewhere in the direction of the constabulary kitchens, but as far as she could tell, no one was at work along the foreshore as yet.

She strolled leisurely along the beach. The sheer island that stuck up out of the water held no menace for her as it had in the dream, and for the first time since she had arrived, Emma saw the beauty of the settlement of Newcastle, thankful that she could wake up to the sunrise.

Two soldiers stood ahead of her, and she bid them good morning as they surveyed something on the sand.

'It's a body, miss. Don't step too close. It's not something a lady ought to see.'

'Goodness me,' Emma said, though she halted in her tracks, unable to look away.

'They wash up all the time. It's the work of foul play more often than not, though he may have drowned because of the shipwreck or the construction of the pier. Dangerous work, but still, someone's got to do it.'

'A few less for the crown to feed, though,' the other man laughed.

Emma stared, taken aback. When she looked at him more closely, she thought she recognised him as one of the two who had so roughly escorted the convict away from the shore just days before, and Emma admitted to herself that it was not charitable to dislike the man. Judgement of a soldier who took a few minutes to complain was not her right.

'What was his name?' Emma tried again not to look at the body laying face down in the beach sand.

'Freeman, I think.' He screwed up his face in thought. Emma stared up at the soldier, and repeated the name after him. He seemed sure of it.

'That's right. It'll take three men to move him. Can't tell me they don't get adequate rations. Look at him,' he said, as he prodded the body with the toe of his boot. 'He's a giant.'

Emma turned away. Her stomach churned. She had never seen death, not until she had arrived in Newcastle. Here, death was commonplace.

Life was cheap.

She heard the two soldiers behind her discuss the weight of the body in the sand.

'I won't be moving it. I'd only pull a muscle. My back has only just righted itself. I helped carry big Jenny out of the natives' camp. Aye, she's feisty. I won't heft *this* whale.' Emma wondered why big Jenny didn't want to leave the natives' camp, but was not game to ask.

'No need though. We'll get a couple of the convicts to do the work. That's what they're here for, after all.' Emma realised that, whatever her misfortunes, they were nothing compared with those of the men and women convicts who lived a life of drudgery from one day to the next and dragged up their children beside them in the best way they knew how. She'd already learned that they laboured from first light till sunset, except for the latter part of Saturday. Sunday, their only full day's respite, was set aside for the salvation of their souls. And for many of the convicts, she surmised, the Ten Commandments were hard to follow when they lived with the devil in a hell of their own making. Although her aunt's distaste for the felons of the settlement was understandable, Emma pitied their lot.

It wasn't easy to flee from the bounds of authority, people told her, for with five roll calls a day, it was next to impossible to escape. That's if the blacks didn't track them down, which they invariably did. There were none better at the task than they, and they relished it, happy for the remuneration that came their way, especially in the way of tobacco, blankets and corn. When they stripped the captured convicts of their clothing, to bring them in shamed and naked, they broke any tenuous friendship that may have been possible between the two. It was common knowledge that the convicts who had been brutalised by transport and all that went with it often brutalised the natives. When the blacks made good others' misfortune and traded escapees for food, the prisoners they had worked against beat them sooner or later, and some used their women when they got the chance. Still, the natives had long memories. Often escapees would escape the bounds of authority, only to be speared when they unknowingly trespassed onto tribal lands.

Emma shook her head in an attempt to turn her thoughts to other matters, and the upcoming social event fought for prominence in her mind over the sight she just witnessed. She had little interest in the parsonage supper planned that evening. Her gown, which she had yet to choose, seemed of little importance when she thought of the man who had saved her life only to be washed up with the flotsam and debris of the sea then jabbed by the toe of a hob-nailed boot like so much useless driftwood.

When Emma arrived back at her uncle's cottage, Phoebe held out gowns for her so she could select one. For Phoebe it was the festive event that she had looked forward to for months.

'I don't feel like going to the parson's supper, Aunt. I'd much rather stay at home,' Emma said. 'I can assure you that I would be quite all right by myself.' She pictured the drowned convict blanketed in damp yellow sand and blinked back tears.

'But dear, you must come, certainly you must,' Aunt Adelaide protested. 'You have been invited by name. In any case, I wouldn't dream of leaving you alone. Wily convicts have been known to break and enter before, and it would be beyond me to enjoy myself knowing that you were here unprotected. Whatever would Gideon say? He wouldn't stand for it, I'm sure.'

'Up until a few days ago, Aunt, Gideon Quinn hadn't even met me. I don't think his concerns would be that grave.' Emma wanted to use the excuse that she had nearly drowned only days before. It should be understandable that she didn't feel inclined to attend a social event, yet she knew saying so would only seem churlish. How could she explain to the woman that she didn't have the mettle to tell people that she was betrothed to Officer Quinn? She was spared further words when her aunt left to look after her own attire for the event.

'Try this gown on,' Phoebe said. 'It will fit you admirably, I'm convinced.'

'It is a lovely gown. I'm grateful to you, Phoebe,' Emma told her truthfully. 'If it were not for you, I'd still be in my shift.'

'I would wager that the commandant will be a mite disappointed if he doesn't see you at the rectory dinner. I am sure you caught his eye down by the foreshore.' Phoebe sounded pleased with her observation as she sat on the cot that had been made up for her cousin. Emma shot her a glance.

'Fiddlesticks, cousin; you dream.' And then after a moment, 'Did you tell anyone that I went to ask his help?'

'Of course not, Emma. I wouldn't do that to you,' Phoebe protested. 'Still, why bother about helping the convict in the first place?'

Emma stared at her cousin as she considered her answer. 'Perhaps it is because he helped me first.'

A sly look crept into Phoebe's eyes. 'Is he handsome?'

Emma turned away. 'I can't say that I noticed. In any case, he's dead now. Soldiers found him washed up on the shore.' It wasn't true; she had noticed him, and his demise was made all the more poignant.

'Oh well, you couldn't have married him in any case.'

'I never thought to do so.'

'Are you in love with Gideon, Emma?'

'We've only just met.' Emma was rational but she was annoyed.

'But do you believe in love at first sight?'

'Well, if I do, then it hasn't happened. The man is as a stranger to me, and I can tell you that it will take more than a passing glance to be swept away by such a romantic notion.'

'Then it's time to get to know him, Emma, and tonight is a wonderful start.'

'And I will have all my married life to accomplish it.' Emma sighed wearily.

'If I didn't know better, Emma, I would say that you didn't want to marry Gideon at all,' Euphemie said as she looked in at the door, a smug smile on her face. The girl had not grown in kindness over the last two years.

Emma considered the gown spread before her in thoughtful silence. Outside the window, the water met the shore like the ticking of a clock, and the measured seconds fell heavy in the cottage bedroom.

'We don't have to talk about it,' Phoebe apologised in her sister's stead. 'Matters of love are a private thing.'

Emma nodded, as she felt no desire to disclose her admission of dread.

She remained weary from the previous night. She had pitched and tossed like a capricious yacht as she lay in bed and considered her marriage with dismay. She was far from English shores without a penny to spend or a stitch of clothing to her name, reliant now on her uncle for her very existence. Not only did she feel beholden to him for his care of her, she was honour-bound to wed a man both her uncle and aunt had sanctioned as a worthy match, yet for whom she could stir no interest. It had been a long while before Emma was claimed by tiredness and forgot her dilemma in blissful sleep.

She steeled herself back to the present and turned to give Phoebe a smile of reassurance as she squeezed her hand.

'I thought for one moment then we would stop being friends,' her cousin said, visibly relieved, as she made herself more comfortable on the bed.

'Not at all,' Emma said. 'You are my *only* friend.' That assertion turned Phoebe pink with pleasure. There was a longing for friendship in her cousin that Emma was beginning to understand very well.

'I would consider myself adequately recompensed if you would reconsider going to the rector's supper,' Phoebe said and giggled.

Emma graced her with a fond smile.

'Then go I shall.' Yet even as she said it, her attention drifted back to that morning on the shore, to the body of the man who had rescued her.

FOUR

The convict watched the candle-lit spectacle through the open shutters. Hidden in the shadows behind tea tree and she-oak, he heard strains of music, and within the open parlour, tapers glowed and flickered as if to the rhythm of the wings of the moths that flitted near the glow of the naked flames.

In the early summer night, brass buttons shone, china teacups clinked, and Tobias Freeman saw the 'petticoat miss', and thought that no butterfly, in all its fragile beauty, could compare with her angelic face.

He decided to call her that, in his mind at least, although until that moment he had never wondered for her name. It would serve no purpose, he was well aware, but curiosity held him captive. He cursed himself for a cur as he remembered her gratitude on the shore and how he had shrugged off her kindness with callous disregard. It seemed a long time since anyone had cared that much.

Only he knew the reason for his angry response to her naïve touch, yet desire had been kindled by one innocent move, and as he watched her, that hope became a flame. He was drawn to watch her, and only the occasional blink of his eyes testified to his not being asleep on his feet.

The commanding officer came into view. His companion talked

in a conspiratorial whisper.

'She's betrothed to old Gideon. First you'll have to grapple with him.'

The commandant looked at his friend, the soldier's red hair a violent clash with the choleric complexion. 'She's begging to be rescued.'

'Out of the frying pan into the fire.'

'Gentleman's honour,' his better assured, 'I intend only light-hearted flirtation.'

The soldier shot his commanding officer a dubious look. The commandant shrugged. 'All's fair in love and war.'

Tobias knew to whom they referred. His fingers twitched at his sides in annoyance to hear her spoken of in such a light-hearted manner. He watched them wander off.

'What are you doing here?' hissed an old convict who sneaked up behind Tobias. 'Your life will be worth nothing if they find "Peeping Tom" at the window.' But he sidled up to the shutters to peer round the curtains at the sight inside.

'That makes the two of us, then,' Tobias noted wryly. The old man Kevin, squinted inside the room. He wondered whether the wiry Londoner could withstand a flogging were the 'cat' presented to him.

'You won't achieve anything staring after that young lady, Kevin said. 'Filthy overseer was right, you know. A lady like that wouldn't look twice at the likes of you.'

Tobias glanced away and the moment of dreaming gave way to reality. He didn't need to be told, and it rankled. 'Doesn't hurt to look.' Kevin's few teeth shone strangely white beneath the moon.

'I'll give you that, mate.' The two men crept back to the bushes and crouched down. They watched as the young woman stepped out onto the porch on the arm of the commandant to take in the cool of night, at least what little breeze there was. It was clear to Tobias that thoughts of flirtation played in the commandant's mind when the officer bowed to take her hand and seal his admiration with a kiss.

'Would you Adam and Eve it?' Kevin whispered.

'What?' Tobias frowned. Didn't the man ever stop talking?

'I said would you believe it?'

For a moment the woman glanced in their direction and it seemed that she held his gaze from where he hid with Kevin in the brush. Tobias heard Kevin's warning beside him and tried to focus his attention on the words, but for a moment they held no meaning.

'We're going to be seen, mate,' Kevin hissed.

'You think so?' He sounded almost hopeful. Kevin stared at him, nonplussed.

'Use your loaf and put your shirt up around your head. It'll be the best protection it's ever given you,' came Kevin's urgent warning. As the two men yanked their worn clothes up over their faces, the commandant's attention met them full on.

'What, in the name of the king, are you doing there?' the commandant called, as he strode over to make out the reason for the commotion of leaves.

'Just having a quiet moment with the young lady with me, sir,' came the clipped and measured tones from the darknesss. The commanding officer smiled his understanding, hardly realising he was being duped by a convict.

'I see. Pardon me. As you were.' But stepping back he suddenly stopped, as though the truth had dawned.

Yet as the commandant opened up his mouth in indignation and affront, Kevin sprang from the bushes. His fist caught the man full in the jaw and rendered him senseless even before he fell. He lay like a toy soldier in the dust.

'We've done it now, lad,' Kevin growled. Tobias stared at the wiry Londoner with new respect. There was more strength in those fists than he would have given the man credit for.

He then glanced towards the parsonage. The young lady stared in their direction. She hesitated, but stepped down from the porch.

'Get his jacket off,' Tobias ordered. 'I'm going to put it on.'

Kevin squinted up at him as though he were mad. 'Use your loaf, mate. Don't you think someone will know someone's stolen his clobber? And you strutting around like some cocky rooster.' Tobias ignored him and yanked off the commandant's boots. The breeches hardly fit him like a glove, but well enough to pass muster. 'Don't allow him to wake for a while.' Tobias nodded over his shoulder, his tone the perfect parody of a soldier.

'Here she comes, mate.' Kevin's whisper was harsh. He gave a dumbstruck look as Tobias walked from behind the shrubbery and met the young lady. Tobias offered her his arm.

*

The man she thought was the commandant led her down the garden path and clicked shut the white picket gate behind them. Emma glanced up hesitantly and her hand shot to her mouth to still her gasp of surprise.

'You're alive.'

'Aye,' he nodded, 'for now, at least.'

'The commandant?'

'He is otherwise occupied with a convict who has nothing to do on a Saturday night other than hide in the bushes.'

'What are you doing wearing his clothes?' Emma whispered as she glanced back at the manse. Laughter tinkled through the open windows like silverware on china.

'I am about to take the air with the landed gentry's niece, and it was hardly fitting, miss, that I should be in the garb of a government man when one such as you appeared before me.' Emma felt herself colour deeply at the audacious compliment. She looked up in sudden breathless nervousness. Emma saw his eyes glitter and the butterflies in her stomach fluttered madly at the consequences of being in the company of a convict; both for her and him.

'As a gentleman you should be aware of the fact that a young lady is first asked before being led down the garden path by a perfect stranger.'

The convict swept her a gracious bow and displayed a military bearing that looked as though it had been born to him.

'But then, miss, I am neither perfect nor a stranger, and certainly no gentleman. I've no more chivalry than most of the soldiers in the barracks.'

'You forget yourself I believe, sir. You cannot know any of the regiment, for you have been here no longer than I.'

'I heard enough in the garden to know you were destined as the sweets course, that's for sure.' Emma frowned at the coarse insinuation.

'Considering that I am betrothed to Officer Quinn, I hardly imagine that the commandant had any such thing on his mind.'

'Aye, then perhaps it was not undisguised lust I saw on his face.'

Emma flushed with indignation at his words. 'I wonder if your thoughts are somewhat the same sir, for the appraising eyes you fix on me have an altogether familiar stare.'

'I beg your pardon, miss. I never realised I was staring.'

They stood silent for a moment.

'Can you waltz?' the convict asked.

'You are asking me to dance?'

'That I am,' he said with a bow from the waist.

Emma took the hand held out to her, but glanced away from the parsonage, away from Gideon Quinn who stood at the open door. She could not see his features, but she could make out the indecision in his stance. Would he cut in on her dancing partner in displeasure? Yet he mustn't have seen the commandant as a rival,

34

because after a moment's thought he retreated. Emma had feared he would surely see through this man's disguise.

As the strain of the single violin reached them, he took her in his arms and began to sway in time to the music. Emma noted that the convict's movements were both strong and fluid.

'I will say nothing against you,' she said.

He nodded.

'Aye, I know.'

'What you are doing is folly, to say the least.' She said. He didn't justify his actions, so Emma continued. 'Do you know what will happen to you if you're caught?'

'Aye, I do.' For the first time Emma saw him smile. She was surprised to see that his teeth were strong and white, even as she wondered at his apparent unconcern.

'It's been a while since I danced,' he admitted, and Emma stared at him, slightly open-mouthed. 'And it's nothing short of boring in a cottage with Kevin.'

Emma smiled. There it was again, that bold look in his eye.

'I would like to know your name.' Emma was suddenly loathe for the music from the rectory parlour to end when she knew that she ought to have been scared senseless. Perhaps it was fear that quickened the rhythm of her heart.

'It's better I don't tell you that,' he replied.

Emma nodded, but she was disappointed, displeased even, though she knew her reaction was infantile.

At that moment, she watched two young soldiers walk out of the building, their faces filled with puzzlement until they saw what appeared to be the commandant back in the dance, and in a most unconventional spot. The young men smiled and nudged one another conspiratorially.

'You don't know my name. You never saw my face,' her dancing partner whispered.

Emma looked up into his eyes. She knew without a doubt, that neither the encounter nor the face of the man before her would ever be forgotten.

The music ended in the last notes of the melody, and as he bowed and took her hand, Emma felt the warm, firm pressure of his mouth through to her skin.

'Goodnight, Commandant,' she said.

He nodded wordlessly and had already walked away into the night before she thought to turn to watch his departure. She hesitated for a few moments to take in what had just happened. As soon as Emma returned to the brightness of the rectory, she realised that every eye was upon her. From the corner of her eye she saw that her uncle and aunt watched her curiously. She flushed, as well she should. Unexpectedly, the hairs rose on her arms. She wrapped her shawl round her shoulders. She was offered a cup of tea. The china trembled in the saucer.

Minutes later a cry went up and silenced the chatter in the rectory. Emma managed to set down her tea with studied decorum before she spilt it.

'Excuse me doctor, the commandant's injured.' The same two young soldiers she'd seen before appealed to the surgeon, who turned around, a frown on his face.

'Yes, sir. It appears he was attacked as soon as he left the building. Bludgeoned or punched—we can't tell which—and his clothes stripped off him for good measure. All he was left with were his gloves.'

'Oh, mercy!' Aunt Adelaide threw her hands over her mouth.

'You've got the culprit?' Emma heard the doctor ask before they were out of earshot.

'They're after him now sir, he can't have gone far. Won't be surprised if he's strung to the gibbet for something like this.'

'I doubt it, unless the commandant's been killed. How bad is he?'

'Nothing that a toddy and a vinegar and brown paper compress won't fix, sir, but he's pretty shaken.'

'Rope-able, more like,' said the other one, 'but far from done in.'

'You say there was one convict responsible?' the doctor asked.

'More likely than not. If there had have been more they would have killed him for sure. Once they get the smell of the blood, it sets them off.'

Emma stood rigid, clutching her shawl as she took in what was being said. She saw the commandant come from around the corner of the building and her heart lurched. She watched as he snatched the long coat that was passed to him, shook it, and shrugged it on as he walked.

Bruised and dishevelled, dark eyes intent, he walked towards her slowly, yet with purpose. She held her breath, and with startling clarity, she realised that unless she spoke up she was an accessory to the crime.

'Phoebe,' her mother hissed as the commandant approached, 'get away from the shutters. You won't see any clearer from there than you can with those spectacles.' As if to verify to truth of the statement, Phoebe tripped on a chair to sprawl undignified at the commandant's feet. Though an ill-timed, embarrassing manoeuvre, Emma appreciated the decoy it provided, even though poor Phoebe was spread out in a rather unbecoming way.

The commandant helped her cousin to stand, with a grimace either at the pain of his injuries inflicted by the convicts, or the deadweight of Phoebe, who it seemed, had momentarily lost her senses. She peered through the lenses of her glasses with a smiling blush. Emma noticed that her aunt was clucking in nervous embarrassment as she waved her fan violently back and forth in an attempt to draw a cooling wind against the heat of her flushed cheeks.

Yet it was not Phoebe, but Emma herself to whom the commandant made his next address. Emma held her breath, aware of Gideon standing by her side. The butterflies took wing again in her stomach.

'Miss Colchester, you have been fortunate. How did you manage to escape? I have let you down immeasurably and ask your forgiveness in what seems my full disregard. Are you totally unharmed?'

Emma assured him she was, though her legs had begun to tremble as violently as the cup in its saucer.

'I realise the lateness of the hour and will not at this moment put you too much to task, but did you see the felon who caused this indignity to my person?' he asked.

Emma blanched white and thought desperately for a response closer to truth than a barefaced lie. She struggled to think. 'Think, Emma, my dear,' Gideon said. 'What kind of features did the offender possess?'

'Wicked features, I'm sure.' Her aunt sounded positive about that. Emma saw her her glance at the commandant's lack of attire and she began to fan herself all over again.

'I was frightened,' Emma nodded reluctantly. She understood the need to warm to her task a little, though all the time she wished that Gideon would not use her Christian name. She *was* scared now, that was certain.

'To be sure, to be sure.' Gideon nodded compassionately. 'But Emma dear, what did he look like? Did you not see his face?' Emma thought furiously and shared what was neither the truth, nor yet a falsehood.

'The lighting where we danced was very poor and he made sure to keep his head down. His grip was like a vice.'

'You danced with the felon?' Gideon said, and then stared round him at the company, who thankfully had almost dispersed. 'I thought it was the commandant.' 'And so did I, at first,' Emma agreed, and this she could say in all sincerity, because for a moment, his disguise had fooled her too. After all, she had assumed the convict had drowned. The commandant grimaced. 'How was the ruse accomplished?' he asked.

'To be honest,' Emma said, 'I am not entirely sure. I watched as you walked away from the manse and round the building. I thought I heard raised voices, but shortly thereafter you returned, and for a moment I thought nothing of it, but it was not you after all.'

'Why did you not refuse the scoundrel?' Gideon said.

'If I did not, he may have done me some harm.'

'It could well have saved your life,' Phoebe said.

Her uncle spoke for the first time all night. 'You did what was necessary, certainly. It only makes me wonder that you didn't give the cry the moment the man left the vicinity.' Everyone seemed to think this a pertinent observation, and they turned as one to face her, curiosity plain on their faces.

'He said his eye would be kept on me,' Emma whispered, though she hated each abominable word. Her aunt and cousins breathed in tones of shock and indignation.

'Yet surely if you had spoken out, the man could have been punished before he could have done any harm,' Euphemie said.

'Not if he escaped with the natives to the bush first,' Phoebe put in.

'Murdered in our beds we'd be,' her mother agreed nervously. Phoebe's eyes were round as though horrified at the thought.

'You are lucky to be alive.' Gideon seemed to choke on the insolence of the prisoner who had dared to touch her. 'The convict will be punished,' the commandant assured her with a smile that was clearly meant to set her at ease.

'The convict will be hanged!' Gideon said. His superior officer glanced at him. It was enough. Gideon was silent. 'If we find the individual responsible for the bold act, then he will be duly penalised, but unless we are sure of the person or persons in question, we must be sure not to make a mistake.' The commandant did not have to raise his voice to assert his authority.

Emma's uncle was not so easily appeased. 'Even if the wrong felon was charged and brought to justice for the crime, it would show others that disrespect would not go unanswered.' 'No flogging will be given until after Miss Colchester identifies the man responsible.'

'I'll have the convicts assembled directly, sir,' Gideon assured him. The commandant shook his head. He held up a hand. 'The problem will wait until morning.'

'Begging your pardon, sir, but Miss Colchester may not remember as much after she has had the leisure to sleep on it,' Gideon said.

'Miss Colchester has been through enough this evening, Officer Quinn, and I for one look forward to my bed. I am certain that Miss Colchester would wish for the same,' the commandant stated pointedly. 'Come, Emma dear,' Aunt Adelaide soothed. 'It's high time you had some rest. What an ordeal you have had during these past few days, and how brave you have been through it all. Sleep is the best medicine.'

'Allow me.' Gideon nodded at Aunt Adelaide and took Emma's hand solicitously. Emma's teeth clenched in a bid not to pull away. Although his hand upon her flesh was deceptively gentle, she was sure Gideon meant to remind her that he was in command of *her*, at least.

'Of course,' her aunt nodded in thankful agreement. 'We are fortunate that you are here.'

The grey-haired officer bowed.

'My duty is done very willingly.' His assurance didn't comfort Emma in the least.

'Emma dear, I know I said that we could have as long an engagement as you wish, but it worries me that I cannot protect you as readily and fully as I would like. Your safety is my only regard.' Emma heard Euphemie snicker, but pretended not to hear.

40

'A husband's duty is to safeguard those he loves.'

'You are not my husband yet, Officer Quinn,' Emma reminded him.

'Never my surname,' he said. She heard the smile in his voice. 'Please, only Gideon. Let us begin as we mean to continue, for in matrimony, Christian names are nothing short of endearments when spoken by husband and wife.'

Emma cringed. Euphemie and Phoebe nearly choked on laughter. Emma's warning stare had the desired effect as Phoebe's white gloved hand pressed against her mouth.

As the girls lay in their beds later that evening, the lapping surf covered their voices as they whispered in the darkness.

'What was the convict like, Emma? Was he very horrible?' Phoebe whispered quietly.

'No,' Emma said after consideration. 'He acted the perfect gentleman.'

'Except for his vice-like grip,' Euphemie reminded her.

'Yes, except for that,' Emma confirmed quickly, and she remembered how large his hands had been, and how rough with calluses.

'Was he an appalling dancer, then?' Phoebe asked.

'As a matter of fact, he was very good.'

'I'm sure you must have been frightened Emma,' Phoebe said, 'but I must say, it is frightfully exciting now that it's over. Still, it's just as well that you didn't get a good look at him. I imagine him to have been rather ugly, and that wouldn't have done at all.'

'Quite so,' Emma agreed quietly.

She heard Euphemie's whisper, sharp and short, as they listened to the sea and the sound of one another's breathing. 'Emma, the commandant is not for you.'

Emma blinked into the darkness and considered her response. 'I am well aware, Euphemie.' Her smile felt counterfeit. 'My future is a settled thing, as you know.'

She recalled the look on Euphemie's face after she came in from the garden at the rectory. The other girl seemed to coolly analyse the emotions Emma knew must have been mapped out on her face. It seemed that her features had given away a secret she was hardly aware of herself.

The coltish Euphemie from two years ago had grown into a woman, it seemed, and Emma wondered whether she had cast her line for the commandant and now feared Emma to be fishing for him as well. But it was his counterfeit that had commanded Emma's emotions in the rectory garden above the whispering sea.

In the last moments before she slipped into sleep, she paced out the measure of the dance in her mind.

*

It took Tobias Freeman a similar length of time to drift off to sleep. When he did, he dreamed again.

His stomach growled in hunger as he walked through the belt of trees, and even though he hadn't reached his father's croft, he could smell the potatoes frying in the pan. He released a tired sigh, and looked forward to a cool draught of water to quench his thirst.

Tobias didn't hear the commotion until he had passed what had once been the gamekeeper's cottage. When he heard the strangled scream he took a step back. There was something familiar in the timbre of the voice. His stomach churned afresh, but now out of fear.

When he threw wide the splintering door of the abandoned cottage, he saw his young sister, Molly, lying there. Her face was contorted with her weeping, thighs slick with her own blood and shame.

He spun to face the brazen farmer. He hardly bothered to bow his head as he retrieved the waistcoat he had flung to the floor in his haste to appease his lust.

Tobias hit him full in the mouth, once, twice, again. The blows

felled the man so that he toppled heavily and hit his head against
the hearth. Tobias heard the dull crack of bone and knew at once, as
blood pooled on the hearth, that the farmer was dead.

'You'll still be lovely, Molly,' he whispered. He tried to make
his voice bright, as he carried her through the trees. 'This will pass
for sure.'

She said nothing.

He blamed himself for what had happened. He had meant to
walk home with Molly after the afternoon milking, aware of her
fears of the farmer, but he had finished his own work later than
usual, and he had been too late. It was all his fault. Tobias awoke
with a start. The dream was always the same. It had plagued him
since his conviction. The man he killed had been one with friends
in high places, and those friends had no more scruples than the
deceased, and they made sure Tobias paid for his death. Now he
was branded a murderer. Transported as a convict, his name was
forgotten and he became something closer to an animal. Not for the
first time, he wondered whether that was true. Sweat and emotion
wet his cheeks. He wiped his face with the back of his hand and
wished he were home. He fancied he almost smelled potatoes
frying. Stretched out in the warmth of the uncomfortable night, he
thought of his family, especially his sister, Molly.

Yet in the dream it hadn't been his sister's face that had stared
up from the flags of the cold stone floor. It had been that of the
petticoat miss.

He saw her now in his mind's eye, back on the day they had
washed up on the shore, and he remembered the flush of her cheeks
and the whiteness of her throat, the wet shift as it clung to her body.

In his imagination he could almost believe he held her pliant and
warm, and that he'd found peace in her arms, as he lay in the dark
alone. It was small solace as he waited for the daylight to come and
with it the drudgery of reality.

Tobias lay on his back. Scored as it was by the cat it gave him no rest. He tossed fitfully, the painful itch having given way to infection. For the last two days he had ignored the wound, hoping that it would heal. His throat was parched and he longed for a drink of water, but he knew that he would have to wait until the morning to slake his thirst.

When he awoke he could hardly stand. In a fever, he swayed like a giddy dancer. He stepped outside and shied away from the light when the sun, which shimmied like crystals over the water, glanced off his crazed vision.

As though drunk, he relieved himself and then drank greedily while he sopped water down his chest. The hard bread nearly choked him. He had no appetite for it, and it clung dryly to his throat and lodged there for a moment just before he brought it back up, accidentally splashing the overseer's boots.

'Filthy scum!' the man hollered then he kicked Tobias in the stomach as he bent double to retch in the blinding sun. Only when someone helped him up was he able to stand, and as he turned to utter some kind of thanks, he saw that it was the commandant.

'That's enough, Hodge,' the commandant told the overseer quietly. 'Can't you see he is sick? He is a man, not an animal. Get him over to the line-up, and if he doesn't improve by this afternoon, then have him taken to the hospice.'

The overseer nodded reluctantly. 'Aye, Commandant, I'll see to it.'

Tobias only saw them vaguely through blurred vision. But as he teetered on unsteady legs, he noticed the surgeon's niece from the night before, the one who had stolen through his dreams, and he vaguely wondered why she was there. The commandant answered the question.

'Miss Colchester is here to discern which of you thought to assume my identity, strip me of my clothing, and harm my person.

Don't think to avert your faces, but stare straight ahead that the lady may ascertain if you're guilty.'

He steeled himself to stand still. He felt his body teetering as she passed by him, even though he did his best to stand tall, out of pride in front of the young woman if nothing else. She never glanced at his face. He sensed every move she made. Though the sun glimmered cruelly over the sea, and blinded him with its early morning light, her glance was the last thing he remembered before he passed into unconsciousness.

*

Emma turned to the commandant. 'There is no one here I recognise. They all look the same.' She didn't notice the convict's condition until she heard a soft sound and turned to see the man on the ground. The jaded men glanced around at him as if he were no more than a stray dog in need of a good feed.

'Get that man to the hospice, Hodge,' Emma heard the commandant order the overseer sharply. She watched as they dragged the convict to the cart that held a newly made coffin then threw him down beside it, heavy as the dead. Although her stomach was empty, it churned inside her.

'I'm sorry I have been of no help at all.' She smiled pallidly. 'I understand,' the commandant said.

She walked back along the foreshore with the battered commandant, whose spirits seemed high, regardless of the trouncing he had taken the night before.

'Is the colony of Newcastle all that you thought it would be?' he asked, as he turned to look at her.

The wind fanned the tendrils of hair around her face. 'It is nothing as I imagined.' Her face warmed as she realised two naked natives watched them darkly from the mangrove trees as they passed.

'Would you go home if you could?'

'I am bound to Gideon Quinn.'

'And if you were not?'

Emma gazed out to sea, and her eyes followed the flight of a lone gull. 'I don't know. It really is a long way home on one's own with a promise made and not met.'

He turned to her, his words quiet, yet earnest. 'Then I beg you, Miss Colchester, tread carefully. The king's soldiers may well wear the saddle, but it is often the devil that holds the reins.'

FIVE

Emma opened the whitewashed gate and brushed past the sweet flowering lavender. Yet the perfume of the flowers that she crushed underfoot had dissipated by the time she passed the open midden that served the colony. Blowflies hovered and settled over the excrement in a blanket of contented industry.

Emma hurried past. In her other hand she carried a hessian bag that contained an assortment of withered carrots, eyed potatoes, and slowly rotting onions. Beside this motley hodgepodge was a bone that had been intended for the dog. With these things Emma planned to make broth for the infirm at the hospital. She entered the hospital and began at once.

Although the building always seemed to smell little better than the midden, situated as it was so close to the night-soil dumping area, the aroma of vegetable broth began to change the feel of the place.

It was not until late in the day that a salt breeze drifted off the glimmering water and through the unglazed windows. It seemed to lessen the smell of sickness and apathy that clung to the patients, and Emma's smiling ministrations helped soothe away listlessness as she rolled bandages and ladled soup.

'Emma, dear,' her uncle said with a frown, 'you should not be troubling yourself in this place. It would have been far better for you to have gone with your aunt and cousins to call on the reverend and his wife.'

'Although I had every intention of doing so, I remembered what you told me about the dietary privations of the convicts.'

'If your aunt is not happy, do not be surprised. She is of the strict opinion that felons are only that and deserve no privileges.'

Emma nodded. 'I had also thought to share the Word of God with each one, when I remembered that man does not live by bread alone.'

Her uncle chuckled and shook his head.

'You are your father's child. That much is certain.'

'Surely this occupation is as modest as any I might employ in the colony? And can do no harm to anyone, but only good.'

'You waste your time. What little faith they may still possess has been hidden by the vice of years.'

Emma considered this a moment in thoughtful silence. 'The Lord Jesus tells us that faith the size of a mustard seed is all we need.'

Her uncle conceded with a nod. 'I suppose I cannot argue with that.'

'What ails the man with his back facing us?' Emma had hoped, but she had not really expected, to see the convict. Her heart skipped a beat and she put a hand to her breast to still its flutter.

'His back is poisoned with the cut of the lash. The flesh around the wound is sorely inflamed and needs to be bathed in brine again before another poultice is applied to draw out the filth. It can take as little as forty-eight hours for a wound to become septic. He has slept with a fever most of the afternoon. He's been calling out to someone called Molly, and of course, like most of them, he's asking for his mother. His mind is wandering.

'The poor soul. Should I bathe his back?'

'I don't know that I can allow you to do that, Emma. His wounds are not for a young lady to tend. The inflammation is ripe and foul smelling. The wounds will need to be drained and dressed each day if he's to survive this. If infection continues on to septic shock, the internal organs can shut down. I don't think that it's the duty a young lady should assume. The obligation is not yours to take on,' he told her reasonably. Emma listened to her uncle's words in dismay.

'The man is ill and needs care. As you say, if he is to survive, he needs help. If I were the one burning with fever in a trundle bed, I would like to believe that I was of enough worth for someone to care for me.'

'Of course, niece, but then, you would not be in such a compromised situation.'

'Perhaps I have also been lucky. I have never known privation or want. I have never had to cling to life with both hands as I tried to haul myself out of poverty.'

'You have sailed through newly chartered waters to marry a man you had never met to help your family through the benefits of a good marriage,' Uncle George reminded her.

Emma smiled weakly at his praise, suddenly fearful that she would start to cry. Her lot had not yet become any easier, no matter how hard she thought about it.

'The thought to serve these people is a noble one, you may be sure of that but … just don't tell your aunt,' he warned her.

Emma smiled. 'I can only hope that she doesn't ask.'

I can understand your interest in healing, my dear. It's a noble profession, and after all, someone needs to do it.' He smiled. 'Yet you are like your father too, and he would be proud of your selfless desire to minister to the convicts.'

'You think so?' Emma said, gladdened at the thought.

'There is no doubt about it, but I wonder if there can be any headway made with these men and women. A wound can heal, but a life ill spent is one gone to waste.'

'I have heard it said that wherever there is life, there is hope,' Emma reminded him. 'If bones can break and knit together, if a wound can heal, then so can a heart. All it takes is the desire for change.'

'I suppose that's true, Emma. The apple does not fall far from the tree. You are your father's daughter. Do what you will.' He smiled and shook his head as he walked away to continue other work.

Emma bent to her task. The warm salt water she applied bit sharply into the convict's open wound and Emma cringed every time he groaned in his sleep. His rest was fitful, and at the insistence of her sponge, he awoke with a great start of pain. Emma jumped and spilled the basin over her skirts and onto the floor.

Her uncle watched her mop at the muslin, his wordless curiosity and concern evident, his glasses perched precariously at the end of his nose.

'It's all right,' she assured him with a glance over to where he stood. 'It's only water. I can easily fetch more.'

He nodded, but Emma knew that it was only her welfare he was concerned about. She smiled, and his frown eased before he continued his own tasks.

'I'm sorry I woke you,' she apologised to the convict. 'Your wounds needed to be bathed, and shortly the doctor will have a poultice to help draw out the infection.'

Emma's hands trembled slightly as she bent to retrieve the basin. She felt her cheeks colour so furiously that she felt foolish.

'Molly,' he said, 'Molly my love.' He breathed the name like an elixir of life, and then leaned forward to take up Emma's hands and press them to his lips. Emma shook her head in confusion, and with a glance behind her, was glad that no one was there.

Drawn to the thankful convict's side, Emma was unsure how to react. She stood there hesitantly, and even as she smiled at him, she watched his glazed expression became lucid. The cool eyes slowly cleared to focus steadily on her face. He seemed to realise his mistake.

'I'm sorry,' he rasped. 'I thought you were someone else.'

Emma nodded and smiled wordlessly. She understood his embarrassment, but not her own chagrin that she was not who he wanted her to be.

Gently she released her hands, and it was he whose cheeks flushed, though Emma knew that it was the fever. Her blush was due to other emotions.

'You have nothing to apologise for,' she said solemnly, and when he said nothing she continued. 'Do I remind you of Molly?'

He considered her, and then with a smile, shook his head. 'No not really.'

Emma smiled in turn, and he studied her without speaking, then his gaze held hers momentarily before Emma glanced away.

'Do you think you could take a little soup?'

'Aye, perhaps, but then, the last time I tried food, it didn't go too well.' 'Let us try a little and see how we fare.'

When she returned with the soup she helped the man to sit up, but his arms would not support his weight. Nor was he able to recline on his back, and so lying on his side, he tried to use the spoon with a shaking hand. The liquid made it to the skirt of Emma's muslin before he could transport it to his mouth.

'Beg your pardon, miss,' he said, clearly humbled at his incapacity to help himself.

'Compared with the waves you braved at the mouth of the harbour, spilt soup is of no consequence to me,' Emma assured him with a firm smile and a hand that waved away his request for forgiveness.

Then, as he leaned on one elbow, the bowl in both hands, he clasped it to drink thirstily. Some liquid strayed down his chin and Emma wiped it away with a yellowed square of linen. He looked down at himself like a self-conscious boy.

'You were thirsty,' Emma noted.

'Aye, I reckon I was.'

51

His head fell back against the pillow in exhaustion. Even as Emma watched, he closed his eyes and sleep claimed him. While he slept, Emma ladled out more broth for those well enough to take it. Afterward she rolled bandages that had been draped over bushes to dry in the white sunlight, then she walked back to her aunt and uncle's house.

'Someone has been in while we were away, I am certain of that,' her aunt said that evening at the supper table, 'for before I went away there was a neatly stocked cupboard, and yet when I returned, husband, all was in disarray. The dog will have to make do with scraps from the table tonight, because there is no bone for him to have.'

'Who would want to eat a dog bone?' Cousin Phoebe wondered out loud.

'Someone who isn't as well fed as you,' Euphemie said with a snicker. 'Felons,' her mother said, 'or natives, you may be sure.'

Phoebe stared, her eyes wide with the fearful implications. Emma could stay tight-lipped no longer.

'It was me,' Emma admitted. 'I took them. It was to make a broth for the sick in the hospital.'

Everyone stared at Emma. She struggled to explain as Uncle George looked fastidiously to his own plate.

'Primrose will have to do without her bone,' Aunt Adelaide scolded. Emma refrained from personal opinion that the spaniel could quite easily do without a meal or two.

'And do they not feed them, these convicts?' her aunt enquired incredulously.

'Emma has travelled halfway around the world to be here with us, and we can count ourselves honoured that she is willing to lend her hands in healing. If she wants to strengthen the colony with nutritious food so that we are not overrun with maladies, then she is to be thanked.'

Emma's Aunt Adelaide appeared mildly horrified, as though she hardly dared to think of the consequences of a settlement filled with the sick. 'I am at a loss to understand your interest in men's work. I suppose you can be spared to help your uncle George on the morrow, yet do not stand too close to them, Emma. I advise your uncle of the need to keep his distance from them all the time.'

'Which is a hard request my dear, considering that I am a doctor.' Her husband smiled tolerantly, but Aunt Adelaide's thoughts had apparently jumped to something else.

'The reverend's wife has proposed that the ladies of the parish make Christmas gifts for the unfortunates and that includes the poor children of some of the women, as well as those in the infirmary. We have been knitting scarves for months now.' She beamed, pride in her generosity evident in her face. 'It was my idea, you know.'

'Though I daresay, dear, that they may find woollen scarves a little warm in this southern land. There won't be any snow,' her husband said. 'Christmas is only days away.'

'I am aware of that, husband,' she told him reproachfully. 'After all, it is the thought that counts.'

'It is a heartfelt thought, certainly,' Emma's uncle agreed, and turned the conversation. 'We were recently worried that bush fires far to the west, near the Sugar Loaf Mountain were going to engulf us all in smoke,' her uncle told her.

'We thought we'd be sitting in ashes,' Phoebe joined in. 'The sun was like a fire ball and the heavens were covered in smoke as far as the eye could see.'

Aunt Adelaide stood to open the knock at the door. 'Please do come in, Officer Quinn, You are just in time to share dessert.'

'My favourite course,' he told her agreeably. He smiled at Emma. She returned the smile briefly before turning away.

Aunt Adelaide continued the conversation. 'Everything smelled of smoke. There was no escaping it. That was the week before you arrived, Emma dear.'

'And what an arrival,' Euphemie said, as a rare smile twitched the corners of her mouth.

'A long-awaited one,' added Gideon. 'If I may be so bold.' He lifted his glass in salute to the subject of conversation. 'I would like to propose a toast. To new beginnings.'

'Here, here,' Uncle George agreed, lifting his glass. The rest of the family echoed the sentiment.

'While we are on the topic, I wonder if I might have a private word with Miss Colchester concerning our future plans?'

'Why of course,' Aunt Adelaide said. 'Emma, you must so look forward to the building of your house at Wallis Plains, for after all, every young lady dreams of a home of her own.'

Emma blinked, perturbed. She did not relish the thought of moments alone with the king's officer, but felt that she could hardly say as much. Instead, she took up the thread of their earlier conversation and hoped she did not appear rude.

'Uncle, as to work within the hospital, what would you consider to be most helpful to you?'

'I do not know that I am comfortable with the notion of you acting as unpaid help in the hospital,' Gideon said. 'It would not appear seemly.'

'My sentiments exactly,' her aunt agreed, and Emma realised too late that it had not been a wise topic to bring up after all.

'Not only that,' her betrothed continued, 'but it is essentially the task of the female convicts to carry out those duties. Why should you, Emma, stoop to such a thankless task?'

'They may mistake you for one of the women serving a term and shave your head as they do the women convicts.' Euphemie pretended horror at the notion, but Emma was aware that her cousin had little love for her and probably relished the idea.

'Heaven forbid!' Aunt Adelaide cried.

'I think, Euphemie dear,' said her father, 'that you are being a little too dramatic.'

'Emma could never be mistaken for a convict,' Phoebe said. 'She is far too beautiful and kind.'

Gideon bowed his thanks at Phoebe's compliment. He raised his glass in Emma's honour.

'Thank you, Phoebe.' Emma smiled and her aunt and uncle murmured their agreement, but Euphemie, Emma noticed, said nothing. Emma looked at her plate in discomfort and wondered if she had done something to make her cousin feel so disagreeably about her, or whether Euphemie always acted this way towards others.

When Gideon bowed and held out his hand, Emma found herself taking the hand he offered to be led away, with her aunt's encouraging murmurings at her back.

The grey-haired officer had barely closed the adjoining door when he brought Emma's hand to his lips in an ardent outpouring. Emma fought not to turn her head away. Yet if Gideon saw her lack of enthusiasm he did not show it and pressed his mouth damply to her other ungloved hand in turn, before he drew them both to his chest.

'So when is it to be, Emma my dear? Hold me in suspense no longer. Let us make a date for the wedding that will seal our future as husband and wife.'

Emma put her hand to her head in confusion, unable to think, let alone make any decision that would last the rest of her life.

'The last few days have been so very busy, and in truth, I have had little time to contemplate the idea.'

'Yet it is a decided matter, this union, and because I am here we can think on the best time together.'

Her hands remained captured in his clammy ones, and it was with willpower alone that Emma didn't snatch them away to wipe them on her skirt. She struggled to find some way out, yet saw no solution but to relinquish her wishes and begin plans for the wedding day.

'There is yet the house to be started,' she said, in an effort to stall for time.

'There is the beauty of it, my dear, for I have already begun on the plans I had drawn up to show you, and I have workers on the task from dawn until dusk.'

'I see.' Emma's voice was no more than a whisper in the still night. His words, enthusiastic, rushed to meet hers, and she was swamped by dread.

'So I propose one month after Christmas, say, the twenty-sixth of January.'

'But that is not enough time for the house to be made ready, surely.' It was far too soon.

'Rest assured that it will. I will make sure that the job is done.'

Emma nodded in wordless misery.

He grabbed at the response and sealed their decision with a chaste kiss. He smiled when she pushed him away in breathless confusion, and seemed enchanted by her innocence. He clearly intended to hold on to her with all his might.

'I have other good news for you,' Gideon announced. Emma hardly dared to guess. 'There is a trunk just outside the door with your name on it. It was washed up on the beach. It looks sound enough, and you may be able to salvage a few things.'

Emma stood and genuinely smiled for the first time since his arrival. 'Thank you. I had thought it lost.' The thought of something hopeful lightened her heart.

*

As Gideon walked back to the barracks and whistled tunelessly through his teeth, he saw the astuteness in his decision to take to wife a woman as young as Emma. A youthful wife was so much more agreeable to a man, even one in mature years as he was. He could mould her to his needs, and educate her as to his wants.

One thing rankled a little, and that was the dear girl's adamant wish to help in the hospice. For now he would let the foolish notion be—he had the promise he needed—but shortly he would have to nip the idea in the bud, because it simply would not do. Her time would be taken up with him. Let her relish her last days of privacy to play nurse to the infirm and pore over her Bible, or whatever else she did. Her future rested with him, and he was content in that.

*

The petticoat miss's face was the first thing Tobias's eyes alighted on in the morning. As she read from 'The Good Book' to one of the convicts on the other side of the room, the Word did not seem to lift the attitude of grief he saw on her face.

He wondered at it, wanted to ask her what was wrong, but it was none of his business, and nothing could be gained from his curiosity. Still, as she walked softly across the room to where he lay in silent regard, she had a smile for him. Pleasure stirred within him, and the gesture, though small, warmed the emptiness that resided in his heart.

'Good morning, miss.' He was struck by his own gratitude at her being there, yet he had the presence of mind not to show it. His words to his own ears sounded cool. Of this he was glad. There was no place for attachments of the heart here. He knew he would do well to remember it.

'You seem much recovered this morning,' she said.

'Aye, I'll be out of here soon.'

'I am glad of it. You were very ill yesterday.' The warmth in her face made him wonder if he wanted to stay ill or get better faster.

*

Emma was pleased that the convict had improved so much, but at the same time, she would miss him. She quickly cast aside the question whether her reasons for spending time in the hospital were as selfless as she had first thought.

'I forgot to thank you for nursing me yesterday,' the man said, and his thanks gave her pleasure.

'Perhaps you will allow me to read to you from the Bible?' she asked hopefully. If she judged by his face, it seemed a clamp tightened over his heart.

'It's been a long time since I was comforted by words of The Good Book.'

His eyes flashed a challenge, and Emma took a steadying breath of courage.

'Perhaps the load would not be so hard to bear if you knew you have a friend in Jesus.'

'There are no friends to be had in this line of trade, miss.'

'You are mistaken,' Emma said, saddened at the depths of his bitterness.

'Aye, do you think so?'

Emma nodded, filled equally with compassion and dismay.

'Can you not see the blood on my hands?' He stared at his outstretched palms, as if he could see the darkness of his sin.

'If the Lord of heaven and earth can forgive, then so must I.' The words of Isaiah came to Emma. 'I, even I, am He that blotteth out thy transgressions for mine own sake, and will not remember thy sins.'

He stared at her with a look of hope before he turned his head away.

'If you repent …' she began.

'Repent? I don't repent of anything.' He spat the words resentfully, but he did not look at her.

'Our heavenly Father who loves you forgives us much. Now you need to learn to forgive yourself.'

His head snapped around to confront her with a look. Still, he said nothing, and Emma saw that her words pared too close to the bone.

She stood up quietly. She knew he saw the tears of compassion in her eyes, yet he apparently could not bear her mission of mercy, and so she set the Bible on the side of the bed and left without a word.

*

Later that day, Tobias Freeman opened the book, and read the words inscribed inside on the flyleaf.

> *Courage sister, do not stumble,*
> *Though thy path be dark as night,*
> *There's a light that guides the humble,*
> *Trust in God and do the right.*

In the top corner he read her name, Emma Colchester, and after he opened the Bible to the words of the Gospel, he read until all light faded from the sky. He tilted the book to squint this way and that until further efforts shed no light on the pages.

The next morning the sun rose, deceptively gentle on the calm waters, visible a ways outside his window. The sea breeze blew tentatively through the unglazed windows of the hospice, and Tobias ate heartily, as if the breakfast were fried potatoes and black pudding, instead of the same greasy salt beef and coarse bread of every day.

He knew that he would be sent back to work at the foreshore and could only hope that in time he might be allowed to go with the timber cutters to fell the cedars that grew in profusion in the valley. The lumber was sought after for furniture and the like. It would mean a certain amount of freedom from settlement life, and although he might lack the skill, he did possess the strength. He had been told though that natives were in the habit of ambushing the convict timber cutters; that the men had to carry weapons for their own safety. There had been men grievously wounded on more than one occasion, and although this was a sobering thought, the idea of a certain amount of freedom was inviting.

It was with reluctance that he allowed these considerations to push away the thought of the girl with whom he had danced.

Yet he was sure he would remember that evening for the rest of his life. If anyone had told him that the best thing that ever happened to him would take place when he was an exile transported to the colony of New South Wales, he would have laughed at the notion. Yet here he lay and reminisced as though he had waltzed with the girl of his dreams.

He told himself that if he ever had the chance to speak with her again he would address her by name, but now that he knew her as Emma Colchester it didn't help him as he expected it would. When he reminisced about her thoughts of friendship and perhaps of something more entered with it. Still, he knew that could never be. He picked up the holy book as he sat on the edge of the bed and opened the cover, and then ruminated on the freedom of which she spoke.

When he heard the guards' voices, he knew that they had come to enquire about, and then to collect him. They glanced over at him and then back at the doctor as they listed the report. Tobias looked down at the book on the bed, and then after a moment's consideration, slipped it into the waist of his breeches just before he was escorted away.

SIX

Christmas Day blazed with a molten bauble in the sky. The church was packed with humanity, for the most part ill washed, ill-dressed and unpleasant smelling, Emma noted. Only the vast bunches of ruddy blooms seemed to give the congregation a show of true festivity. Mrs Brown optimistically called the shrub 'Christmas Bush', and it was crammed into any vase or pail that had come to hand.

Emma smiled as the children of the few women convicts danced around as if it were the best celebration there ever was. They did not see the humbled souls, the fallen men. All they saw was the festivity in Christmas morning. Emma watched them a while, her heart warm. She looked forward to giving them each a twist of paper holding a few boiled sweets, and as she did, the gospel of Matthew came to mind.

'Whosoever therefore shall humble himself as this little child, the same is the greatest in the kingdom of heaven.'

If it were as easy to have men accept the love of God as it was for the convicts' children, reaching them would be uncomplicated indeed. She prayed for patience to accept these men and women as Jesus would have, by being an example of love.

When she looked behind her as more people filed into the place of worship, Emma's eyes alighted on the convict she had nursed at the hospital. *Perhaps if I did not find his face so charming,* she thought, *I would not have been made to start.* But with a sharp intake of breath, Emma realised he was looking straight at her.

His cool stare arrested her, and he looked, for want of a better word, hungry. He probably was, she considered, and then she blinked as her breast rose and fell in agitation. Emma looked away.

He should not have been staring. Certainly it was rude to stare. A gentleman did not gaze at a young woman for moments at a time. But then, Emma reminded herself, the man behind her was not a gentleman. It wasn't his fault that he had no manners. Staring was nothing to a man like him, she supposed, and yet Emma herself longed to glance back. She toyed with the lace at the neckline of her day gown, impatient for the service to begin, and then remembered that all men were equal, that he had saved her life, and that he knew how to waltz as well as any gentleman.

Temptation ruled her, and Emma glanced back one more time. Now *she* was being rude, for had she not been taught as a child not to sit and gawk as the congregation came to sit in the pews? She looked anyway and tried for cool composure, as if she searched for someone else, but she felt her cheeks flush shamefully. He stared as before, but this time his face held the trace of a smile.

Emma asked herself what ailed her. She questioned her rapid heartbeat and the heat in her cheeks, and wondered at the desire to be hidden behind the Christmas bush and to maintain her inquisitive perusal of the man at her back without anyone noticing.

She turned away to stare studiously at the small panes of glass in front of her and tried to aim a heart of thanks for all she had been given. Emma prayed too for Gideon Quinn. She asked for spirit enough to surrender her will, because every fibre of her being struggled for rebellion against union with him.

Emma looked up to see her affianced slip in beside her and her aunt and cousins. He took her hand without a second thought, it seemed, and Emma averted her glance from the flakes of dander that had fallen from his iron-grey hair to rest on the red wool of his coat. She idly considered that it was probably the only snow that would fall all Christmas Day. Emma reminded herself that careless thoughts such as that were neither kind nor fitting for a young woman about to make a promise of marriage, and nor was bitterness in the lot she had chosen.

'I'd like to invite Officer Gideon Quinn and Miss Emma Colchester to the dais,' she heard Parson Brown say. 'Before the witness of this congregation they forge a bond. By the Church they are blessed, and by their promise they are sanctified.' She asked herself what was worse: making a vow she didn't want to keep, or breaking a promise already made? As the parson took their hands and joined them as one, Emma felt ill.

Emma wished she had the gumption to tell the congregation that she had changed her mind, that her resolve was failing her, and that she did not care about this man. She reminded herself for the umpteenth time that she had made her choice. Nothing, it seemed, would postpone the intentions Gideon had for her life, and Emma swore her commitment to their engagement. He clasped her hand, his eyes fixed upon her, and Emma swallowed uncomfortably, all too aware that the dark-haired convict at the back of the church watched along with everyone else.

Yet if she made a promise to Gideon out of mere duty, rather than love, she knew she was a liar. Did dishonesty make her a felon?

*

Tobias, standing at the back of the congregation, saw the clasped hands of Officer Gideon Quinn and Miss Emma Colchester from behind and was filled with envy.

His fingers twitched with the powerful need to push Quinn off the dais. He knew he had no right, but then, right had very little to do with it.

Whereas, moments ago, his being had thrilled at the sight of Emma Colchester, now the disappointment nearly nauseated him. All he wanted to do was leave the church.

From the first time he had seen her, Tobias had felt the attraction she held for him, and he was equally aware of the fruitlessness of his hope that he could win her.

It was only more suffering he had to endure, and it was of the kind that was hardest to bear. The words of The Good Book had only opened his heart to hurt, it seemed. And if the poor inherited the kingdom of God, then why was it that he, who owned nothing, felt like he was living in hell?

Yet the hope that she would turn and see him as a man, even without those trappings, consumed him. Aye, he knew how foolish it was, but when she appeared before him in his mind's eye, his daytime labour was lighter.

Still, he was lonely at night. The dream would return. Sometimes it was Molly, and other times it was Emma who needed his protection. Then day would dawn again to the fact that no matter how strong his frame, he wasn't at liberty to shield anyone, certainly not Emma Colchester.

*

After the service Emma waited as the worshippers at the front of the church filed out first. The convict turned to look at her; she saw him in the periphery of her vision, but Emma kept her head averted.

She knew that Gideon was no fool. It would not take him long to figure out that the convict had been the one masquerading as the commandant and that she shielded him for reasons wholly unacceptable for a young woman engaged to be wed. If it were his decision, the convict would be given up to the noose at the slightest provocation.

Out in the sunshine, the children took the sweets with wide-eyed pleasure as Emma handed them out. They rewarded her with smiles that lit up their bronzed, freckled faces, and laughed with undaunted enthusiasm before they ran to climb up the boughs of ancient coastal banksia trees. She watched the girls collect the cylindrical seedpods and pretend they were dolls. A tiny child wrapped her 'baby' in the sweet paper with small sticky fingers and brushed away the fine hair that clung to her sugary cheeks.

Yet it was the convicts, forced to stand in ragged lines of apathy as they were doled out the ludicrous scarves, that Emma felt for the most. Their overseers ordered them to voice their thanks for their gifts. Their mumbled words were given in a monotone of surly indifference.

'I can honestly say that I have never seen a more disagreeable lot of individuals,' Emma heard her aunt say to the reverend's wife. 'I think that next year we shall instead give something only to the children.'

'I am sure they were grateful even though some of them did not appear so,' the lady said.

'I suppose that we should not expect them to know how to behave in society. Doubtless they were never taught any manners. Now when I was a girl …'

'Yet we do not give to the convicts to gratify ourselves,' Emma reminded her aunt. 'If their show of appreciation is not all we would have them display, then perhaps we need to question our own motives for giving the gifts.'

With her words of criticism Emma gave full vent to her irritation. It wasn't lost on her aunt. The woman was so angry she stormed away. Now Emma had to give out the useless woollen scarves to the convicts with the reverend's wife, and this punishment proved more effective than any retort that Aunt Adelaide might have given her. Emma felt so foolish.

'It seems that we miscounted the number of mufflers we would need, Miss Colchester dear, because a dozen still have no gifts, and only one article remains to be given.' But this task was made easy, because the men, when they heard this, walked away without too much disappointment at all. 'Would you like it?' the reverend's lady asked the older man Emma had met first at the hospice.

'Well, missus, it's like this: if I don't have any shoes, there's not much point getting dollied up in a scarf.' He chuckled and Emma smiled at his quip.

'But this fellah here,' he added with a gesture to the Irish giant from the brig, 'he'd like nothing better than a soft piece of knitting from the young lady.'

Emma's mouth parted in shock. The black-haired convict called Freeman stared down his talkative friend and the reverend's wife clucked, although whether from displeasure or otherwise, Emma wasn't sure. In any case, the lady handed the muffler to Emma, who had no choice but to smile and offer it to him.

As she handled the article, which was small, narrow, shoddily knitted and inadequate for the neck of anyone above the age of five the man took it as invitation to step forward.

'Commandant Morisset has your Bible,' he said.

Emma looked at him stupidly. 'A very merry Christmas to you, too.'

He blinked at her, as though uncomprehending, then tried again.

'I said the commandant still has your Bible.' He looked at her meaningfully, and the penny finally dropped.

'He may keep it,' she assured him, 'if he thinks it will be of aid.'

'Yet you will have none to read yourself.' He frowned.

'It was given as a gift.' Her face searched his in all seriousness.

'Then it will be accepted as such.'

'I am content in that,' Emma told him with a small smile. He almost returned it, but then seemed to think the better of it, and nodding his leave, walked away.

Emma turned to see the vicar's lady standing beside her once more.

'The commandant has your Bible?' Mrs Brown blinked and

fanned herself in the heat.

'It's of no consequence.'

'My husband expects some articles when the ship comes into port, and I am sure, Emma dear, that he will have a Bible for you. One good turn deserves another.'

'Thank you. I would appreciate that.'

The woman looked down at Emma's hands, which still held the muffler.

'You didn't give him the scarf.'

'How forgetful of me.' Emma shook her head and wondered what on earth she had been thinking. But that had been the problem. When he stood before her, she hadn't thought of much else at all.

'You can catch him up, dear.'

'Oh, I couldn't possibly do that.'

'Why ever not, Emma dear? It will be of no use to either of us.'

Emma looked at the vista from Prospect Hill: the wattle and daub huts with their whitewashed walls, the similarly coloured picket fences like so many soldiers, and forward and beyond to the cool sea water that beckoned, deceptively calm as it lapped the sandy shore.

'You may keep your clothing on, madam, but you will drown in your good manners.'

'Of course, you are correct. If you are sure that no one will mind me doing so?'

Her fiancé chose that moment to join them, and the reverend's wife told him what Emma had forgotten to do.

'On no account must you chase after the convict, my dear Emma. Give the gift to me and I will take it to him presently.' Emma passed it to him, both relieved and disappointed that she would not get a chance to speak with the man again. With a courtly bow the officer strode from them with the scarf in hand.

Emma left Mrs Brown and walked in the breezy sunshine down

to her uncle's cottage. She expected her aunt to be in an ill humour, but thankfully she was too preoccupied in advising the maid on the best way to cover the roast mutton so that it wasn't 'blown' by flies.

When she spied the potatoes and onions that went with the meat perfectly roasted in the drippings, Emma realised then how heartily sick of salt beef and salt pork she had grown. Dried peas had been soaked overnight, and a wonderfully sweet-smelling pease pudding filled the basin to its brim. A large jug of ale made with hops and malt sat on the table, and in the parlour a huge pot of Christmas Bush graced the room.

'We may not be in England now, my dear, but it is Christmas Day even so, and make merry we shall,' Uncle George said as he poured a tankard of ginger beer that overflowed onto the lace cloth. It was like the water that foamed cold against the shore.

'You either chose life, or a watery grave.'

Emma watched her aunt fuss over the spilled beer and was momentarily washed back to the moments in the harbour. She could almost taste the briny water as it burned her throat, smell the salt of the waves, and hear the cries of the men on the clipper. She realised then that she held her breath and took a draught of ginger beer as her aunt passed it to her. She drank deeply to quench her parched throat.

'How strange it seems not to wonder if we will have snow,' Emma breathed.

'I despise it,' Euphemie said.

'The snow?' Emma asked.

'No, the heat.'

'And I perspire so.' Phoebe fanned her face and rolled her eyes.

'Still, it gets hotter than this, does it not, ladies?' their father asked as he prepared to carve the mutton with zeal. His eyes shone with anticipation at the fresh-roasted meat. Both girls groaned at the thought of hotter days to come, and Emma knew they secretly wished their mother would permit them to wade in the water without stockings or boots. They longed for the waves to smack against their calves as they gasped at the pleasure of it. At that moment a waft of sea air drifted in through the open window. All the women sighed. Emma was glad of the breeze to cool the cottage, made more unpleasantly warm because of the morning's cooking in the kitchen adjoining the little house.

'I have asked Officer Quinn to lunch with us today,' Emma's uncle announced, and she felt herself wilt at the knowledge. Still, he was her betrothed, and all of the colony could attest to the fact.

As though aware of her reticence, Uncle George poured Emma another draught of ginger beer, and she drank it in a gulp without thought, then coughed and spluttered as it burned her throat.

Aunt Adelaide passed her a napkin. 'A lady never quaffs her ale at a gulp.'

Emma flushed. She had never had ale in her life, and she already sensed that the sweet, hot ginger beer was as heady as any she could care to drink. Had she known the drink was intoxicating, she would have not had a drop, putting down the cup with resolution.

*

Gideon made his way along the foreshore from the barracks. His iron-grey hair was slick with pomade, his red coat bright as a cut and his brass buttons in full gleam.

Normally he would disdain to walk along the sand. It clung to the boots and the seawater dulled the sheen, but today, even though it was Christmas, and even though the surgeon had invited him to lunch with them, he ignored it. As he walked he undid one or two buttons to pull from his coat a scrap of knitting, badly worked and desperately plain. He threw it into the outbound tide without a backward glance. It floated on the sea like a bobbing seagull as he strode away.

*

Emma wondered idly, as she covered yawns after luncheon, whether the convicts had any more variety to their midday meal on Christmas Day. Their own meal was not finished yet, and Emma wondered how hard it had been for Aunt Adelaide to procure the fruit for the plum pudding. Emma knew there had been no milk available for custard, but Aunt Adelaide had made do with flour, which was at least plentiful, and had concocted a sweet blancmange. Emma thought it the best thing she had eaten since she had left home. The whole household then sat in the small parlour.

'This, my dear Emma, is for you,' Gideon said, his voice softly familiar as he handed Emma his Christmas gift.

Emma untied the string, and then the brown paper it was wrapped in, as tentatively as if the gift were a snake. But the thing felt weighty, and of course, did not move at all but sat steadfast and heavy in her lap.

'Oh, Emma, how beautiful,' Phoebe whispered at her shoulder, looking on in rapture.

'Aren't we the lucky one?' Euphemie said sarcastically, even though Emma caught her look of unreserved admiration, for the trousseau was everything a young woman should care to have. Tablecloths, tea towels, napkins, a set of linen sheets and pillowcases, and last but not least, the more intimate apparel that forced Emma to blush; corset, chemise, petticoat, nightgown and bloomers.

'The finest linen to be had from Ireland,' Gideon told her. Emma could not help but finger the finery in pleasure. Though the items were pleasant to look upon, she did not relish the thought of when they would be worn. She folded them with quiet ceremony.

'Not a thing has been forgotten,' she said, and she admitted to herself that his taste was impeccable. She knew she would not be left wanting when it came to her nuptials and marriage thereafter. If it had been another man, a man of her choosing, there would have been no doubt to cloud her smile. *'Now lie back against me, and kick like fury else we're lost.'*

She felt as if she were floundering still, and struggled to put a smile on her face, though she felt nothing save the fear of drowning. 'Emma dear, are you well?' Aunt Adelaide asked.

Emma took a deep breath and nodded with her sunny smile. 'I am overwhelmed.' She meant it. Yet she hoped only she was aware of the double entendre. The others chuckled. Gideon preened. But all that Emma could think of was the duplicity of which she had been a victim.

'Merry Christmas dear,' Gideon said.

For the life of her, she could not answer him back. If she opened her mouth she feared she would burst into tears.

'I must away,' he said to the company, 'for the convicts will be rowdy this evening, and I must be there to nip trouble in the bud should it arise.'

When the door closed on his departure, Emma sighed in relief.

'Shall we walk on the beach, Emma?' Phoebe asked after a nap in the sultry warmth of their shared room.

'I shall stay and read,' Euphemie said with a yawn before she curled into a corner chair.

'Girls, you should stay indoors. You heard what Officer Quinn said. There could be unrest in the colony this evening,' Aunt Adelaide said.

'Rest easy dear.' Emma's uncle calmed his wife as he looked up from a newspaper that had been read and re-read, a paper which told events that had happened in England six months previously.

'After all, mother,' Phoebe said, 'it is daylight yet, even though it is almost now time for supper. We shan't be gone long, and after such a delightful Christmas luncheon, however are we to get up an

71

appetite for supper if we do not stretch our legs?'

Emma's aunt smiled at the compliment.

'I thought you were always hungry, Phoebe.' Euphemie smiled sourly as she looked up from her book. Phoebe looked a little crestfallen but chose not to respond.

Emma was not disappointed that Euphemie was content with her own company, and she, for one, looked forward to only her cousin Phoebe's.

The setting sun lit the shore. It gleamed off the water like a yellow topaz. Emma felt a breeze tussle the soft ringlets that framed her face and neck, and in the distance she could hear the sounds of native song, accompanied by the clack of hardwood sticks. It was music foreign to both of them as it rose and fell with the incoming waves. The natives had a campfire burning, Emma could see, and it shimmied as sinuously as the body of the dark dancing girl visible through the mangrove trees.

'I have gooseflesh all over my body,' Phoebe breathed. She sounded excited by the faraway snatch of song.

'I do not know what to think of this strange and beautiful place,' Emma said. She had been beached, as it were, on some island, primitive, beautiful, and dangerous.

Closer still, an Irish bodhran struck a rhythm for dancing, followed by the notes of a tin whistle, quick and lively, and it set their feet to faster motion as they followed the music's melody.

The many Irish men and women danced with their hands at their sides, their feet alone sang the pleasure, while the handful of Scots danced with arms up flung and stepped the quadrants of some imaginary sword. To Emma, their hearts seemed left behind with ancestors across the leagues of the ocean.

'Have we stepped into a fairy ring, do you think Emma?' Phoebe said, clearly enchanted. 'I feel as though, if I set my feet to dancing, I will never be able to stop.'

'You and I both,' Emma agreed.

A campfire burned. The light shone on the faces of the dancers slicked with sweat. One or two groups of aimless redcoats looked on, derision written on their faces. Yet even still, a couple of soldiers were not above flirting with the convict women, and Emma heard that if it wasn't for Christmas Day falling on a Saturday, the commandant wouldn't be turning a blind eye to the holiday spirit.

'Curfew in half an hour,' one of them said. 'I'm sick of watching their shenanigans.'

'That's the problem with the Irish,' his companion said, 'they can't shut their mouths and they won't stop their feet.' The soldier smiled as the others laughed at his quip. Emma knew people said that the Irish were as keen to exercise their tongues as they were to dance.

'Did you hear about the two on the cutter whose water ration was stopped?' Emma heard another one of the redcoats say. 'They died drinking their own pee.'

'They probably thought it was whiskey.' Another raucous laugh, and as the melody momentarily stopped, a laughing Kookaburra joined in from up high.

Emma gave Phoebe a meaningful look and took her hand, then they moved away from the foul-speaking soldiers, whose sole entertainment for the evening seemed to be the denigration of the Irish.

'Would you say it is true, do you think?' Phoebe screwed up her face in distaste.

'I suppose any of us, if we were thirsty enough, would do the same thing.'

'I would rather die first.'

'Let us be thankful that we are not, and probably never shall be, in such a terrible situation,' Emma said.

Phoebe nodded wholeheartedly.

73

'Have you come to see your china plate?' The unexpected voice startled them. Emma turned to find the old convict she had ministered to in the hospital. Emma glanced at Phoebe and both blinked without understanding.

'I beg your pardon? I'm sorry, but I think I missed what you said,' Emma replied, her brow wrinkled in confusion.

'I asked if you'd come to see your mate?'

Emma flushed, with sudden full understanding of what he meant.

'We heard the music and came to see the dancing.'

'Not much fun in looking when you can be doing.' He chuckled. 'But perhaps you'd rather be dancing with your old aunt.' Phoebe looked indignant and was about to flounce away. Emma stayed her with a restraining hand.

'My aunt?' Emma asked, perplexed.

'The commandant.' The bandy-legged Cockney looked up at her and winked before he walked off.

'What a singular man,' Emma said, almost to herself, as a humorous smile touched her lips. This time Phoebe looked perplexed, but directed her look at Emma.

'He spoke as though you were his *china plate*,' Phoebe stated.

Emma looked at her and both girls broke into laughter.

'What do you think they are eating over there?' her cousin asked, never able to forget the needs of her stomach for long.

'I can't tell, but it smells like scones.'

Phoebe's expression seemed to melt at the pleasure of the thought. 'Oh, how I long for a cream tea.'

Emma smiled. 'I am not sure that the convicts are rationed with jam and cream.' Phoebe put her hand over her mouth to stifle a giggle as the black-haired convict walked towards them. 'Hush,' Emma whispered, hardly knowing where to look.

The man had singled them out in the crowd and strode

purposefully to where they stood. His gaze measured the distance. Two soldiers watched him as he passed. He looked past them as though they weren't there.

Emma felt her face flush. He nodded at both young women in turn, Phoebe, then Emma, before his eyes rested on hers.

'Kevin said you were after staying for supper.'

'He did?' Emma scanned the faces in the crowd, but the matchmaker had gone.

'Aye, he did.' He stood unsmiling as he waited for her response. She was tongue-tied and had none.

'So what are we having for supper?' Phoebe asked, ignoring Emma's pointed look, and the direct stares of the soldiers who dogged the convicts' every move, 'Kangaroo and damper. The fresh meat was worth the trade.'

'You and the natives are friendly towards each other?' Emma said, unable to keep the interest from her voice.

'No, but a few of the lads traded their scarves. It seemed like a good idea at the time.' He looked apologetic and Emma bit her lip and tried not to smile.

'Is damper anything like a scone?' Phoebe said.

Then he did smile and showed teeth as white as sea-washed shells. 'I believe it is.'

SEVEN

The men took the damper from the coals with as much reverence as a Christmas pudding, Emma thought, even though it had been shoved among the ashes and could not have looked much worse. Someone tapped on it and listened. It sounded hollow. She noticed a few smiles at this, and it seemed that this was a good thing. Taken from the fire and broken into pieces, it would taste indeed much like a hot scone, she decided.

The kangaroo was similarly praised, and was every bit as black. Emma and Phoebe looked on from a short distance away, watching as the meat was uncovered from the depths of the smouldering coals, and wondered how long it had cooked, because it broke apart at the touch, bone and steaming meat exposed. The men gave it a generous handful of salt, and hoed into it with hands as grimy as any Emma had ever seen.

'Would you like some?' the younger convict asked the girls.

'That's generous, but we will have supper when we return home,' Emma said, sure that the handful of ravenous faces that looked up were not disappointed. The man nodded.

Emma was all too cognisant of the social impropriety of them being in the company of convicts. She was sure that if Phoebe's mother and father were aware of the company they were mingling with, they would be greatly displeased. She was uncomfortable being there, and yet she wanted to linger still

'You can't say no to a cup of sweet tea and damper, ladies, surely?' Kevin walked over and offered a drink to them, hot and steaming, before Emma could think to say no. Phoebe bit her lip thoughtfully, glancing at Emma. Then she shrugged and dunked the bread into the sweet black tea. 'I like it,' she declared. But neither Emma nor Phoebe was inclined to sit among the convicts, and stood apart, surveyed with suspicion by the indentured men and women, and looked on in surprise by the soldiers.

A small group of women, with heads of hair as short and spiked as the long-tongued echidnas, were not so placid. Emma suspected the women saw her and Phoebe as 'gentry', and the two received no smiles of welcome, dressed as they were in their light muslin dresses, their long hair coiled with care. Emma understood their dislike and felt compassion for them.

The convict stood with his back to the female convicts, and she thought that perhaps he too was aware of their animosity towards her and Phoebe. The stares of the redcoats dogged their every move as well. For two young women to engage in conversation with those who would be considered colonial riff raff was hardly the done thing. But Kevin appeared not to give a fig and kept up a steady flow of chatter. For this Emma was glad, because the giant with the black hair had a face far too charming and she could not, for the life of her, stop her gaze from lingering on those eyes.

Then Emma heard the sound of the bodhran again, and inexplicable though it was, she wanted to dance with the man beside her and did not care who saw her. Pixie ring indeed, she thought ruefully. And he seemed to know it just as surely as if her toes tapped the rhythm beneath the hem of her dress. For he didn't ask for her hand, shameful, ungentle behaviour that it was, but put down her empty cup and grasped her hands, and she danced with him like a hoyden in the dusk. Phoebe looked on, hands pressed against her cheeks as though she flushed shamefully for Emma's indelicate behaviour, even if Emma did not.

'You have not yet told me your name.' Emma smiled as he spun her round and round.

'Nor have you told me yours, miss, though I know it all the same,' he said with quiet confidence.

'You have the upper hand, sir. Yet though you prudently call me "miss" in one breath, you twirl me with abandon in another.' She was forthright this evening, and wondered at herself. 'If you knew it, you would address me as such, would you not? Do you tease me?'

'Perhaps I do,' was his enigmatic response.

Emma frowned, unable to comprehend his meaning at all.

'I cannot dance with a gentleman on the green without knowing his name,' she insisted on a whisper, as though it were a sin.

He considered her and then let go of her hands. 'My name is Tobias Freeman.'

'Why do I feel as though you did not want to tell me your name, yet you carried me through the waves against your shoulders and took my hands and pulled me into the dance?'

He seemed inclined to ignore the question, but she waited still.

He finally spoke. 'Because when I lie awake in the middle of the night, it will do me no favours to imagine you whispering my name.'

Emma's mouth formed a small circle of surprise then parted in shock at his words.

'And that is nothing I should tell any lady, is it now, miss?'

'I don't suppose it is.' She turned and saw Phoebe, who had let down her guarded misgivings it seemed, and danced with one of the redcoats, a youth with a flash of carroty hair. 'But still, is that so bad a thing?' she asked.

'Aye, it is, because it is all I can ever have of you, when I would do more than give you my name on your lips.'

Emma blinked, shocked. When Kevin stepped in to take a turn with her, she was glad, as she felt embarrassed by the dark-haired convict's assertion.

'I hope you've washed your hands, Kevin.' Tobias winked. Kevin squared his shoulders in mock offence, but when he turned back to face Emma he grinned and wiped his grubby hands on the legs of his breeches.

'I'm pretty light on me feet, don't you think, miss? Better than that big oaf before me. Still, he does show some potential. Now, what I'm trying to figure out is whether he's in love with you, you're in love with him, or whether it's both of you that have been bitten.'

'I cannot care for him. I am betrothed to another, as well you know, and even were I not; our social situations are so different …' She let her voice trail away.

'You're saying he's not good enough for you?' Kevin sounded offended. She hardly knew what to say.

'Newcastle is for second offenders. Who knows what is in his past? I grant you, he is more than comely, and yes I am drawn to him, but how to respect someone with so much violence in his past, much less entertain thoughts of a shared future friendship?'

Kevin dropped her hands, as though *she* were the off-cast of society.

'Well, I'll let you in on a secret, for what it's worth. He ought never to have been convicted to begin with, and at Sydney Cove, he took the blame for another bloke who stole bread for his young family with hardly a penny to see them through from one day to the next. Said the man had more to lose, since he had a family and all that. Not many men I know would do what he did. Does that officer of yours show the mettle of a man like young Toby? I wonder.'

Emma gasped and spun away, then lifted her skirt a little as she walked away to hide her emotions. Then she ran, the prick of tears in her eyes.

'Emma?' Phoebe called as she followed in her wake. 'Emma, what's the matter that you ran off like that?'

'I cannot say, Phoebe.' Emma shook her head. 'Please, don't press right now.'

'Of course not.' Phoebe reassured her as she took hold of her cousin's hand, and they spoke no more about it as the sun sank into the ocean and covered their voices with the night.

When she prepared for bed that evening, Emma wondered what kind of man took another's punishment on his own shoulders for the sake of someone else's children.

She had been shocked at Tobias Freeman's confession, that he would openly tell her his feelings. She had thought him to be uncouth and raw. Then Kevin had put the man into perspective. She saw her arrogance for what it was. But why she had stood outside and cried beneath the stars, she did not care to analyse, because how she felt would not make an ounce of difference anyway.

Both men had been as blunt as old spades, and Emma wondered if any sly rum had been obtained. There were illicit stills to be found, and apparently there were those within the ranks not averse to selling convicts and free settlers watered down alcohol, or grog, as they called it. Not all the convicts were without money. Some traded where they could, or worked extra hours for pay. The wet barracks might be set aside for army personnel, but it seemed that there were other ways to obtain liquor in the colony, for all that Newcastle was a harsh place, and its discipline more so.

Phoebe's voice intruded in on Emma's thoughts. 'Will you look at all the laces Mama has in her trunk tomorrow, Emma, so that we can begin to plan your wedding gown?' Phoebe asked.

Emma blinked, puffy eyed in the darkness. 'Soon, Phoebe, soon.' She stared a moment at the moon in the black southern sky and wondered if they were still dancing above the surf, and then realised that they would have gone in now after curfew sounded. She also wanted to know if he was lying in bed and thinking about her.

*

'What did you say to Miss Colchester to make her run off like that?' Tobias asked, mild challenge in his voice.

Kevin set his jaw. 'Just a few home truths that fancy miss of yours needed to know.'

'Don't call her that.'

Kevin looked taken aback. 'So it's like that now, is it?'

'Like what? It's not like anything at all.'

'You Irish are so testy. You need a thicker skin, Toby, mate.'

'Aye, that's true and all.'

'She's got in deep.' Kevin nodded knowingly.

'What?' Tobias frowned, not sure if he knew what Kevin was going on about.

'Your … I mean, the young miss. She's knocked you fair and square in the breadbasket.'

Tobias wondered why the Londoner didn't just say what he meant. But all the same, he knew.

'What do they call you?'

'Nothing you'd like to hear repeated.'

He was condemned for the term of his natural life, and nothing short of a miracle would change that, no matter what he hoped or prayed to the contrary.

Kevin said nothing more about the matter.

'Well, I am off to bed,' Kevin said, his tone a little miffed. Tobias suspected it was because the man had stuck up for him somehow, and thought all Tobias cared about was the surgeon's niece, a woman who probably looked down on him. 'Goodnight Kevin.'

Tobias sat at the table bowed over the small Bible. The tallow candle burned low, and Tobias had to tilt the book this way and that to catch all the words before him.

81

'I am the light of the world: he that followeth me shall not walk in darkness, but shall have the light of life,' he read.

He peered at the scripture again. John, chapter eight, verse twelve.

How hard it was to trust when the days and years spread out before him would be filled with captivity. Harder still not to think of the petticoat miss, with eyes like none he had seen before.

'Oh, Emma,' he whispered, with no one to hear him except Kevin, whose steady snore rose and fell like the waves that lapped against the shore. The candle gutted and extinguished, and left a warm pool of cooling wax on the stand. Tobias sank further onto his arms in restful sleep at the table.

He was startled awake when the door hit the cottage wall with a bang. Kevin and he had missed roll call.

'What do you think it is, Christmas? Get up and get out for roll call!'

'As soon as I've used the chamber pot,' Tobias told the soldier while he slid the Bible away before it could be seen.

'I said now!' The redcoat was irate.

'We're coming, we're coming.' Kevin stifled a yawn, stumbled bandy-legged out of the hut, and pulled down a hat over his head as he went.

It was stinking hot in the morning light, warmth which promised a long, dry summer, and Tobias was glad of the cover of his shirt as it fluttered in the wind and stopped the fierce sun from burning his back. He hoped that the heat didn't get worse than this. His breeches pulled snug against the muscles of his thighs, and the woollen hose prickled his shins. He stood in the blaze and waited to hear his name.

'You missed out on the dancing last night, Quinn,' Tobias heard one of the young soldiers jibe.

'What dancing?' the officer asked.

'Some of the convicts had a bit of a jig. That young lady of yours was down here as well. Spinning like a top, she was.'

'Are you speaking of Miss Colchester?' Quinn said, his ire ignited.

'Don't know what she's called, but it was your girl all right.'

Tobias turned to glance at the redheaded soldier from the evening before. He had twirled Emma's plump cousin on the rise of the hill at sundown. The same young man now looked on at the interaction and then back at Tobias. Tobias wondered where the conversation was headed.

'And who was she dancing with?' Quinn said. 'She was never dancing with a convict, surely?'

'It would appear that Miss Colchester is not averse to giving her dancing card to the government men,' the commandant noted, and Tobias thought that Quinn would explode, his face grew so red.

'My apologies; I meant nothing more than a jest.' The commandant smiled wryly.

'Harming the reputation of my affianced is no jesting matter to me. And have you considered sir, that the individual with whom she danced may well be one and the same individual who battered you at the parsonage the other evening?'

This apparently gave the commandant pause for thought.

'It was him.' The loudmouthed young soldier broke in again as he pointed at Tobias.

The roll had not even been called and now every face turned to Tobias where he stood, unable to hide.

If he admitted to dancing with Emma Colchester, he put her in the path of ridicule. If he confessed to dancing with her at the parsonage, he might well get Kevin involved, and he was not prepared to do that. Yet if he denied that he had done anything of the sort, he was a liar and did not even have the dignity of an honest man, never mind a free one.

'I can vouch that it wasn't him,' The copper-haired officer told the commandant.

'You can?'

'Aye, Commandant, I can, because it was me who was taking a twirl with Miss Colchester's cousin, so sir, I think I would know.'

'Are you sure about that?' Quinn demanded. 'Look at him closely. You! Take off your hat.'

Tobias did as he was bid. His hair fell dark and heavy down to his nape. He brushed it back from his face with his hand.

The soldier appeared to consider him and squinted this way and that.

'I'm not mistaken sir. He isn't the one.'

Tobias noted that a few of the convicts who stood around looked unsure, but none ratted him. No one was about to take Quinn's side over one of their own.

'I will go and get Miss Colchester,' Quinn said, 'for if anyone ought to be asked their opinion, it's her.'

The commandant held up his hand. 'Officer Quinn, I do not think that Miss Colchester would thank us for waking her from sleep, only to question her integrity before all these men and women, do you?'

Gideon pursed his lips; his anger clearly simmered even still. 'You are right, Commandant, but you had the clothes stripped from your back just the other night, and if it is indeed the same person ...'

The commandant nodded thoughtfully. 'I understand what you are saying, officer, but Miss Colchester has already been in front of a line up, and she could not find the man responsible for the act. I hardly want to put her through it again. Surely you see that I am thinking of the young lady's name?'

'Of course sir,' Quinn agreed. Yet from the tone of the elder man's voice, it seemed that it was the commandant who had Emma's reputation at heart, Tobias decided, not Gideon Quinn.

The roll was finally called and the men and women of the colony went about their daily tasks. Tobias pushed the woollen hat back down upon his head as the red-haired officer strode past.

'God bless Ireland,' Tobias heard him say quietly with the hint of a brogue. He looked up, squinted thoughtfully, and wondered if he had in fact seen the soldier wink as he walked away.

The bells tolled the start of a new day. They sounded in the morning for work to begin, and then in the late afternoon for the workers to finish. Their iron voices proclaimed the beginning of toil or the end of it, the time for meals, the Sabbath day, or the news of yet another death. Tobias heard it and it felt like a yoke about his neck as he trudged to the constable to be given his orders.

'You are to go to Limeburners' Bay,' Tobias was told, and he wondered what on earth that was.

Kevin looked at him with compassion. 'If you're lucky you won't get more than two weeks. It was because you danced with *her*, the young miss. That's why they're sending you there. He doesn't believe it wasn't you, regardless of what the blood nut said in your favour. If you hadn't been seen dancing ...'

'And I'd do it again Kevin, never fear but that I would.'

The old convict looked at him as though he felt sorry for him. 'But still ...' Kevin shook his head, much like a father who worries for his son.

'I did nothing wrong.'

'You clapped your meat pies on his girl, and he knows it, for sure.'

The Cockney said some funny things, half of them indecipherable, but eyes rhymed with pies, so Tobias guessed that must be it.

He frowned at Kevin's back, as the man hurried away before one of the constables saw him. For if anyone was found unemployed after the bell had sounded, it would mean twenty-five lashes with the cat o' nine tails.

'I cannot dance with a gentleman on the green without knowing his name.'

Aye, he had his eye on a woman who could never be his; yet for all his common sense in knowing it, it made not a jot of difference.

In the morning he would go the lime-burners' camp, and who knew when he would return, if ever, for there was no one who cared for him. He felt powerless.

Humble yourselves, therefore, under the mighty hand of God, that he may exalt you in due time. Casting all your care upon him, for he careth for you.

Yet if this were true, why did he feel so alone? Still, he hung on to those words he had read, for he felt it was the only hope he had. So as he passed the day at labour in the heat, Tobias repeated those words, for they somehow served like a comfort he could not explain.

As the men rested on their pallets that evening after the nine o'clock curfew, Tobias stared up at the ceiling.

'Be sure to be careful when you're at the lime-burners' camp,' Kevin said.

'It's not a place that folk go to take the water then, is it?'

'No, mate, it's not. I heard the overseer killed a bloke with a hand-pike and wasn't even charged for the crime. Your life is worthless here, mate and the only one who cares about it is *you*.'

'And here I was thinking that you were going to sing me to sleep with your tears.' Tobias smiled wryly. 'Thanks Kevin, I'll be sure to remember your advice.'

'One good thing though, and it's this: you get vegetables twice a week, I'm told, and that's twice more in a week than we get here.'

Tobias went quiet as he considered the days. 'She won't know where I ever went.'

'Limeburners' Bay isn't paradise, but I didn't say it was purgatory, either.' Tobias offered no reply.

Kevin continued, 'Go and tell her, then.'

'Eventually she will be Quinn's wife,' he said, by way of defence.

'Is that why she comes running whenever you crook your little finger?' Kevin asked slyly. Tobias scoffed.

'It's true.'

'Are you asking me to dance?'

'Sure, and she's going to want me to throw rocks at her window at night just to let her know I might not be around town for a while.'

'You don't know if you don't go and find out.'

'It's past curfew.'

'And you leave after first light.'

'She may not even know I'm gone, man.'

Now Tobias heard Kevin scoff. 'You don't believe that any more that I do. I might be old, but I think my eyes still see pretty well, and I've seen the way she stares at you.'

'Like what?' Tobias asked, intrigued.

'Like you were ... I don't know ... a plate of jellied eels.'

Tobias pulled a face. 'Is that appetising?'

'It's the best, mate.'

'Nothing else springs to mind?' 'Pie and mushy peas.' Kevin grinned.

Tobias smiled with a nod of challenge. 'Leg of mutton?' Both men laughed into the darkness of the cottage. 'Black pudding? Potato cakes?'

'Now you're talking! So what are you waiting for?'

'A good square meal, I'm thinking.'

'That's not going to happen anytime soon.'

'Letting the lass know I'm up to my neck in love with her isn't going to make her run after me down the aisle, either.' His heart sank.

'Why not, I'd like to know? Government men have been given permission to wed before now.'

'Aye, but she's no convict now, is she? I'd have to be in the horrors to even consider such a notion.' 'We're in the horrors now, aren't we?' 'I mean that it'd take more than a tipple of rum to make me think any such thing.'

'So you don't want to go and see her now?'

'Aye, of course I do.' The man was frustrating him.

'Well, come on then, mate. What are we waiting for?'

In spite of himself, Tobias smiled at Kevin's enthusiasm. 'Miss the night life of London, do you?'

Kevin chuckled. Yet Tobias glanced out the window, surprised he would even consider a tryst with Emma. They hurried out in silence.

The sky was black and the clouds hid the moon, and for that Toby was thankful, suddenly hopeful that any constables who were at their posts were fast asleep.

'There are only two windows on this side and two windows on the other,' Tobias whispered when they reached the house. 'How are we supposed to know which window is the one?'

Kevin blinked at him as though he were stupid. 'We look, of course.'

'The house appears to be dark.'

'Here, give me a leg up so I can see.'

'What were you convicted for, anyway?' Kevin turned around with a grin. 'Peeping Tom'.

Tobias looked heavenward and shook his head. 'So you do this kind of thing for fun. And what am I supposed to do; I'd like to know? Whisper her name?'

'Exactly. Tell her it's the commandant.'

Tobias sighed but lifted the man up. 'I can't believe I'm out here with your backside in my face, when I could be fast asleep by now.'

'Shush, here comes someone with a candle.' Tobias looked up, listened, and waited. 'Would you Adam and Eve it?'

'What?' Couldn't the man just say what he meant?

'It's her!' And then Kevin frantically waved at the window.

Tobias heard her drop the candle. Nothing happened. Then a dog stirred within and Kevin cursed.

'Blimey, there's a pan licker inside.'

Tobias let down the skinny Cockney, who was becoming heavy

anyway, and spoke softly but clearly in the voice of an Englishman, as he told her it was the commandant. Then she appeared in the window, her anxious face pale as the moon, before leaving the house and passing around into the garden to meet him.

Kevin had crept around the other side to keep watch in the shadows, probably enjoying himself like nobody's business, Tobias concluded. Here he had been concerned for the man's safety.

When Emma turned the corner, she gasped, regardless of the fact that she knew he would be there. She held the dog in her arms. She hushed it, calling it Primrose, and set the animal down. Primrose sniffed at Tobias and cocked his leg in dismissal, aiming at the shrubs nearby.

Tobias took hold of Emma's arms in a gentle grasp. As he looked down at her, he could not help but notice that she was ready for bed and head to toe in fine linen. Her unpinned hair curled around her shoulders and down to her waist, and he forgot for a moment why he was there, except to look at her.

Neither of them spoke for some time. When Tobias realised that he was in fact gently rubbing her arms from shoulder to elbow, he moved his hands away as if burnt.

'What is it, Tobias?' she whispered.

He pulled her gently to him, desperate to hold her in his arms. She did not pull away. He kissed her hair then and her brow, before he could stop himself, and then, to his wonder, she didn't push him away.

He didn't notice how long he held her. He didn't count how many times she rose on the tips of her toes to accept his kiss. He only memorised the feel of her hair against the touch of his hands, the fragrance of her skin, the softness of her form as she nestled against him.

'I have to go. Someone may wake,' she whispered reluctantly. Tobias raked a hand through his hair.

'As do I. By that I mean I am leaving the colony. I don't know when I'll come back. I can't say if you'll ever see me again.'

'Where are you going?'

'Limeburners' Bay.' He stopped to consider what more he was going to say.

'I just wanted you to know, that's all. I'll be thinking about you, for however long I'm gone.'

She smiled then, he saw through the dark, but it was not a joyous smile. 'You know that I am to be wed to Gideon Quinn?'

He nodded and looked down at his feet. 'I wish you didn't have to.' 'So do I, Tobias, with all my heart.' Emma reached up to touch his cheek. He felt forlorn. She looked surprised at his strength of emotion, yet at her touch he took her hand.

'Goodbye, Emma,' he told her, and watched her go safely inside before he turned to leave. He almost wished he had not come to bid her farewell. Almost.

EIGHT

Tobias at first thought that Limeburners' Bay was a beautiful place. Water lapped and foamed on a sandy shore that stretched for miles on end. Towering sand dunes rose perhaps twelve feet high, and further up the banks, waving sea grass gave way to mangrove trees and then on to coastal banksias and ancient paper-barks. But as he entered the camp he saw it was a lonely place, and it was also cruel.

He encountered men half starved, with nary a scrap of clothing— save for part of a ragged shirt they wrapped around their loins could have been natives, their backs were so bronzed. Yet unlike the blacks, these men were not comfortable in this country at all.

Tobias never thought that he would miss the Coal River, its monotony of bells and its rules, especially not in comparison to his green country of birth, but he suddenly knew he was wrong. For the men here were mere animals, underfed, poorly clothed, and provided with hardly any shelter at all.

'Is this where we sleep?' he asked as he settled in.

'Aye,' one of the other convicts replied.

'All of us?' The man nodded. Tobias shook his head as he surveyed the spot. It wasn't even fit for a cow byre. The slabs of the shanty were so widespread he could have galloped a horse between the slats. A pile of mouldering seaweed carpeted the floor.

The other man nodded then continued. 'When its cold we gather the weed and cover ourselves with it. The stuff makes you itch like like mad at first, but there is little you can do about it. At least it's a bit of warmth. Although eventually you get so tired, you just sleep regardless. There's worse than the seaweed to concern yourself with.'

'What like?'

'The lime; it's caustic and it burns and itches like there's no tomorrow.'

Tobias looked around him. Trees and bush grew thick as far as the eye could see. It was a wild place, and the colony seemed almost homey compared this desolate spot.

'So what did you do to deserve a stint here?' the convict asked.

'I danced with a girl.' Tobias sat near him. The man laughed. 'Pull the other one, mate. When has that ever been a crime?'

'She's betrothed to an officer, and he didn't like it.'

Tobias's companion shook his head. 'Do you know the name of the officer?'

Tobias pursed his lips and nodded. 'Quinn.'

'He's *old*'

Tobias shrugged. 'He's still betrothed. To a girl who could be his granddaughter.'

'So he thinks he'll get rid of you here for a while, while he goes off and marries her.' The convict shook his head. 'No justice. If he's going to the trouble of sending you away for just dancing with her, she must be a beauty.'

Tobias smiled and nodded. 'Aye, she's grand. She's not for the likes of me.'

His companion clapped him on the back.

'If you can avoid carrying the lime to the boats, it'll make it easier on you. Whether you can, though, that's another matter. That stuff burns like the very devil.'

That night, as he tried to stretch out in the hut, he understood for the first time how bad mosquitoes could be. They peppered his feet and hands and face until he scratched like a flea-bitten dog. He watched the stars in the southern sky through the cracks in the lean-to. As he recollected the moments he had snatched with Emma Colchester, he wished that things were different for him.

At the opposite side of the shelter a boy of sixteen cried for his mother like a baby. Tobias turned to the dark shape of the man beside him ready to ask the question. The man answered the unspoken thought before Tobias could open his mouth.

'The boy stole a handkerchief for his ma's birthday and was sentenced to seven years in Sydney Cove,' he whispered. 'But it seemed he couldn't stay put, and tried to scarper off all the time and so he was sent to the Coal River. But that didn't work so they told him he could do a stint here at Limeburners'. Apparently they told him they were going to make him learn to respect the king's authority.'

'Poor lad,' Tobias was filled with compassion.

'Aye,' returned the voice in the darkness.

The next morning Tobias smelled smoke in the distance, pleasant and seemingly remote. By midday the smoke that filled the sky obscured the sun, and it glowed like a red ball of fire in a hazy sky more brown than blue.

Tobias and the other men ignored the distant bushfire and continued to gather shells and pile them, to light the kindling and watch the tendrils of smoke rise as they added logs before the oyster shells were scattered over the coals for burning. By late afternoon they could hardly tell if their eyes burned from the bushfire heading towards them or from the fires of their own making.

'Unless the breeze changes direction, we're going to end up like roast mutton,' Tobias overheard one of the constables say.

'Not me,' said the one they called Blue, 'because I'll be in one of the barges, heading back to the Colony. They can burn alone.'

Tobias had learned that Blue was the overseer who had been handy with the hand pike. The other government men knew to avoid him. When they couldn't do that, they were sure not to anger him. Life was hard but it was still worth living, and no one wanted to become the next fatality. Tobias followed their cues.

Just after they stopped for tea, as they listened for the approach of the flames, a kangaroo bounded through the bush. It was a big buck, and flames leapt from its fur as it sprang towards their camp.

'Stone the crows,' someone said and then stood up as the kangaroo fell on its side. Two of the constables ran to smother the flames with sand, not to preserve the life of the animal, for it was too late for that, but so that they could roast it over the open coals.

'Fresh meat for supper,' Blue said.

'It won't need to be skinned, at any rate,' one of the men quipped, and all the while Tobias and the rest kept an eye on the encroaching fire that crackled beyond them not far from sight.

Only the thunderstorm that came down on them that evening saved their camp. The rain fell hard and heavy, and as Tobias crowded with the men into the shanty to sleep, the rain blew between the cracks of the slab walls and pelted him across the back. He wondered what was worse, the heat and the smoke that filled the lungs, or the cold rain that trickled down his back so that he shivered until the dawn.

*

In the days that followed, Tobias did as he was bid. He collected the shells of oysters, whelks and pipis from middens that he was told the native Worimi people had deposited over thousands of years. Basket after basket he helped to heap the shells on the burning logs. Like everyone else's, his eyes became red, inflamed, and itchy from the burning lime, and it was impossible not to rub them. Between the streaming eyes and the never-ending mosquito bites, Tobias could barely rest, even when he was allowed to.

But lugging the baskets of un-slacked lime through the shallow water to the moored boats was the worst, because when the lime sifted from the basket onto the healing welts of his back, it burned holes that were excruciating to the touch. They began to weep and fester, and before long he almost reached the point of tears himself. Nothing would relieve the inflammation. One day, he nearly gave out.

'You've deliberately rubbed lime into your eyes,' the constable accused. Tobias didn't bother arguing, because the *Lady Nelson* had come for the cargo and was taking him with it to the convict hospital. Let them blame him; it made no difference.

The youngster who had stolen the handkerchief tried to persuade them to take him back to the colony, and even went so far as to climb into the waiting rowboat, but they yanked him out with rough hands and hauled him over the shoals. Tobias turned a jaded eye to see Blue aim a swift kick as though the boy were no more than a dog. Dimly he heard him yelp.

The first thing he perceived of the settlement was the peal of bells. Their hollow voices sang the news of the ship's arrival. They neared the wharf and Tobias fancied that the bells told Emma that he had come back after all. He stood up in his feverish state and watched for her on the foreshore until, light-headed, he swooned on the deck in the burning sun. He felt a wooden pail of saltwater pour over him as though he were rum-drunk.

'Wasn't this one in before?' he heard Emma's uncle ask no one in particular as Tobias was deposited unceremoniously onto the cot. 'I seem to remember him, I'm sure. Ah, yes, his back was badly scourged. He was working with the lime-burners, you say?'

'Yes, sir,' someone replied. Tobias, his mind hazy, couldn't tell who.

'Well, he was lucky last time that his life was spared. Unless this infection is brought under control, he won't make it. The lime has eaten into his back. Look at it. And I have a mind to have you tell the commandant that this man must not be moved until I say so. And that won't be for some days yet, if at all.'

*

When Tobias came to he heard the surgeon's apologetic voice. He was speaking to him in kind tones.

'I am sorry to hurt you, son, but this must be done, regardless of the discomfort,' the surgeon told Tobias as he patiently picked up the tin basin from the floor. 'What do they call you?' the surgeon asked him, coaxing Tobias to lie on the pallet once more.

'What do they call you?'

She had asked him the same question.

'Freeman,' Tobias mumbled from his position face down on the bed.

'Well, I'm not sure if the name is an unfortunate pun or whether it bodes well for your future in the colony. I'm sure it is the latter,' the surgeon assured him. 'Why were you convicted? That is, if you don't mind me asking.'

'Murder.'

'Oh, I see.' It was the last effort at conversation the man addressed to him for the entire day. But at that moment Tobias didn't care. He fell to sleep and dreamed he was eating potatoes.

When he awoke, that was exactly what he was doing, or at least the liquid that dribbled into his mouth tasted like potatoes. Whether the stuff *contained* potatoes was another matter entirely.

'I am glad to see you awake,' Emma said before she wiped his mouth as if he were a baby. The late afternoon sun shone through the large open windows, and a sea breeze tickled the ringlets at her nape.

'Some might call it heaven,' he whispered, and he gave her the flash of a smile.

'When you have eaten this, we will turn you onto your stomach to bathe the wounds on your back.'

He grimaced at the thought, closed his eyes for a moment, then started awake, to realise that he had been dreaming and his back was stinging as the surgeon once more bathed it. The liquid that dripped into his mouth had been salted water from the surgeon's sponge making a trail over his collarbone and down and around his chin, nothing more.

'We need to get you to drink something,' the man told him. Tobias nodded with the realisation that he was indeed parched.

'Do you have any soup?'

The surgeon frowned quizzically. 'I don't know that we do. My niece enjoys coming to help nurse the patients here, but her affianced is not keen that she should do so.' Tobias was now well awake. He knew full well to whom the surgeon referred.

'Does she know that I'm here?' Tobias asked hopefully. The man looked puzzled.

'Why would she know you're here?' he asked. Tobias didn't know what to say, and decided to keep his thoughts to himself.

*

As he sat at the table for the noon meal with his family, Emma's Uncle George chuckled over the tale as he added a pickled onion to his plate, and expressed his thanks for their own supplies from the small kitchen garden.

'What condition is the patient in?' Emma asked.

'He's lucky they brought him in when they did, or else he might not have recovered. If the commandant wasn't so free to administer the lash, there would be a lot less infection in the colony, and if the food rations were more abundant, there would be far less sickness, not to mention apathy. How can a man work without sustenance? This particular patient was in the hospital just recently, and then he was sent to work with the lime-burners, and that reversed the healing altogether.'

'But he will live?' Emma asked, making an effort to keep her voice even.

'Convicts die all the time, Emma,' Euphemie said, as though she were a dullard not to understand that the life of a convict was cheap.

'But still...' Uncle George gave his eldest daughter a sharp look. 'They know what to expect if they disobey society's rules.' Euphemie shrugged.

'They have no one to blame but themselves,' her mother said.

'They have often known hardship which we have no notion of, dear. Desperate men do desperate things, and until we have walked in another's shoes, it is all too easy to judge. We all of us have things for which we are ashamed,' Emma's uncle told his wife quietly.

Aunt Adelaide went stony white and spoke no more.

Later, as her uncle unlatched the gate, Emma hurried to him, cautious so not to be overheard.

'Uncle, I wonder if I may take anything from the garden which is blighted or too old for use that I might bring it to the hospice to make broth? I thought I had better ask this time.' Emma smiled.

'We have little to spare that would be of any use, but perhaps if you have a mind to do it, you may ask if anything might be spared from the parsonage kitchen garden as well. Yet you know,' her uncle reminded her, 'that Gideon Quinn is not happy for you to help nurse the patients in the convict hospital, and I must say Emma, that I understand his qualms.'

Emma said nothing to this, but her uncle seemed to sense her disappointment and continued. 'Doing good works for your fellow man is no sin in my book, my dear, and I would be pleased for your companionship in the ward whenever you choose. Only,' he looked down in consideration, 'I don't believe there is any need to make your involvement widely known.'

Emma smiled and touched her uncle's arm. 'Thank you.'

The sweet smell of the lavender nearby rose to her nostrils, and Emma stooped to pick a few spikes the pushed them through the buttonhole of her gown. Then she was going to see to gathering vegetables from their own kitchen garden and from the parsonage, and even any discarded peelings from the commandant's kitchen, if they had not gone to the fowls or swine.

Euphemie found her with her hands in the soil.

'I wonder why you waste your time, Emma, when you could sit in the parlour embroidering or reading at your leisure.'

Emma wiped her hands on her apron. 'Part of the reason I came here, Euphemie, was not only to be married but to give, if I could, some help to those who need it, namely the convicts. To be a listening ear …'

'I heard the parson's wife tell mother that you had given the commandant your Bible as a gift. Allowing him to call upon you in the dead of night in the shrubbery …' Euphemie's words were cool, but malice flashed in her eyes. Emma looked down at the sparse offerings in her bunched-up apron.

She could not refute it. She had given her Bible to another, but it wasn't to the man Euphemie thought, and it would be folly to try to explain otherwise. If the commandant found out, he would think her a liar, but if she divulged the real circumstance behind the gift of the Bible, and why Tobias Freeman had referred to himself as the commandant, then his sentence would indeed be hell on earth. Gideon Quinn would make it so, she was certain.

As to the stolen kisses, there was nothing to do but bite her tongue. She flushed in the knowledge that Euphemie had watched from the cover of darkness while Emma had stood on tipped toes to wantonly kiss Tobias Freeman.

'Why do you insist on throwing yourself at the commandant when you are betrothed to Gideon Quinn?'

'It is not as it seems, Euphemie. Please do not think so.'

'I sincerely hope not, for your sake, because I do not think that Officer Quinn would be pleased to think that his affianced was indulging in some underhanded flirtation.'

Emma clutched her apron in anger as she watched Euphemie walk away. Still, there was nothing she could say to anyone, certainly not to her caustic cousin. How the girl would laugh if she knew who the commandant really was.

But if Gideon found out, would he still want her to make good on her promise to marry him? She believed so. Her betrothal had been made with pen and ink; in fact, it was more binding because of it. It proclaimed Emma as his in black and white, until death.

As Emma walked up Prospect Hill towards the parsonage, she allowed herself the liberty of a few hastily dabbed tears. It was a windy day, the breeze whipped the waves into white horses in the harbour, and should anyone see the moisture in her eyes, they would think that dust had blown into them. 'Let's see what we can give you,' the reverend's wife said as she led Emma inside. 'There isn't much in the way of vegetables dear, unless you want the potato peelings from last night.'

'Why, that is just what I need.' Mrs Brown chuckled. 'Now, there are some odds and ends. A few bruised potatoes, some onions which are growing mouldy and which ought not to be fed to the chickens.'

'I will take anything you are willing to give.' Emma accepted a mutton bone with alacrity.

'Now, when you have made your soup, dear, be sure and come for a cup of tea.'

Emma didn't know how long she would be at the hospital and knew then that the parson's wife would be sure to tell everyone of Emma's vegetable foray. If it reached Gideon, there was little she could say to defend her actions, and with this in mind, she decided that she'd better not go anywhere near the barracks kitchen garden in case it lead her straight to him. Emma put the basket into her other hand, surprised at how heavy it had become with scraps that people would only have thrown out or given to their pigs, heedless of the needs of men. One man in particular took hold of her thoughts, and it was not so much in the light of charity.

*

When Emma entered the ward, her first task was to wash and cut vegetables, and in this, she garnered the help of the convict helpers in the hospital kitchen. She remembered having seen these women around the campfire. They were sullen, until she brought out the potatoes and onions and mutton bone and told them what she intended to do with the food. When they understood that they too could share the broth, they grew far more tolerant towards her, and went so far as to chat about the weather, the food and their families.

'So how did he dance?' one named Mary asked with a wink. 'Like a gentleman?'

Emma looked up from her task with a puzzled frown, and then understood the woman's question. She smiled in return. 'Yes, I believe he did.'

'Ah, but did he behave like one? Now that, Mary, my dear, is another question,' another asked.

'And the answer remains the same,' Emma said, and then she flushed and smiled as she cut the scraps of lamb from the bone.

Mary studied Emma. 'Why do you come here and associate with the likes of us? Dancing on the beach with convicts, when ladies like you normally wouldn't be seen dead with government men?'

'Whatever good anyone does, he will receive the same from the Lord, whether slave or free.'

'Aye, but it's easy to say when you're no slave,' one named Bessie mumbled with half a smile.

'I am a bondservant of the Lord.'

With that Emma smiled at them, and although the women's faces showed they weren't entirely sure of the meaning behind her words, their attitude towards her changed. Regardless of her own wish to see Tobias, Emma made sure she finished all the work she could do for others first. That, after all, was why she was here in the colony and in this hospital, she reminded herself, not for the gratification of her own wants. Still, she was pulled by the tide of desire. In the midst of it all she thought of Gideon and her promise to him. She would carry it through. She had to; it was right in the eyes of the law.

Yet what was right and true in God's eyes? That she wed a man to whom she had been betrothed through deceit? Was she meant to love and esteem him, this grizzled veteran? She pondered this as she headed through the room.

Emma's heart thumped like a parade ground drum alight with anticipation, yet it was not for a glimpse of Officer Quinn, but for Tobias Freeman, convict, a man to whom she could give nothing, certainly not herself.

She knew he watched her as she worked. All the way through the ward, the light glanced off the ocean to stream through the lofty windows and into her face as she walked towards him. He was gawking way beyond the laws of decency, but his expression looked as though he saw a vision of an angel.

Emma glanced at him again. She smiled tentatively, but the look he gave her was almost fierce. Emma remembered then, with a start, that this man was a convict for a reason.

What had he done? True, he had taken the blame for the father who had stolen bread in Sydney Cove, but before then, before that time, what had Tobias done?

Emma understood then that she had allowed a handsome face to cloud her judgement. Yes, she was to love these men and women, but that didn't mean that she was to fall in love with a pair of Irish eyes.

She chastised herself. No, this man was not for her. It struck her that this was not the first time she had felt the need to tell herself this.

'My uncle, the surgeon, tells me that you have been asking for soup?' Emma said.

'I would have asked him for *you*, had I thought he would grant it,' he told her, his voice soft. Emma flushed and gestured at his back.

'May I see? After you have eaten something I will bathe it for you.'

He shook his head. 'I don't want you to see it.'

'Why not? It needs to be done!'

'Let one of the others do it, the surgeon, his assistant, or the convict women who help here. Anyone but you.' Emma frowned and began to walk around to the other side of the bed. He grabbed her hand and held her to him. Emma looked at him askance.

'A man has his pride, and to see your pity is more than I can bear. Already I cannot be a man as I am treated like an animal; and I cannot court you as you will soon wed another.' He then sat up and the sheet fell away to expose the breadth of his muscled chest. Emma's eyes unconsciously traversed the planes of his torso over the tracing of dark hair then travelled up to meet his own.

'Will you meet me behind the church when I get out of the hospital?'

'I cannot.' Emma shook her head. 'It isn't right.'

'Aye and it isn't right that I love you, but I do. I am in torture for want of seeing you, and I cannot sleep for fear that when I wake up you'll wear his ring.'

Tears formed in Emma's eyes as she put her hands on his shoulders.

'Lie down and let me bathe your back, Tobias, for it is all that I am permitted to do.' He smiled sadly and shook his head in defeat as he did her bidding.

Tears sprung to her eyes, and as she washed his poor ill-treated flesh, she wondered what damage they had done to the heart of the man.

NINE

Gideon Quinn gave a quick rap at the door. He brushed at his sleeves for clinging specks or stray hairs, but he was spruce as usual, he told himself.

The lady of the house is slow to open the door whenever the indentured help isn't here, he thought wryly. He knocked again.

'Good evening, madam. I am a little early to dine, but I thought it would be a good opportunity to spend time with your niece. Or should I say, my fiancée.'

'She isn't home from the hospital yet,' Adelaide said. He let her see his displeasure. She went on. 'You will remember that it was allowed that she could help in the hospice today.'

'Yes, but it is now time to dine and she ought to be home.'

Adelaide said nothing. Gideon followed the woman into the cottage.

'Your niece, madam, is not acting in a manner appropriate for my soon-to-be wife. I would suggest you be more cautious with what Emma does with her time.'

'I cannot stop the girl from doing what she likes. She's not my daughter. Perhaps, Officer Quinn, you ought to see to your affianced yourself.'

Gideon's heat rose. 'When you coaxed Emma to accept my hand, you told me that you would carry it through, but we are not wed yet, and still I have said nothing of your former folly. But I expect your help, Adelaide, and I will not be opposed.' He cocked his head to listen. 'Here is your upstanding husband now, my dear. Shall we be done with pretence and tell him our secret?'

Adelaide hissed in fear as sweat broke out across the bridge of her nose. Even now she was an attractive woman, much like a full-blown rose.

'I will take care that Emma is more circumspect. Now speak no more about it. He is coming through the gate.'

George entered the room with an affable smile. 'Ah, Officer Quinn, you have beaten me to the table, it seems. I hope that there is more mutton and that you two have not dined without me.'

'You are the head of the household, George, and I wouldn't have the meat carved by anyone but you,' Adelaide crooned.

He chuckled and pushed his glasses further up the bridge of his nose.

Gideon looked around. 'You have not brought Emma with you?' he asked, more in accusation than question. He stepped out onto the porch and looked up the road. She was nowhere in sight.

'She was just finishing up and said that she would be here presently,' Adelaide's husband smiled affably.

Weak man, Gideon thought, *ragged from work and ruled by women*. That his neice was helping at the hospital obviously cut the surgeon's workload, but if the man thought that it was fitting for a girl to play nursemaid to felons, Gideon did not. She ought to be at home. That was a woman's place.

'I will go at once and escort her home,' Gideon said.

George and Adelaide exchanged glances. Adelaide looked as though she was about to shed tears, and turned away to prepare the table.

'I suppose I ought to have asked her to walk home with me,' George admitted.

'Oh, do you think so? A little late now, is it not?' Gideon gave the doctor a hard stare.

'Emma told me she would be here to join us for dinner presently, and it's no more than a hop skip and a jump to the hospital. It's not a long walk.'

'It's not an issue of safety, but one of principle. Her behaviour should be beyond reproach.'

'I would be very surprised indeed if Emma did anything untoward,' her uncle flushed. Gideon had offended him.

'Perhaps, George, you should think walk home with the chit at your arm in future if you want to continue with her as hospital help.' He looked at the surgeon before he walked out the door. The man's look of shame told him his words had sunk in.

He was furious. Emma made a fool of him before others, and cuckolded him when she cavorted with people she should not even consider associating with. He saw to the house under construction for her on the fertile riverbank of Wallis Plains, and yet she did not show any interest in their plans whatsoever.

He'd designed a grand place of yellow sandstone with shutters upstairs and down to keep out the extremes and high ceilings for the heat to rise in the heights of summer. There would be a fireplace in every room in readiness for frosty mornings and the winter chill, and yet she did not care.

Only the convicts interested her, with their wounds and their syphilis and their ill-begotten children, and she loved them as though they were her family. That she could think to join hands with such as them and dance on Christmas Day as though he would not give a fig. Well he did, and he would put a stop to it.

He was intent on speaking to Emma about her disobedience. He was overheated in his red woollen coat and his beige breeches grew uncomfortable against his skin. As he entered the convicts' hospital he felt disgruntled already. When he saw his betrothed caressing some felon's back, he grew livid.

'Emma, remove your hands from that … that *person's* back at once!' he ordered. Emma started at the sound, and the man she tended turned and slowly sat up.

'Gideon. I didn't hear you come in.'

'That much is obvious. This is no Turkish bathhouse for leisurely gentlemen that you should give massages to just anyone.'

Emma wiped her hands on her apron. 'You are correct,' she said. 'This is in fact a place of rest for the sick.'

'Well, they can heal without your care, because I will not have you play the role of servant, so come with me.' He grabbed her hand and pulled her towards him.

'And who are you that you think you can pull upon a lady's arm as though she were nothing more than a bag of potatoes?'

'A man soon to be her husband,' Gideon spat.

'All the more reason why you should treat her with all the respect due her.'

'It seems we have an Irish rebel in our midst,' Gideon scoffed. 'Perhaps you had better be about your own business instead of worrying about other people's. If you don't have enough labour, be sure that I will find you more to do. Believe me, you will have so much on your plate, Irish, that the *last* thing you'll be concerned with is potatoes.'

*

Emma saw the darkness fall over Tobias's face. 'Hold on a moment, aren't you the one I gave orders to be sent to Limeburners' Bay?'

Tobias said nothing and Gideon asked, 'Why have you returned so soon?'

'Infection,' the convict answered. Gideon showed his scorn.

'Infection? That's ludicrous. This place is becoming too lax as far as I'm concerned. Why, the commandant panders to you convicts as though he cannot abide your displeasure.'

'If Tobias had been left at the creek he may have died. Look at his back and you will see the damage the caustic lime does to flesh that has been flayed,' Emma said hotly.

'Oh, it's *Tobias*, is it? Pardon me sir, for not having been formally introduced.' Gideon gave a mocking bow.

Tobias clenched his jaw and remained silent.

This only seemed to make Gideon angrier. 'Did you dance with this *gentleman* on Christmas Day, perchance?' His eyes locked on Emma's, and she knew she could not lie.

Tobias spoke up on her behalf. 'You were told by the constable that she did not. He vouchsafed for her reputation, and assured you that she did not.'

Gideon sneered. 'Half the constabulary are convicts themselves who have merely made good of their position, albeit most of them with better manners than yours.'

'Come, Gideon, let us both return now for supper,' Emma said as she placed a placating hand on his arm. 'This man is nothing to you, and like all the rest of the patients here, I have tended to his wounds.' She would not see Tobias in more trouble if she could avoid it.

'Certainly, Emma, and I sincerely hope that you stay away from compromising yourself in this place in future.'

Emma nodded. 'I will come here no more, if you wish it,' she assured him calmly as she walked away from Tobias with scarcely a backward look. Gideon gave her a sideways glance. He led her down the road on his arm, then after a few moments, spun to face her, grasping her arm.

'Emma, I don't understand why you would want to act as nursemaid in that place. I fail to see what motivates you to spend time with those reprobates. You embarrass me and you damage your reputation by being there. Why, your name was even suggested as one of the hoydens dancing with soldiers and convicts.' He looked at her, waiting for a reply. Emma remained silent. 'The fact that those men and women are beneath me is beside the point. I have an image to uphold as an officer in the king's army, and as my fiancée, so, my dear, do you. I expect you tow the line.'

'I apologise if I have hurt you,' Emma began.

Gideon snorted. 'See it doesn't happen again.'

He turned away and they stopped at her uncle's cottage gate. 'The work on our house is in progress, and in the next weeks I will head up river to take supplies and make sure that the overseer is getting the job done in the manner I would wish. I would like you to come, but I don't think that your Aunt Adelaide would care to travel up Hunter's River as chaperone, so unfortunately, you won't see the house until we are wed. Still, it will be a wonderful surprise, will it not?'

'I look forward to seeing the house,' Emma said, dragging her thoughts away from the convict, from the direction her heart would have her take.

She was curious about Wallis Plains. Emma had heard that it rested on the river's fertile banks, pockets of cedar-studded rain forest interspersed with lush pasture that spread out in all directions. She was told that dairy cattle and their calves grew fat and glossy on the flats. Homesteads too were shooting up as quickly as new saplings.

She would miss the convict settlement—the bustle of its beachfront, her cousin Phoebe, and other acquaintances in the community. Yes, and she would miss *him*. She thought that everyone in her uncle's house must see it written plain on her face—her duplicity and the feelings she harboured in her heart for which there was not a hope.

Even over dinner, these thoughts continued until she realised that she had begun to daydream and asked her aunt to repeat herself.

'I said that tomorrow we will go the general store and buy notions to make your wedding gown. The time is fast approaching when you and Gideon will be wed, and we must begin on it as soon as possible.'

Her aunt's adamant tone brooked no argument, not that she could have said anything in front of Gideon. But it was true; it was time to start on the wedding gown, and her heart dived to the pit of her stomach at the thought.

Phoebe, Emma saw, hardly noticed her cousin's reticence to talk of such things as silk and lace, but Euphemie watched Emma like a sleepy eyed cat. Emma was aware that the secret kiss with the *commandant* was something of which only Euphemie was aware, and as the other girl smiled, Emma suspected she was content in that knowledge and what she could do with it.

'The *Prince Regent* will sail into harbour tomorrow, Father tells me,' Phoebe said. 'There will be all manner of things from Sydney Cove: newspapers and the Ladies' Journal, oranges and apples from the Hawkesbury River. Perhaps even letters from England.'

'Fresh fruit,' Aunt Adelaide said. 'Shall we walk down to the wharf when she comes into port?' Phoebe asked in excitement.

'Certainly we shall. It isn't every day that a ship sails into the harbour with luxuries from home.'

'While I'm working within the colony it will be good to know that you are suitably employed.' Gideon smiled with a nod at Emma's aunt that showed something like commendation.

Her aunt reciprocated with prim thanks. 'I will make sure of it,' the woman said, and Emma felt as though she was not the only one keeping secrets. There was something cryptic in the way Gideon and Aunt Adelaide conversed.

'Emma dear, I wonder if you will step onto the porch and bid me goodbye?' Gideon said. Emma flushed, ill at ease. Everyone watched for her response. She could do nothing but calmly stand

and smile. 'Of course.'

The night was balmy, the air still, and Emma could hear the waves meet the shore. She looked over her shoulder to watch them lap the sand to foam palely beneath the moonlight.

'Emma, look at me.'

She turned to meet his eyes. She found it uncomfortable to stand so intimately with him where no one else could see them, and when he took both her hands and began to kiss her palms in admiration, Emma squirmed. His mouth was damp, his breath hot with ardour, and eventually Emma pulled away.

'Oh Emma, don't tease me,' he said. He took her about the waist and clasped her to him, then pressed his mouth to hers so hard that she thought that he would feel her clamped teeth behind her lips, shut tight as they were.

'I'm sorry Gideon. I must go in; the insects are biting my arms.' She shuddered at his touch, and he apparently mistook it for a squeamish constitution where bugs were concerned and chuckled.

Her lack of response didn't seem to bother him; in fact, he probably expected a chaste girl of gentle breeding to be demure. Yet while his expression appeared pleased that Emma knew how to behave, something glimpsed behind his eyes seemed delighted that he would be the one to lay claim to her.

'Forgive my enthusiasm, my dear. It's just that I cannot wait to see us wed. There are few women in the colony, as I'm sure you know, and to have secured your hand will be my blessing in growing old. Many men would envy me my good fortune, and my appetite grows apace whenever I see you.'

The thought of wifely duties towards her vigorous grey-haired husband would indeed be a labour of marriage, for she would have to work to suffer the touch of his hands.

After she escaped him, Emma walked into the bedroom she shared with Euphemie and Phoebe and went straight to the ewer and basin and washed her face in the tepid water. Patting her skin dry, she turned to see Euphemie curled up on the chair. She started, and her cousin smiled slightly so that Emma wondered if the girl had watched Gideon plaster her hands and lips with kisses.

'The commandant is having a dinner party.'

'Oh?' It was the first time Emma had heard of it.

'Yes, but we only received the invitation today. I want to ask you to make sure you avoid the commandant, not seek his conversation. There are sure to be many other people with whom to chat.'

'Why, of course,' Emma assured her. She did not care one way or another to whom she spoke or sat next to during dinner. 'Do you have feelings for the commandant?'

'Not at all,' Euphemie said, 'but I am free to be courted, should the right man come along, and you, for all your midnight trysting, are not.'

'Will you meet me at the church when I get out of hospital?'

She had not shied from his kisses, but had risen up to meet them, almost as if she had an appetite for them, and yet the feeling was not like hunger.

'I am not interested in the man at all. Good luck to you.'

Euphemie got up from the chair. 'I am pleased to hear that you have changed your mind. He is far too young for your tastes anyway.' She snorted as she went through the door.

Emma stared after her, hurt and annoyed. Her face flamed with impotent anger. Euphemie had rubbed salt into the wound, and there was nothing she could do about it. Gideon could be her grandfather. She blinked away a tear at her cousin's hostility, as she got ready for bed and prayer. Scripture floated through her mind as she fought to put the incident out of her thoughts.

Forgive us our debts, as we forgive our debtors.

Emma tried to sleep and listened to the breath of the sea as she wondered what kind of man Tobias Freeman was. He had taken another's crime on his shoulders and received the punishment of transportation to Newcastle. It was inconceivable that he had done something so honourable only to gain no reward but a name as black as the Coal River seam itself. Yet who knew it but Kevin the old convict and herself?

Emma asked herself if she would look foolish bringing Tobias's good deeds to the commandant's attention again. Perhaps he had forgotten that Tobias had saved her from drowning? Was the commandant aware of why the Irishman had been transported from Sydney Cove to Newcastle? Many convicts were pardoned for exemplary behaviour, and this gave her hope. She smiled at the thought of Tobias Freeman throwing off the 'slops' of a convict and dressed instead in neat breeches and jacket with a trim cravat. She wondered whether he would remain in the area as one of the free settlers who arrived on these newly chartered shores or sail away for Ireland, his birthplace.

It occurred to Emma then that his future did not concern her, whether he was a felon or free settler. But she was struck by her own foolishness and by shame and hurt, for she knew that he was far more to *her* than either of those things. Tobias Freeman was the man she loved.

Emma wondered at her felon heart. In all her life she had never fought convention, had never questioned doing what was right. She knew she ought to exercise caution regarding Tobias, yet she had thrown caution to the winds, when in reality she knew little of him.

With a heavy heart Emma stared into the darkness and tried to will herself to sleep, but it was hours later that she fell into waves of forgetfulness. Morning arrived all too soon.

'There are bound to be all manner of things heading off the brig,' Phoebe said early that morning as they headed towards the harbour. 'Perhaps there will even be some new settlers come with their families.'

'I cannot imagine why anyone would want to leave a perfectly good country like England for a place like the Coal River,' Aunt Adelaide said, patting her hair in the breeze. 'It is not always the new start they might think it is. They will find a hard life.' 'I think this is a beautiful place,' Emma said as they walked into the sun, the breeze at their backs. The harbour bustled and teemed with ships and open boats that bobbed atop the water like seagulls.

'I am inclined to agree with Mama,' Euphemie said, 'and were I given the chance to sail back home, I would surely do so.'

'You and I both, my dear,' Adelaide agreed, 'for this is a wild and lonesome corner of the world.'

Emma supposed in some ways her aunt was correct. She gazed at the tall trees that stretched for miles and miles to line the shores and then grew off into purple-hued and exotic mountains in the distance. Even the birds were strange in this place. They screeched from high in the branches then swooped down to flash their brilliant colours of red and orange and blue and green. It seemed to Emma that every hue of the rainbow had been splashed on these parrots. Yet with nothing spared for the beauty of their plumage, it seemed that no thought had been given to their song, for their voices rang raucous and harsh.

The convicts were drab in comparison, she mused. Grey jackets and washed out calico breeches hung from most men, and very often in tatters.

'Why, the clothing on some of these men and women is literally rotting off their backs,' Emma shook her head.

'They are issued with clothing,' her aunt assured her.

'Then they do not hand out clothing often enough. Why the broad arrows on their slops? What do they signify?'

'That they are the property of the government,' aunt Adelaide answered.

'The convicts or the clothing?' Emma asked wryly.

'Why my dear, both.' Emma glanced at her aunt, and saw that she spoke in all seriousness.

'Ah, here is parson's wife now. Yoo-hoo, Mrs Brown!'

The parson's wife met stood waiting at the wharf waving her handkerchief like a white flag, almost lost among the bodies on the busy foreshore.

'There is no room to move,' the woman said cheerfully, when she finally finished flapping her hankie and put it in the sleeve of her dress. Her face beamed a jolly pink beacon of welcome. Emma returned her smile.

'I cannot wait to see if there are any ladies' journals on the shelves of the general store,' Phoebe said before she rose up on her toes to watch sailors file down the gangplank with all manner of boxes. Emma saw Phoebe catch sight of the redheaded constable who had twirled her on his arm on Christmas evening before the campfire, the sun sinking into the sea. She watched as they exchanged smiles.

Emma noticed that Euphemie had also intercepted their looks and looked at her sister in silence. Phoebe pretended not to notice. Emma did not blame her cousin and tried to hide her own smile.

Euphemie flounced away to join arms with her mother and the parson's wife, and Phoebe pulled Emma aside. 'There is the commandant making his way towards us, Emma. He already has the *Sydney Gazette* under his arm.'

Emma caught Phoebe with a smile fit to beat the band at the red-haired lieutenant walking beside the commandant, and Emma smiled herself at her cousin's hushed excitement. 'And the name of your lieutenant?' 'Rory,' Phoebe whispered. 'That is to say, Lieutenant Ferguson.'

Emma put the tips of her fingers over her mouth in fear of giggling, as Phoebe herself was about to do.

'Good morning, ladies,' the two men bowed.

'Good morning, Commandant.' Emma and Phoebe curtsied, and

were then introduced to Lieutenant Ferguson, the commandant not realising that the two were already acquainted. Phoebe blushed pink.

'I see you have the *Sydney Gazette*, Commandant,' Emma said, as Phoebe and the pimply soldier glanced shyly at one another. 'I wonder if there is any noteworthy news.'

'Indeed there is, Miss Colchester. I was just speaking to Lieutenant Ferguson about the bushranger hidden somewhere in the scrub who steals from settlers' homes and holds them up as they cross his path.' Emma's eyes widened. 'He is one of many convicts who abscond and take to the bush. But the natives get most of them in the end; that's if we don't catch them first.'

He said this with confidence, as though to put her at ease, but Emma wondered at the new place she would call home—Wallis Plains—and was not a little perturbed. A young woman alone in a grand new home was bound to pique a passing renegade's interest, and she found one more reason for trepidation at the days to come.

'I am told you are to hold a dinner party, Commandant?' Euphemie said as she came upon them, all smiles and sugar, sickeningly sweet.

'Certainly.' The commandant bowed slightly and a dark curl fell over his forehead. 'Our Newcastle colony is poor of women, and we men must enjoy your presence whenever we are able. I pray, you will all three come?'

'Have no doubt, Commandant, I will be there,' Euphemie assured him. Phoebe and Emma agreed to the same.

'Then with the promise of a wonderful evening, I look forward to your company very soon.'

TEN

Although the general store was expansive, there was not much to recommend it to young ladies with a penchant for fripperies and lace, thought Emma. True, it offered calico and twill— heavens, Mr Tucker even kept a small bolt of lawn 'for the finer ladies of the colony'— but beyond that, the store seemed bereft of anything like what the other ladies had hoped would grace Emma on the day she wed. Why, she could be bedecked in calico print, but how inappropriate when her undergarments were of such exquisite stuff.

Phoebe showed no interest in camphor, saltpetre, turpentine or brooms. Euphemie and Aunt Adelaide had often bemoaned the fact that, although there was plenty of space for a table and chairs, the storekeeper had not thought to provide tea and cake should any customers wish to take tea. Everyone said that, although there was much they lacked in the way of foodstuffs, there was no shortage of tea. Uncle George always said that tea was a refreshing beverage, no matter the weather, and in this country at the end of the world, Emma had found, one was always thirsty.

'It grieves me to say it, Emma dear, but I believe we will have to make do with Phoebe's 'coming out' gown for your wedding. Gideon has shown impatience to see you wed, and there is not nearly enough time to send to Sydney for either fabric or a gown before your nuptials. Why, it may take months for the articles to arrive, and I know for a fact that Officer Quinn would not be pleased about that.' Aunt Adelaide was obviously disappointed for Emma.

'I had intended to wear the pale grey silk I brought with me on the ship,' Emma said, 'and need nothing more than that.'

'Fiddlesticks,' her aunt replied. 'If that is the gown you had considered wearing to the parsonage supper then it is nowhere near grand enough for you to wear on your wedding day. Doubtless you will wear the same gown to the commandant's dinner party, so you must have something else.'

'I have not seen Phoebe's debutante gown, but I am sure that if Phoebe is pleased to loan it to me, then I shall be happy to wear it.'

'Of course we shall have to take it in a little, but that is no bother. We will have it finished in no time, and it will look well on you, of that I'm sure.' Aunt Adelaide smiled, and Emma felt thankful for the generosity of both Phoebe and her aunt.

'Mr Tucker has both linen and lawn, so we will buy a good amount of each so that we may get to work on doilies and pillow shams and tablecloths. Do you crochet and embroider well, Emma dear?'

'Tolerably well.'

'Wonderful, because my efforts are appalling. Still, I do try, and that is all one can ask for, is it not?'

Emma watched Aunt Adelaide bustle around the store, and when the woman saw a pair of dainty hook-and-eye boots she asked Mr Tucker to take them down.

'These belonged to Governor Macquarie's wife. Had them made especially I am told but they were too tight, so she brought them here for me to sell.'

Aunt Adelaide appeared impressed. 'They are exquisite, Emma, and looking at your dainty feet, I am sure that they are just the right size for you.' Emma did as she was told and began to untie her boot in the hope that the delicately pointed shoe would indeed fit, for she had never owned anything half so lovely. It was no wonder the boots had remained at the shop for such a long period with their tiny size.

They were the most comfortable shoes she had ever put on. But then, as the daughter of a deceased clergyman, Emma had not known much in the way of extravagance of any kind at all. Doubtless, her mother was far more comfortable now thanks to the helpmeet payments Gideon sent, and for this, Emma was glad.

'How marvellous,' Aunt Adelaide said, as she clapped her hands. 'Our morning's shopping has not been wasted at all. They do look well on you, Emma.'

'Thank you, aunt.' Emma smiled then lifted her skirts to ride high on the calf so she could admire first one shoe and then the other.

At that moment Tobias Freeman burst through the door. He glanced at Emma and she dropped her skirts with haste. In his arms he carried a small child, and Emma recalled her as the little girl whose curls had stuck to her cheeks as she ate the boiled sweets on Christmas Day. Her head had lolled back, and she looked as pale as death, her pupils like pinpoints in the blue of her eye.

The convict pushed past them with nary a word of polite good day and strode to the counter, where he stopped.

'I want you to see what you have done! You sold Mary infant drops for Katy, and they have made her sick.'

The storekeeper grew red and began to bluster. 'There is nothing wrong with the tonic. Mothers buy it for their children all the time for the summer diarrhoea.'

Tobias Freeman stood with feet braced, furious at the shopkeeper's dismissal.

'I tell you, this child is sick, and it has nothing to do with trips to the outhouse. It is a poison, and you are to take it off your shelf before any more children and babes are made sicker because of it. I want you to give me a bottle of infant drops to take to the doctor so that he can know what kind of poisoning to treat this child for'

119

'I'll do no such thing. It's only opium. Where did the child's mother get the money from to procure the stuff anyway? She probably came right in here and stole the medicine, for all I know. That's if she didn't engage in immoral activity with some soldier to pay for them.' The shopkeeper was derisive, but he stepped well back behind the counter, away from the hands of the brawny convict who, his face showed, might well beat him senseless if his hands were free.

At this, Tobias caught sight of the vials of infant medication on the shelf to his side, took one and swept the others off onto the floor. They broke where he stood.

'How dare you, sir!' Mr Tucker thundered. 'What will mothers give their children now to settle them at night, I ask you?'

'How should I know? Sell them ginger beer, but do not sell that poison in your store!'

'You ought to be about your work. You'll be lashed for your tardiness. I'll be sure to tell the commandant about the havoc you've wreaked in this store.'

'If my *tardiness*, as you call it, saves this child, then I will pass the lash-master the cat myself to save him the trouble. I thought if you saw her you might care. But if you think that your profits are of more value than the life of a child little more than a baby, you do exactly what you threaten.'

Then he turned to Emma and addressed her for the first time. 'I take it your uncle is at the hospital right now?'

'As we speak,' she said. Tobias nodded and strode from the store in the direction of the hospital at the point of a run.

'You're nothing but a low down thief!' Mr Tucker cried out, showing more courage now by emerging from behind the counter to yell in the direction of Tobias's hurrying figure. 'They're all tarred with the same brush,' he growled. The blood rushed through Emma's veins as though she had run a race. That a man could dare the hungry cat for such a noble act made her hold her own head a little higher, and when Mr Tucker made his excuses for such wild behaviour, Emma spoke up.

'If my own words were half so daring in the bid to save the life of a child, then I should be glad that I had done my Father's work.'

Mr Tucker blinked and closed his mouth.

'Aunt Adelaide, be sure that Officer Quinn's purchases include the price of the infant drops. I would not want Mr Tucker to forfeit his profit because of accidental breakage.' With this, Emma took off the boots and set them on the counter. 'Wrap these as well, Mr Tucker. We will take Mistress Macquarie's shoes.'

On the way home, Emma wondered at her boldness, and Euphemie, for the first time, looked at her with something akin to grudging respect. Yet Emma's prayers were for Tobias and the little girl he had carried.

She fervently wished that she might be of some assistance in the bid to save the child, but she had given Gideon her word and didn't think it right to break it. Certainly a small life was at stake, and yet she was of the opinion that Gideon would not consider the offspring of a convict a reasonable excuse for reneging on her promise. As they reached home and entered the garden gate, Emma's glance travelled the distance to the hospice.

*

As soon as he saw little Katy's face, George knew what the trouble was. He opened her eyes and saw that his suspicions were right, even before the convict told him what the child had been given.

'I won't wait. I am going to pump her stomach right away. Get hot water and the tin bath. We need to rub her limbs vigorously with warm and cold water alternately.' The man he knew was named Tobias hastened to perform his bidding with but a quick look of question.

'This is a new invention. It rids the body of poison and can easily be inserted through the oesophagus without discomfort. First

121

we are going to give her tepid saline water, and then we will pump it carefully out, continuing the process until the stomach contents run clear.'

'Will it work?' Tobias asked with a note of doubt.

The surgeon wiped his brow. He had begun to sweat. 'I don't know. I've never used one before.'

'There's a first time for everything.'

'Just so,' George said, and pushed his glasses up the bridge of his nose to ready the expensive new apparatus.

They worked on the child until the sweat ran from their faces and dropped onto the floor at their feet. Although Katy lay pale as a corpse the men continued. The perspiration trickled in rivulets down George's chest and back in the sultry room. It seemed a long while before he finally smiled in relief.

'She'll live,' George assured Tobias as he let out a sigh and dropped into the hard-backed chair. The stomach pump had been worth the outlay, no matter what dear Adelaide had told him to the contrary.

Tobias smiled. 'I'll tell her mother straight away.'

'You were right to bring her to me when you did. Even one drop more of the tincture would probably have done her in. Those infant drops are a dangerous remedy, which I would never prescribe. How did you know what the problem was?'

'A brother of mine was not so lucky. A hungry tummy and medicine in easy reach was too much temptation. It was a day I cannot easily forget. When I saw little Katy, and smelled the sweet stuff on her breath, I knew. I remembered as if it were only yesterday.'

George nodded with understanding, and then took out a paper and quill to write a note, which he handed to Tobias.

'Give this to the overseer. I would not see you flogged for the good deed you have done this day.'

'I only brought her here.'

'And it is just as well that you did. Tell Katy's mother the child can rest here. I will see that she is fed and given plenty of liquids and time to recuperate.'

Tobias nodded and the surgeon put out his hand.

'Good day, sir,' he told Tobias, before he let himself out the door and walked down Prospect Hill.

*

Emma was pinned into Phoebe's 'coming out' gown. She thought it sat well on her and was indeed the prettiest thing she had ever put on. The empire styling was tucked under the bust in soft gathers and caught up in a rosy ribbon that echoed the colour of the rosettes around the hem and swooped down at the back to fan the ground. Small gathered sleeves showed the creamy softness of her arms and the wide neckline exposed the same.

'Phoebe, it is exquisite,' Emma breathed.

'And it is not on loan,' she told Emma firmly. 'It is yours to keep.'

Emma smiled and squeezed her cousin's hand. 'Bless you.'

'You already have,' Phoebe said, 'the moment you stepped from the sand.'

Emma looked up and glanced out the window.

'Why, what is it Emma?' her cousin asked in concern.

'Will you wait here, Phoebe? There is someone I must speak to.'

'Of course.'

Emma left the house and, as she lifted the skirt of the gown, hurried down the road.

*

Tobias Freeman was coming from the hospice when he heard Emma's footsteps and turned. They both stopped short.

'Good afternoon Tobias.' Emma smiled tentatively as she caught

123

her breath. Her breast rose and fell, and Tobias steeled himself not to glance down at the milky expanse of bare flesh, nor let his eyes roam over her form, sheathed in a wondrous gown. He failed at the attempt and became aware he must have looked as hungry as he felt.

'How is the child?' Emma asked, then coloured beneath the honesty of his gaze.

Tobias came back to himself and spoke. 'She is going to be all right.'

Emma smiled and he couldn't help but respond in kind. 'That's wonderful news.'

He nodded and felt his smile widen. 'Where do you go in that gown?'

'Nowhere at present. I am merely being fitted.'

'I think you're fitted just grand.'

'You are staring, sir.'

Tobias had the grace to flush. 'Pardon me, miss.'

Emma realised that her aunt would not approve of her standing in the street talking to this man and in this attire. Gideon, she suspected, would be even less impressed.

'I believe there is a special Epiphany service at the church. Will you be going there?' Emma asked, and then felt ridiculous because all the convicts went to service whether they wanted to or not. They sat at the back of the church in the 'Convicts' Gallery'. 'I'm told there is to be refreshment afterward.'

'Aye,' he said, 'I'll be there.'

His closeness grew uncomfortable. So near and yet they did not touch. He was so tall and broad that he seemed to block the heat of the slanting sun.

'Miss Colchester ...'

She shook her head. 'Emma, only ever Emma. Please.'

'Do you recall that I asked if you would meet me when I got out of the hospital?'

'I will never forget, but I cannot do as I would like, Tobias.' Emma shook her head sadly. 'It isn't right.'

He nodded and looked down at his feet before he turned away. She couldn't bear the look on his face, the regret and the disappointment. Emma grabbed for his hand and held it.

'It isn't right that I am betrothed to a man and do not want to be, but neither is it fair that I meet with another man. I cannot do it, Tobias. I must not.'

And though she saw it pained him to hear it, he nodded that he understood. Then he brought her hand to his chest and placed it against his heart, so that she wasn't sure if the tight, quick pulse was his or her own.

'Good day, Emma.' He released her and continued down the track.

As she watched him walk away she saw Mary run to him, grab his arms, then throw her arms around him and sob in a thankful embrace. When he held the unwed convict mother, Emma felt a twinge of jealousy, a feeling she knew she had no right to have.

She would spend the afternoon sewing, and if that did not take up her thoughts, it would at least occupy her hands.

*

'You love him, don't you Emma?' Phoebe whispered as Emma entered their shared room. Emma turned around, startled. Flushed with the truth, she considered Phoebe's kind face.

'Yes, Phoebe, I believe I do.' And Emma, who had never found it either a task or an inconvenience to do her duty, was finally overcome. She would soon wed a man for whom she did not care, and the vow was all the more onerous because she loved another.

Phoebe took her in her arms and they sat down on the bed as Emma wept, for herself, for Tobias and for Gideon, who knew nothing of her dilemma. Then it came to her, the solution and the honesty with which she must treat Gideon.

'I must tell Gideon,' Emma said, almost to herself. 'I will ask him to release me from our betrothal, for both our sakes.'

'Oh Emma, think hard on this,' Phoebe pleaded. 'Consider the consequences of your actions.'

'Believe me, Phoebe, I am. To marry one man when I care for another and to go through with a marriage in which I have no heart is surely wrong.'

'Love is a commitment I have heard it said,' Phoebe told her. 'Perhaps love will grow, who knows?'

Emma looked up at her through tears and shook her head. 'There is something for Tobias Freeman which has taken root in my heart and I cannot pluck it out.'

'Emma, the man is a convict.'

Emma expected to be chastised. She merely nodded her agreement. 'There is no getting around that.'

'Why was he transported to the colony of New South Wales, Emma?'

'I must admit that I do not know.'

Phoebe's brows rose. 'Then perhaps it is something you should find out. For if it was me, I am certain that I should.'

'And Gideon? What of him?'

'Wait a little. Think on it before you rush in.'

'Pray,' Emma finished.

Phoebe nodded. 'Most definitely. Pray.'

*

Adelaide heard the garden gate close and looked up, listening to the sound of footfalls. It was too early to be George home from the hospital. She heard Gideon Quinn's voice.

'Good afternoon, Miss Euphemie. I wonder if I might pay my

respects to your dear mother?' she heard him ask. Adelaide groaned inwardly, rolling her eyes. Then with a sigh, sat up from the bed and put her feet to the floor.

'You do not want to speak with Emma?' her daughter asked in curiosity.

'Unfortunately I am pressed for time, but I look forward to seeing you all at church tomorrow.'

When Euphemie knocked on her chamber door, Adelaide could not hide that she felt put out. 'He only wants to speak to you,' Euphemie said.

'I know,' Adelaide said, and wondered what the man could possibly want.

'I would be cross if I was aroused from my nap too,' Euphemie assured her mother on a whisper. 'Especially by such an odious old man.'

Adelaide pursed her lips but refrained from comment.

'What do you want?' was her quiet demand as she entered the parlour.

He looked askance. 'Is that any way to speak to a future member of your family?' His smile was mild as milk. Adelaide knew better.

'My husband will be home very soon,' she said, with a strong wish that it were true.

He chuckled, seemingly delighted. 'But I am after a different kind of favour entirely than you seem to be alluding to.'

'Why have you come calling, Gideon?' Adelaide asked, flush with the sting of his insult. She knew they both knew better but it bit all the same.

'I need your help,' he said. 'In for a penny, in for a pound, as the saying goes?'

She wondered with dread what he could possibly want this time. 'I have never received anything from you.'

'You and your husband live happily on my good graces.'

127

'You are a man who knows nothing of grace.'

'I beg to differ.' His smile was quickly gone. 'That is why I have come calling today: to remind you of my faith that you will help me.'

*

In the next room, Euphemie's ears pricked and she understood a little better why she disliked the man so much. There were questions for which she had no answer. Had Mama been acquainted with Officer Quinn before they came to the Coal River? She wished she knew. When he and Mama walked into the garden to speak on the favour he asked, she could hear nothing more, but she would be wary of him that was certain.

She spared a thought for Emma, in the knowledge that before long she would share the man's name, his house and his bed. She felt little affection for her sanctimonious cousin, who was prettier than was decent, but no maid deserved to be hastily wed to some conniving old bachelor whom no one else cared to marry. She was only glad that her family didn't have to look to farming out their daughters for want of a nest egg, and for that, she felt a moment's sympathy for the girl who had come to stay.

She decided to join Phoebe and Emma to chat and sew until suppertime— not that she intended to do any needlework.

*

When Emma's uncle came home for supper he told them about the wonderful new apparatus called the stomach pump, which had saved a child from poisoning.

'Even now she is tucked up with a cup of tea and a slice of bread being nursed by her mother.'

'If it hadn't been for that fellow who brought her in when he did, she would not have made it.'

'He swept all the vials of infant medication on the floor,' Aunt

Adelaide said. 'Mr Tucker was so angry I believe that if the convict was not akin to a giant, he would have thrown him to the floor as well. As it was he stayed firmly on his side of the counter.'

'I cannot say that I blame him.' Uncle George smiled. 'Still, the convict was right about the tincture. I have seen many small lives lost due to its use. A bout of diarrhoea rarely kills a child if they are given sufficient liquids, but opium, on the other hand, does. So it is with a happy heart that the girl's mother will go to the Epiphany service tomorrow with many prayers of thanks, I'm sure.'

Just then the bells tolled the end of work for the convicts' day, and Emma looked up from her supper as she wondered whether Tobias would wait for her at the church with the hope that she had changed her mind. She imagined him, standing in the cool sea breeze overlooking Prospect Hill, watching her uncle's house and waiting.

She looked forward to the church service and the luncheon afterwards, and was glad that the government men had this day of rest, that she might look upon Tobias even though she would be on Gideon Quinn's arm.

*

Tobias sat in the candle flame at the table while Kevin snored, but it was so hot in the cottage that he opened the door and stepped out.

The night was still and peaceful, but after his eyes adjusted to the darkness, he caught a movement in the direction of the government store and wondered why anyone was at work so late at night. He squinted through the gloom at the cart being loaded in the distance. Why wait until full dark before loading the dray? It was way past curfew. Whoever was rolling the barrels seemed to be in a hurry, and whoever did it, worked alone, pushing one far back onto the cart before heading into the store to get another.

Tobias knew it had to be rum. Coinage was harder to come by

than 'Nelson's Blood', and the colony thrived on the stuff as a tool for barter. He had heard that when Admiral Nelson had died in battle his body had been preserved in a keg of rum until the body could be buried in England. During the trip homeward the sailors had tapped the keg and pierced the body of Horatio Nelson, and drunk the rum to the last drop, so that when they arrived at their destination, the barrel had been drunk dry, and so, in effect, had the admiral.

Tobias wondered if Emma slept soundly in the balmy night, for he couldn't. He went back inside and opened the Bible to a random page, though he hardly knew what to look for.

'*If any man thirst, let him come unto me, and drink.*' He frowned at that, flipped back a few pages, and found more about drinking. This time Jesus spoke to a woman at a well.

'*Whosoever drinketh of this water shall thirst again: But whosoever drinketh of the water that I shall give him shall never thirst; but the water that I shall give him shall be in him a well of water springing up into everlasting life.*'

Aye, he was thirsty. He wondered what he was required to do. Perhaps he could ask Emma. He yawned and hid the Bible before he fell onto the bed and thought of Emma as she had looked in that gown. In the short space of night, he decided, he could imagine she was his, and he could hope.

ELEVEN

Kevin, like the other convicts, always sat in the gallery above and to the back of the church. The view of the vaulted ceiling was far superior to the one the free settlers got, Kevin supposed, but the area was a sight hotter. Where the government men sat bunched together like sardines it was downright unpleasant, regardless of the sandstone walls. He felt the sweat roll down his back and stop at the waistband of his breeches.

Miss Colchester glided in like some beautiful water bird, and the Cockney saw that young Toby, who sat next to him, watched her with a keen eye.

Doesn't hurt to look, does it, mate? thought Kevin.

But from what Kevin could see, Toby no longer just watched the pretty face, he now *wanted* the pretty face, and Kevin didn't see why he should continue to waste his time over what he couldn't have when Mary stared him full in the face. She was comely. Not nearly as winsome as Miss Colchester was, but she was available, and she had her eye on Toby, that was for sure.

Mary leaned towards Toby then and spoke into his ear. He turned to answer her. The neck of her dress was opened up so wide that a boat could just about steer into her port, but Kevin supposed that that was her intent. Yet only time would tell if Tobias would take her on. As it was, Miss Colchester remained as out of reach as the statue of the saint at the front of the church.

They stood to sing the parting hymn, *Amazing Grace*.

'Amazing grace, how sweet the sound that saved a wretch like me. I once was lost, but now am found, was blind but now I see.'

Kevin heard Toby beside him. That man sang for all he was worth, and he was surprised to find that the man's voice was one of the nicest he had ever heard. It wasn't low and it wasn't high, and apparently they all had different names like soprano and such, but he didn't know them, just that young Toby could easily sing for his supper. Kevin knew that *he* sang like a crow, but since he stood next to the young bloke, nobody would hear him anyway, which was just the way he liked it.

There was tea and bread for everyone after the service. The parson's wife fluttered busily under the boughs of an enormous fig tree and there was no one who was not thankful for its shade from the heat. Few convicts felt free to stand under there with the officers and their ladies, the storekeeper, and the parson and his wife, but Kevin did not intend to move away from the teapot.

'Did you make this, missus?' Kevin asked the parson's wife of the sweet bread. He was in raptures over the fact that he had found a few currants in the spicy loaf, and only wished there would be more where that came from.

'I did. Myself and a few of the other ladies, that is.'

'If I hang around long enough, do you think I could have another slice?'

'We shall see.' She smiled. 'There are many people to be fed.'

Kevin gave her a gap-toothed grin. 'It's a bit like the story of the loaves and fishes the parson was talking about.'

The slice of bread had been a mere triangle, but it was the best thing he had eaten since jellied eels on the banks of the Thames.

He turned to see Mary flirting outrageously with Tobias. The lad might be able to sing, but he was certainly slow on the uptake, Kevin thought. He wished that *he* were a little younger; young enough for

Mary to notice. Not that Toby ignored her by any means, but her banter hardly raised a smile. He was too busy watching Miss Colchester.

Kevin's eyes drifted to what Toby saw. Old Quinn had his hand around Miss Colchester's waist, which seemed a little too familiar. Her parasol was open to shade her face, though, so whether she minded that his hand roamed so freely, Kevin didn't know. He could see Toby's face, and it had grown as dark as midnight. He walked on over to his young friend.

'Gideon, would you mind taking a turn in the church?' They heard Miss Colchester ask the officer. 'It is cooler there, and we can sit in privacy.'

'Certainly, my dear,' he said. 'I am filled with hopeful congeniality.' Tobias looked at Kevin and both men shook their heads.

'Know what I'm thinking, Kevin?'

'What's that, Toby mate?'

'I reckon Quinn looks about as trustworthy as the shark the natives speared yesterday.'

They watched them disappear into the church sanctuary. Mary stood as close as she was able, and it seemed as though her bust was trying to escape the confines of her well-fitted dress. When she saw that her diligence was not going to pay off, she eventually drifted away.

'Even dirty calico can look good on some women,' Kevin mused. Tobias glanced at him and he winked.

'Aye, well I'm a man that doesn't like the plate pushed under his nose when he's not hungry, if you get my meaning.'

'Lordy, I wish I could pick and choose like you, Toby lad.'

Tobias wasn't listening. Kevin watched as he walked towards the church porch, his head to one side. Kevin guessed that he was eavesdropping and shrugged it aside. If Tobias didn't feel guilty, it wasn't going to bother him either. Kevin guessed his fears were for Miss Colchester, and as far as that young woman was concerned, propriety could go hang.

*

'Gideon, I have something to ask of you,' Emma said. She hardly knew how to address what was on her mind.

'Let me help you.' He kissed the tips of his fingers and planted them on her lips, where the gentle pressure parted them. She turned slightly to the side to hide her embarrassment. He stared as she moistened her mouth.

'I have found that I have made an error, and I wish to rectify it.'

'I will help you in any way you wish.' He seemed to hear a noise and turned as though to be sure no one had entered the church. Apparently satisfied that this was the case, he pulled her lightly into the circle of his arms. Uncomfortable in his embrace, Emma stiffened. He smiled and did not seem to mind her shyness.

'I would like you to consent to break off our engagement,' Emma said. At this Gideon's smile stilled and fell. His hands, however, remained where they were.

'My mistake was consenting to become your wife when I had not even met you,' Emma tried to explain, 'and I know now that it was foolish of me, so I would ask that you reconsider our arrangement.'

'Our arrangement?' His voice sounded soft, but his eyes looked cool. 'We ready ourselves for holy matrimony, and you slight it as an *arrangement*?'

'I have no intention to wound you, Gideon, and I am sorry that my forthrightness pains you, but I feel I must address this while I may.'

'What would you have me do, concerning your … *mistake*?'

'I would ask you to release me.' Emma looked at her hands folded tightly in her lap.

'I said I would help you, yet in this I cannot, *will* not oblige you.'

'Why can you not consider it at least?'

He answered her question with one of his own. 'Why can you not marry me?'

'I ... I do not feel for you as I should.' Emma's cheeks burned at the bluntness with which she had to serve him. He turned her to face him then pulled her in another embrace.

'But I can make you want me,' he told her softly, persuasively. 'You are young, innocent, untouched. I am none of those things. I can show you how to love and how to be loved, and when you have felt the physical nature of our relationship, you will grow in your affections, your appetites even.'

Emma blinked and turned away. He pulled her to him. His hands caressed the length of her spine. He held her captive in his ardour, his lips pressed on the nape of her neck.

'Please, Gideon, you forget yourself,' she said. 'Let me go. Please,'

Either didn't listen or didn't hear. She strained away then looked up to see Tobias Freeman.

Feet braced, arms folded, he stood like some avenging angel in righteous anger. He looked down on Gideon in his wrath. The sun streamed through the windows to rest in beams upon his shoulders. Gideon looked up and demanded, 'What do *you* want?'

'I could ask you the same question, but then it would be all too obvious, would it not?' His mouth quirked into a smile, but there was no humour in it. Emma wondered if angels spoke with the accent of handsome Irishmen. He was no angel, but he always seemed to help her when she most needed assistance. She smiled her thanks. Gideon intercepted it, and he stood and straightened his coat while his hard stare flashed between them.

'Why is it that you are always in the way, Irish?' he demanded. 'Why do I find that wherever you are, Miss Colchester is also? Why are you the felon said to dance with my affianced, and you the one to come and save her from me, when all I am doing is what any red-blooded male would attempt with his betrothed?'

'Because you do not treat the lady as a gentleman should,' Tobias said calmly.

135

'And how would you know anything of that, since you are no gentleman, but a convict?' Gideon spat, his voice thick with scorn.

'I have always thought that being a gentleman was not what lines your pockets, but how high you hold your head.'

'Well, I can tell you right now, that you hold your head way too high.'

'Aye and you cannot lift yours from the gutter.'

Emma stood and stepped between them. 'Please, stop this bickering. It achieves nothing.' She realised then that tears streamed down her cheeks. She raised her hands to her face in sudden knowledge, and then in distress, hurried from the church and left both men behind.

She turned the corner where Mary waited, Emma supposed, for Tobias to vacate the church. Emma swallowed her tears and made to pass the convict. She had almost run into the young woman. But Mary was intent on speaking to her. 'He saved my little Katy, Toby did,' the woman said.

Emma's brow clouded then cleared. 'Tobias, you mean?'

Mary smiled dreamily as her hands skimmed down her hips. 'He'd make a good husband.'

Emma flushed; a good husband for whom?

'I wouldn't know anything about that, Mary,' Emma told her, about to turn away. The young woman didn't take the hint.

'And if you were to put a good word in for me,' Mary said, 'I might have better luck attracting his attention.' Emma looked back at her; blinked. The young woman was a little too familiar. Emma hardly knew her, except for having worked along side her in the hospital kitchen on one occasion.

Emma's eyes flickered down to the open neck of the tight-fitting calico dress and considered wryly that there was a lot in Mary to attract any man. 'Mary, I cannot speak to Tobias on your behalf.' Nor did she want to, and her reason was purely selfish. Emma swallowed down on jealousy

Mary was first deflated and then suspicious. 'Why can't you? He thinks highly of you; I know he does. He hasn't spoken about you, but he admires you, miss, I see it in his eyes.'

Emma looked at the ground, and then back up at Mary. 'It is something he needs to consider himself, without any help from me. It's no concern of mine.'

The young lieutenant who had danced with Phoebe, looked over in polite enquiry. 'Is the prisoner disturbing you, miss?'

Mary looked askance at Emma, concern plain on her face. Emma shook her head, smiled a little. 'No, it's quite alright, Lieutenant.'

The soldier looked doubtful and stood by irresolutely.

'I'm sorry if I've spoken out of turn, miss,' Mary glanced at the soldier, shame-faced, and not a little worried. Emma steered to calmer waters and told her truly, 'I am so very glad that Katy is well again. I cannot tell you how pleased.'

That brought a slow smile to the other woman's face. 'Aye miss, she's all I've got in the world.'

Emma walked away, nodding in response to the lieutenant's brief bow, and as she did, she knew that she would not speak up on Mary's behalf concerning Tobias because she was selfish enough to want to cling to him herself. She asked herself if it was a matter of 'if I can't have him, no one else will,' but she would not answer that. She looked instead towards the porch of the church and wondered what was happening within.

*

'You're not in Newcastle to act as guardian angel to Miss Colchester,' Gideon said.

'I would protect any woman I thought needed assistance,' Tobias assured him.

Gideon curled his upper lip. 'Perhaps in the bog where you come from, women are always having their honour taken, and it is a common occurrence among your people. I suppose I should make allowances to you for that, thank you even, for your watchdog charm. But Miss Colchester is under no threat of dishonour from me, I can assure you.'

Tobias's jaw clenched at the slur.

'It's men like you that the lady should be guarded against, and if there are those who would hound our women, it's the king's men, such as yourself.'

Quinn laughed. It was an ugly sound, Tobias thought, and he wished he could wipe the smirk clear off Quinn's face.

'If it weren't the English teaching you lot some manners, someone else would have had to do it. You ought to thank us for sharing the English language with you, if not finer breeding. Why, now your country is almost civilised, especially when it is rid of the likes of you.

'You think that because you're six and a half foot you have the right to act as bodyguard to every skirt in the colony? Let me tell you something, which you seem to be a little slow in understanding: you have no *rights* concerning anything, especially not where Miss Colchester is concerned. I'll tell you one thing more,' Quinn whispered darkly. 'I could have you whipped. I could tell the commandant that you, a mere convict, think you have the right to throw your weight around, and the man would have you flogged. But you'll keep. You see, that's not punishment enough. The Lord only knows that your back's probably so scarred, it's doubtless as tough as old boots. After all, why spoil the fun watching the lash-master give you the cat? It's not enough. I want to see you grovel. I'll wait, Irish, and one day, I'll see you hanged.' Quinn smiled ghoulishly. 'When you stand at the gibbet and soil your own breeches in fear as you wait for the noose, I guarantee I'll be there to bid you farewell.'

Quinn turned on his heel and walked from the church. Tobias shook in his anger, helpless to act and yes, without any right to do so. He dropped down on one of the pews, looked up at the altar, and saw the church from a different perspective than from the convict's gallery. He steadied his hands and cleared his head, for if he walked out into the irritable heat of the day, one more insult from Gideon Quinn could well lead him to throttle the man. He remained where he was until he could think clearly.

Quinn's words had shaken him, and he would be a liar if he said it wasn't so. He had felt anger in his life more times than he cared to count, but he had never experienced such vindictive hatred from anyone. In spite of himself, Tobias felt his innards quiver.

Quinn had it in for him. He had to stay away from Emma Colchester, whatever the cost, because that man would see him hanged at the slightest provocation. Quinn had the power of the Crown behind him, and Tobias had nothing with which to fight back. His strength would have to come from the Almighty above. Did he really believe that? He thought perhaps he did.

When he walked out into the afternoon sun the parson's wife offered him a triangle of currant bread. She smiled at him as though she had known he needed her smile. He doffed his hat and thanked her.

'Now, young man, when I saw you before, I thought that you looked to be strapping-strong, and I am going to see if we might have you work for us in the kitchen garden. What would you say to that?'

'He would say, "God bless you for an angel", wouldn't you, Toby mate?' Kevin said as he came to stand between them.

Tobias smiled. 'Aye I would.'

'Leave it with me and I shall see what I can do. There is one thing, however, on which we must see eye to eye before you even begin.'

'And what would that be?'

'You will be required to come to daily prayers in the house with the family.'

Tobias nodded and said, 'I can do that,' and put the piece of bread into his mouth. He caught the disappointment on Kevin's face over the food.

'Let me beckon the parson a moment,' the lady said as she flagged her husband's attention. The parson shook hands with Tobias, and for one of the first times since he had been in the colony, he felt like a man, not just a convict shamed for his crimes.

'What is your name?' The parson asked attentively.

'Freeman.' Tobias said, but the parson shook his head.

'No, no, I mean, what is your Christian name?'

'Tobias.'

The parson smiled widely then, as if he had received knowledge from the *Almighty above*, Tobias thought.

'Tobias.'

Toby nodded in reply.

'Tobias,' the parson repeated. 'God is good.' He hastened to explain. 'The meaning of the name Tobias is, "God is good".'

Tobias thought on that the rest of the Sabbath day and wondered at the appropriateness of the name for such as him, but then he remembered Emma's words to him in the hospital, when he felt as though he was unworthy of any respect. The memory brought something else to mind.

'I, even I, am he that blotteth out thy transgressions for mine own sake, and will not remember thy sins.'

Tobias wondered if God really was so good that he could forgive him his sins. Emma told him that if he repented, he would indeed be forgiven. Then all he had to do was forgive himself. He pondered the possibility of being of enough worth that God should cast aside all blame and remember it no more.

God is good.

Perhaps he was.

TWELVE

'Emma dear, why don't you and Phoebe come and share a pot of tea with me,' the parson's wife asked outside Mr Tucker's store the following day.

Emma had gone with Phoebe on an errand for Aunt Adelaide and had been chastened by Mr Tucker's stiff reception. Mrs Brown apparently noticed the man's lack of cordiality and mentioned it as soon as they emerged from the store.

'Mr Tucker seems to think that because he is the only storekeeper in Newcastle, he must only be charitable when he feels inclined. I have always believed that a jovial shop owner makes the day a little brighter, and it would not hurt the man to offer a smile once in a while.'

Emma bit her lip and glanced at Phoebe. 'I must admit that I am quite possibly the reason for Mr Tucker's lack of cordiality. I was perhaps a little short with him the other day.'

'Well, it never pays to nurse a grudge,' the woman said, 'and I must say, Emma, that I would be hard pressed to believe anything so harsh of you, coming to know you as I have over the past weeks. Pay no mind to the shopkeeper dear. Why, next time you visit his store, he will have forgotten all about his grievance, I'm sure.' She patted Emma's arm solicitously. 'Now I have a lovely paisley shawl which was given to me by one of our parishioners before we left for

141

the colonies, and I wondered if I might show it to you. I have never worn anything so regal in all my born days, and I cannot decide whether to wear it with my gown to the commandant's ball this evening. Would you mind terribly?'

'We would be pleased to,' Emma said then opened her parasol as the trio stepped off the veranda.

At the parsonage a few minutes later, the women studied the intricate shawl.

'Now I have always thought that a mature woman with grey hair always looks washed out in a similar colour, and that is why I have never worn this shawl. But here, come and see for yourselves; tell me what you think of it.'

Emma touched the shawl with something like wonder. Doubtless it had come all the way from India. It shimmered dully in the light of the parlour window, a soft dove grey threaded with paisley teardrops of pink and blue and gold. It suggested every colour of the rainbow.

'It's wonderful,' Emma said. The rector's wife nodded.

'And yet,' she said, as she pulled it around her shoulders, 'I fear it does nothing for me.'

'Not at all,' Emma told her with all kindness and seriousness.

'It is the same colour as the gown Emma is going to wear to the commandant's dinner party this evening,' Phoebe noted.

The woman's brows rose. 'Why, then Emma shall make use of it. No, no dear, please don't refuse me. Wear it and make me glad.'

'It is also the same colour as your eyes,' Phoebe said. 'Oh Emma, it does look lovely on you.'

Emma turned to the parson's wife. 'Thank you for your generosity.'

The lady smiled and patted Emma's knee. 'I will just take a wedge of this tart out to the gardener. He has been busy all morning.'

'Stay seated where you are,' Emma said. 'I'll go and take it to him. It is the least I can do.'

'Phoebe and I will be quite content to bide with our slices of tart then,' she told Emma thankfully as she took the weight off her feet, 'for my ankles swell like high tide in this weather.'

It was a large garden, surrounded by picket fencing to keep out the kangaroos and possums, as well as any spotted quolls which might think to take one of the hens that liked to fluff their feathers in the dust too long after the sun went down.

Onions and cabbages and carrots dotted the garden. The leaves of the rows of potatoes had begun to wilt with the ferocity of the January sun. Not so the bright-eyed rooster who looked at her askance as she passed him, and hoped, no doubt, that the treacle tart was his to gobble.

Pumpkin leaves, dark and large as dinner plates, spread from the mound of compost like a green hillock, but the gardener was nowhere to be seen.

'I have brought you a slice of tart and some tea.' Emma raised her voice and looked around, mug in one hand, plate in the other.

'Emma.' She started as Tobias materialised from the greenery. She was startled at seeing him, splashing hot tea over her hand. She set it down gingerly on a stump and wiped her hand. 'Are you burnt?' he asked as he glanced down with a frown.

'It's nothing,' she told him then as she patted her hand dry on the hem of her skirt. Without a word he picked up a watering can, took her hand, and watered it as if she too were wilting. 'Thank you,' she told him with a smile and a blush. Receiving the plate, he nodded his thanks.

'Will you sit a moment with me?' He motioned to a garden seat under the shade of a large tree with spreading boughs. It had tiny fruits clustered on it much like small figs.

Emma looked at him and hesitated.

'Please. Just until I finish with the plate,' he pressed.

Emma nodded. She would have thought that such a big man

could easily have devoured the dainty slice in two bites, but he seemed intent on making it last.

'I have been thinking of you. I lie awake and dream of you with my eyes open.'

Emma looked at him and blinked, then looked away as she flushed. She could admit to the same, but she would not.

'You told me that if I confess my sins to God and repent, he will forgive me.'

She nodded. 'That's true.'

'A gentleman farmer died because of me. I knocked him down with my fist and he hit his head.'

Emma turned to him. 'Why did you hit him, Tobias?'

'I hit him because he ruined my sister in his lust to have her, though she wanted none of it.'

Emma felt for his plight. 'What is your sister's name?'

'Molly,' he said. The fondness in his tone seemed to reach beyond the bounds of the ocean.

'That's what you called me when you were feverish in the hospital.' Emma smiled. 'I thought she may have been your love back in Ireland.'

Tobias's mouth quirked into a brief smile. 'Is it a sin to yearn for another man's woman, one who is about to become his wife?'

The burr of his voice was soft with yearning, and Emma felt the pull to be close to him. She resisted the temptation.

'I believe it is,' she told him sorrowfully. He gulped his tea down and set it on the plate with finality.

'Well, if it's a sin to love you, I don't regret it, and I'm sure not going to repent. If God loves me as you told me he does, then he will forgive me for it regardless.'

Tears pooled in Emma's eyes as she stood and smiled at him. 'I am sure he already has.'

'Will you meet me by the church after the supper bell?' he said, his voice raw. Emma shook her head and he took her free hand to waylay her.

'I will wait there every evening until you come. Whenever you hear the bells pealing, they'll remind you that I am waiting.'

'I am not at liberty to love you, Tobias. You will wait in vain.'

'I am a man with time on my hands.' He gave her a wry smile, and when he released her hand, he watched as she left.

'We would have come out looking for you, Emma,' the parson's wife smiled, 'but once we cut the tart, there was no getting us up from the table.' Emma took a filled plate and sat down.

'What were you doing out there?' Phoebe asked. 'Helping the gardener?'

Emma smiled and flushed. *If only I could.*

'I sat and spoke to him while he ate.'

On the way home, Phoebe asked, 'Have you thought any more concerning your dilemma with Gideon?'

Emma sighed. 'I have already told him.'

Phoebe stopped short. 'How did he respond?'

Emma shook her head. 'Rather disagreeably, which is understandable, but what the outcome of it all will be, I cannot tell. He gave me no firm answer, but a good helping of scorn. I have little hope that he will sever our agreement.'

They started to walk again. The white muslin skirts of their gowns brushed the ground and caused the dust to eddy around their hems.

'Were it not for your convict, do you think you would still have changed your mind concerning Gideon?'

'I changed my mind the moment I saw him.'

Phoebe looked at her in surprise, and Emma felt she had to justify herself. 'If I had known how old Gideon was, I never would have agreed to his proposal in the first place. I was sent the miniature and gauged his age to be in his middle twenties at most. Instead

I was dumbfounded to find that I was engaged to some venerable gentleman who could be my grandfather.'

Phoebe stopped again, this time in front of Emma, and clasped her arm.

'You had no idea of the age he was?' She was flabbergasted.

'My assumptions were rather stupid, I see that now, and yet …'

'I am surprised that my mama did not mention it to yours. I had supposed that his being a veteran had been no object.'

'Had my mother known the circumstance of his age, I believe she would have intervened. As it stands, she is leagues distant from knowing anything at all, and I am, as it were, trapped. I might as well be on a desert island, Phoebe, without protection, habitation, or money to call my own. In short, I am in his debt.'

'My dear cousin, I am so very sorry,' Phoebe whispered, one hand on her cheek. Tears of compassion shone in her eyes. 'If you break your engagement with Gideon, you will lose your reputation.'

'Yet if I had gone on without saying a word to try and dissuade him from his course when I love another, I would have lost my self-respect.'

Phoebe clapped a hand over her mouth. 'You told him about the convict?'

Emma shook her head. 'I couldn't; for Tobias's sake, I couldn't tell Gideon. He would make his life a living hell. I know it. Gideon despises the convicts, and to think he has been spurned is bad enough, but to know that I would cast him aside only for a convict to take his place would make him bitter.'

'You are between the devil and the deep blue sea, as the saying would have it,' Phoebe said.

The situation was so dire that Emma laughed, and Phoebe did too. They held one another to stop from falling. Then, just as quickly as it had begun, the laughter stopped.

'What will you do, Emma?'

Emma looked out to the sea, at the ships in the harbour held at anchor against the strength of the waves. 'I will continue to pray. I need to trust that there is a purpose for what is happening in my life now and in the future, and that my days are mapped according to my best interest. For when I cannot swim on my own, I must just hold on.'

*

Later, when Emma sat at the commandant's dining table, she thought it was a coincidence that she was seated beside the commandant, while Gideon was placed at the other end of the dining room, and she wondered why the commandant had not thought it proper to seat her closer to Officer Quinn.

Phoebe sat opposite the red-haired soldier Emma remembered from the beach on Christmas Day and knew that her cousin would be pleased with her lot. But when Euphemie caught Emma's eye, Emma knew that she would not care if it were by happenstance that she sat beside the commandant. Her scorn was spread so thick that Emma could have buttered her bread with it. As it was, Emma hardly cared to talk to the commandant at all.

'Do you like crab, Miss Colchester?' he asked.

'I cannot say, since I must confess I have never tried it.'

'Then you shall this evening. When is the last time you ate apple tart?' 'Too long ago.' 'Then that is something else we shall remedy before the evening is put to rest.'

Even Euphemie stopped with her pointed looks and put herself to better employment as she enjoyed the crab croquettes and fish pie, the roasted mutton and apple tart. The gentlemen drank claret, as well as the ubiquitous 'Nelson's Blood', and there was much flush-faced merriment.

It did not concern Emma at first that Euphemie had her glass topped up with red wine until her cousin grew loud and brash in her conversation. Although Emma did not drink, it was not her place to judge her cousin. But before long Emma knew that Euphemie intended trouble.

'Emma, if I didn't know better, I would think that you changed the position of your name card at the table, just for the pleasure of the commandant's company.' The group laughed at the quip, and Emma was compelled to smile politely along with the rest of them.

'I believe it is the scar running across my cheek which charms the ladies,' the commandant jested. 'It saves me the lack of charisma.'

'Fie, Commandant Morisset,' Euphemie said. 'You charm us all, especially Emma, I know.' Emma glanced at Gideon. He scowled like he'd tasted a mouthful of sour grapes.

'I am sure that it is your kind-heartedness alone that sees your name on the lips of the ladies of the colony, and although I am the envy of many ladies in Newcastle, I did not touch the place card.' Emma smiled but she knew that she flushed as though she were guilty of something.

'Most certainly you are envy of the women in the Coal River,' the commandant said, 'but it has more to do with your winsome looks than any position at this table.'

A few faces leered at their commander's compliment and Emma bowed her head. 'It was for this reason alone that I had your name card placed beside mine,' he assured her.

'Thank you for your compliment.'

'It is mere truth, Miss Colchester. Officer Quinn is a thorn in our sides because of his fortuitous catch.'

'Commandant, it seems that you have not opened the gospel any time of late, for jealousy is one of the seven deadly sins. Emma, you could not have given the commandant your Bible anytime too soon,' Euphemie said slyly.

The commandant blinked, as though he wondered what the girl was talking about.

'I misunderstand your meaning,' he said to Euphemie, but the girl by now was so inebriated that she didn't seem to care what she said or who heard it. Emma glanced at her uncle and aunt, and at Phoebe, and she swallowed her uneasiness. The pink blush spread over her face and neck as she waited for the inevitable. Her damp hands clutched tightly at the napkin in her lap.

The pleading look Emma gave Euphemie did no good. It merely spurred her on as though Emma's profound shame made the mockery all the more worthwhile.

'Why, Emma's Bible which she gave to you,' Euphemie cooed, soft as a turtledove.

'Miss Colchester gave me no Bible as a gift,' the commandant said.'I thought that's what you told me, Emma dear.' The parson's wife leaned forward so that she could meet Emma's look. Emma hardly knew what to say and sat dumbfounded. The commandant looked at Emma, met her eye, saw her flush of humiliation, and saved her, as a gentleman would.

In effect, he lied.

'Oh, that Bible, of course, I remember. Yes, the deadly sins and all that. If there is a deadly sin which we have exercised tonight, it's gluttony.' He chuckled then leaned back, and placed his hand on his stomach in repletion.

'Yes, I believe we have overindulged ourselves tonight,' Emma's uncle agreed, 'and my family and I will have an early night. Doctor's orders.' He chortled, but his eyes did not smile as he glanced at his eldest daughter. There was an uncomfortable silence. Blinking eyes and flickering candles were all that seemed to move for a moment, and then the commandant and the other ladies and gentlemen rose as Emma and her uncle's family left the dining table.

Emma thought that she might well cry.

As they made their way from the commandant's cottage, the lights that glimmered through the windows had previously twinkled in welcome, now those candles resembled nothing so much as looks of censure, and Emma knew that many of those eyes were on her.

She had not had the chance to try to explain the intrigue to the commandant, and did not, in fact, know how she would begin. Then there was Gideon. Yet if she were fortunate, she would not have to mention anything at all. Still, the bold innuendo Euphemie had made was not true at all, for the one who commandeered Emma's heart was Tobias Freeman, convict, indentured servant of the crown, social outcast.

'Euphemie, whatever possessed you to speak in such a way of Emma and the commandant?' her father demanded as he pushed his spectacles firmly against his face with agitation.

'Why, Emma's own admission itself,' Euphemie replied.

'What exactly is that supposed to mean?' the surgeon said.

'Euphemie, why are you doing this?' Emma asked.

'Why?' Euphemie spoke as though Emma were an imbecile. 'Why should you have the attentions of the commandant when you are in fact betrothed to Gideon Quinn? Why must you flutter your lashes in his direction when you cannot have him as you wish? You slink in the garden with your arms around him and your lips pressed against his as though there were no tomorrow, and then have the audacity to give him the gift of your Bible when your actions are anything but those of a chaste woman! Why, I would wager that there was more than kissing that went on that night. I saw things no gentle woman ought to see.'

'Then you saw more than what went on,' Emma said.

'You are a lying fornicator!' Euphemie spat.

Emma gaped in shock. 'You do both him and me an injustice if you think that's what you witnessed.' Emma's voice trembled. 'Nothing more than kisses were asked, and nothing more was given. Nor was it the commandant.'

'Of course it was.' Euphemie sounded bitter. 'I heard him call you, and you cannot deny it.'

'I do not deny it,' Emma said as they entered the cottage. 'I refute none of it. But it was not Commandant Morisset you saw me with, but someone else.'

'Who then?' Aunt Adelaide asked. Emma pressed her lips firmly together.

'That, you shall not know.'

'Because what I say is true!' Euphemie had long since lost her temper, and Emma held onto hers by willpower alone, but as her uncle lit the lamp it was Emma who was under scrutiny.

'The commandant is not who you think he is.' They all looked at her askance. 'What I mean to say is that the name of *commandant* merely hides the identity of the other person involved, and it is unfortunate indeed, Euphemie, that you saw fit to spread your knowledge, which was erroneous at best and damning at worst.'

Euphemie snorted. 'You think I haven't noticed how the commandant looks at you? If you suppose that I will believe you then you must think me a fool.'

'I think nothing of the sort. I am merely telling you the truth. I don't know what you mean when you say that the commandant has looked at me or treated me in any other manner but a courteous one, but I see now why you are intent on causing trouble for me. Still, I tell you I am not interested in the man, and you could have saved your breath to cool your porridge, for I am sure it would have served you better if you had.'

'I rather think that the commandant will want nothing more to do with you now, Euphemie. Emma is correct. You embarrassed all of us, but most especially yourself,' her father said.

Euphemie turned from him back to Emma and jabbed the air with a finger of aggression, desperate and defensive. She seemed fearful that what her father said was true. In the morning, Emma suspected, the girl would wake appalled at her behaviour at the commandant's, but just then Euphemie appeared too livid to care.

'You will end up with a belly full of shame, cousin, and all you will be known for is your deceit.'

'Just as you will be known for your sharp tongue and bitter heart.'

Emma's body trembled in righteous anger, every nerve aflame with the desire to slap her cousin roundly. She would not stoop so low. Instead she addressed her uncle. 'I must go to the commandant to beg his forgiveness for the misunderstanding first thing tomorrow.'

'Euphemie will be sure to go with you,' Uncle George said, 'for her rudeness at his dining table.'

'I will do nothing of the sort!' Euphemie told him.

'Yes, daughter, you will, and if I have to go with you to ensure that you do, then so be it. For when you are under your father's roof, you will live by your father's commands.'

'And what of Emma?' Euphemie said. 'How will she atone for what she has done?'

'The way each of us does every day of our lives: she must take her confessions to God. I am sure that Gideon Quinn will make Emma accountable for what was bandied about in the commandant's cottage like fish wives' gossip, but that is neither my concern nor yours.'

Aunt Adelaide said to Emma, 'In the morning we shall speak further of this. Your betrothal is a binding agreement, and you *will* marry Gideon Quinn, my dear, whether you have had second thoughts or not. After all, the whole congregation witnessed your engagement. I have not forgotten that, even if you have.' And with this her aunt and uncle left her.

The three girls stood in the steady lantern light. Euphemie whispered acidly, 'I would have a care, cousin, for I will find you out. The commandant will take notice of me, because I will make sure of it.' She turned on her heel and left.

'Oh Emma,' Phoebe whispered, 'whatever will you do?'

It was a question for which Emma had no answer.

THIRTEEN

There was nothing to be done for it, Emma thought as she dressed. The longer she tarried, the harder the visit to the commandant would become. He would think ill of her, and she could not blame anyone but herself.

'Will you come with me now, Euphemie?' she enquired of her cousin, who sat in her usual chair at her preferred occupation of reading.

'I will not,' she said. 'I will go by myself, in my own time. I would rather walk alone.' Emma nodded and stepped to the door, and then turned back.

'We don't have to be adversaries, Euphemie,' Emma told her softly.

Euphemie glanced up as though she considered what Emma said, but apparently she did not want to relinquish the fight. 'Your sweetness is hypocrisy, Emma, and your piety a ruse. Because you are beautiful you can pick and choose your men. Still, your lies, your pretence … I, for one, am not fooled. You will get what you deserve.'

Emma shook her head, bemused.

Euphemie went on. 'Revenge is a dish best served cold. I am in no rush.'

Emma stood wordless before Euphemie's promise. A breeze from the open door lifted the ringlets from her nape and a shiver of unease riffled up her spine.

'I will say good morning then,' Emma replied quietly, and walked out into the brightness of the day.

She saw Mary on her way to her work at the hospital.

'How does Katy fare?' Emma enquired.

Mary's face lit up like a beacon. 'She's grand, miss; never been better.' Then she went on. 'You know what I'm going to do about that Toby Freeman? I'm going to come right out with it and ask him to court me.'

'Oh?' Emma felt her face fall and tried to muster a brighter countenance.

'Well, to my way of thinking, if I don't get up the courage, I may miss out. Besides, Katy needs a father.'

'Certainly she does.' Emma had to agree with that. She could not be that churlish. 'Where *is* her father?'

'Who knows?' Mary shrugged. Emma wasn't sure if Mary's words meant that she didn't know who the father was or whether she meant she had no notion where he was at present. Emma put it aside. It wasn't proper to ask.

'Don't tell me you haven't noticed how handsome he is?' Mary asked.

'Tobias?'

'Who else *but* him?'

'I had noticed,' Emma admitted, and then coloured.

Mary looked at Emma's cheeks and laughed raucously. 'And here I was thinking that perhaps a fine lady like you wouldn't look twice at Toby. It just goes to show that bonny feathers don't always make bonny birds.'

It was a truism where Tobias Freeman was concerned, Emma thought. 'Do you get along well together?'

Mary laughed. 'I need a bed partner. Katy needs a father. Whether he likes to sit and smoke a pipe reading poetry every evening makes

154

no difference to me, miss.'

They reached the convict hospital and Mary let herself in at the picket gate and said slyly, 'A girl has ways and means to catch a lad.' With this she winked and turned away.

Emma had an inkling of what Mary meant, and as she walked towards the barracks her heart sank a little further into her shoes. She reminded herself to count her blessings, but was so heart sore she could not think of any. It didn't help that, as soon as she was in the commandant's presence, she had to blink her eyes free of tears. The man mistook the reason and stood from the chair behind his desk and went to her side.

'Why, Miss Colchester, whatever is the matter?' He looked into her eyes and offered his handkerchief.

'Commandant, I have come to offer my apologies, and I find that I am overcome. Please excuse my tears.'

'Won't you sit down? Let me pour you a glass of water.' He turned to pick up the jug and Emma heard the water tumble into the glass. Emma thanked him and drank.

'It's true that I gave my Bible away, Commandant. I was thanked for it in front of Mrs Brown, the parson's wife. However the person I gave it to, thought that it would be frowned upon, if not forbidden that a gift of any kind be given to a felon. Considering the recipient is a convict, I think the assumption was a correct one. I'm only sorry for the embarrassment I must have caused you.'

'As for your interest in me as a man, then, your cousin Euphemie is barking up the wrong tree, so to speak.' The commandant smiled. 'Because you care for someone else.'

He knew it. Emma could not lie. She nodded. The name Gideon Quinn was before them but they knew he was not the man of whom the commandant spoke.

'I would ask that you forgive me for what was said last night,' Emma said.

'My dear, Miss Colchester, I want you to think no more of it. I am only sorry that you were maligned at dinner. It must have cost you some embarrassment.'

Emma nodded. 'You also, Commandant.'

He grinned and shook his head, and the scar on his face was lost for a moment in his smile. 'I do not blush easily, and I consider it a compliment of sorts. It would be even better were it true.'

Emma smiled and stood. The commandant went with her to the door. 'God bless you for your understanding.' Emma curtseyed. The commandant bowed and placed a chaste kiss on her hand.

'And you also, Miss Colchester.' He smiled. As Emma made her way down Prospect Hill, she met Euphemie on her way up. Emma perceived a change in Euphemie's appearance and realised that her cousin wore her hair in a different fashion, that her gown was one of her best, and that rose water had been dabbed on rather liberally. It seemed that not just convict women used their feminine wiles to attract a man.

'Yoo-hoo, Emma dear!' the parson's wife called with a wave of her handkerchief from the parsonage. Emma turned to head in her direction.

Mrs Brown was a small, round woman and always seemed to use the same mode to attract attention. The handkerchief fluttered from her outstretched hand, in the manner of a cabbage moth negotiating its way through the cottage garden. Emma was not surprised that the lady liked flowers so well, for she seemed very at home as she brushed past the lavender and tansy and bachelor's buttons.

Mrs Brown met Emma at the garden gate, opening the latch as she spoke in a consipiratorial tone. 'I cannot help but go over in my head what your cousin Euphemie inferred at the commandant's dinner last night, and I feel the need as a Christian woman to caution you to be careful since you are betrothed to be married.'

'I assure you that I have no interest in Commandant Morisset,'

Emma declared, and it was then that she noticed Tobias, who tended the garden by the porch. His black hair shone, and as he glanced up, his eyes in his bronzed face shone sea-bright. His hair fell around his nape as he put his head down, but Emma had caught his look. Her heart took up a quicker rhythm and she forced herself to attend to the parson's wife, the woman's small brown eyes curious.

'My dear, it will soon be time for you to wed, and a woman's good reputation, once sullied, is forever remembered. I just want you to be careful and am mentioning this for your own good.'

'I agree with you wholeheartedly, Mrs Brown, and I'm not at all put out by your plain speaking. I know you have my best interests at heart.'

Mrs Brown smiled at patted Emma's arm.

'I see you admire my lavender,' the good woman said. 'Tobias, pick Miss Colchester a long-stemmed bunch of flowers. Come, Emma dear, step out of the sun and wait on the porch with me. Tobias will be a little while yet trimming you a nosegay.'

So the woman chatted as they watched Tobias collect the flowers, and although Emma tried to listen to the reverend's wife, she stop thinking of the Song of Solomon.

My spikenard sends forth its fragrance. A bundle of myrrh is my beloved to me.

'I am inclined to give that cousin of yours a piece of my mind,' Mrs Brown said. 'My uncle spoke to her at length.'

'I am glad to hear it. Oh and here is Tobias finished. What a wonderful bouquet you have there. Did you know that Tobias means, "Gift from God", Emma dear? And what a gift he has been to me here just lately, haven't you, Tobias? Now, give Miss Colchester the flowers.' She spoke to him as though he were a rather large boy. Emma had to smile.

'They are the colour of your gown, Miss Colchester,' he said as he stepped onto the veranda to hand her the lavender and doffed his hat. The bouquet's perfume was invigorating, sweet, but she smelled him too, rich as the earth, and the cadence of her pulse beat quick as a drum.

'Thank you, Tobias.' Emma met his gaze for moments too long.

When she arrived back at her uncle's cottage she placed the lavender in a jug and set it by her bed. She would inhale its sweetness when she readied herself to sleep.

She reminded herself again that her future was not hers to give away, nor was her heart. Emma prayed that God's will would be done in her life and that she would continue to trust in his wisdom, even when she felt she stood on sinking sand.

Aunt Adelaide stood at the door. Emma turned from the spray of flowers with a self-conscious flush on her cheeks.

'Where did they come from?'

'They came from the parsonage,' Emma answered truthfully.

'Oh,' Aunt Adelaide said, appeased by her answer. Had she thought that they were from the commandant? Emma crossed her hands in front of her and waited. She was uncomfortable with her uncle's wife.

Why did you fail to tell your sister-in-law that Gideon was in his dotage? Why, with your letter of recommendation to Mama, citing all Officer Quinn's noteworthy praises, did you not mention his age?

'I would like to talk to you concerning Gideon Quinn.'

'Of course, Aunt Adelaide.' Emma nodded and moved aside to close the door as the woman entered the small room. Aunt Adelaide sat on the hard-backed chair and turned her gaze to Emma.

'Euphemie embarrassed herself and everyone else around the table last night,' her aunt said, folding her hands before her. 'Yet I ask myself, why would your cousin try to damage your reputation unless she had due cause?'

Phoebe had entered the room and spoke up. 'Why, Mama, it is

because she was drunk.'

Adelaide turned her stare towards her youngest daughter and pointed a wrathful finger that shook with emotion. 'How dare you speak such slander?'

'I am only being honest,' Phoebe said, clearly realising that honesty was not what her mother wanted to hear, not about Euphemie, at any rate. 'Leave the room, Phoebe, and attend to your sewing.'

Phoebe glanced regretfully at Emma and did as she was bid without a word of argument.

'Are you carrying on with the commandant, or are you not?' Aunt Adelaide demanded. She used her finger like a poker as she stabbed the distance between them.

'I am not,' Emma said, but her aunt had her dander up and would not be so easily mollified.

'You seem to forget that you are affianced to Officer Quinn and that your nuptials will take place within a matter of weeks.'

'I have forgotten none of it,' Emma told her quietly, and raised her chin.

'Do you defy me?'

'Not at all, but I would like to ask you something, if I may.'

At that, Aunt Adelaide calmed herself. 'Of course, you may ask me anything you wish. You are my sister-in-law's daughter in my duty of care, and as such I have the responsibility to be your listening ear for at least until you are wed, and beyond that too, I would hope.'

'Then why,' Emma asked with dignity, 'did you not see fit to tell me or Mama that Gideon Quinn was a man of more than sixty years, when I have only just seen out my seventeenth? Why did you allow me to come all this way without sharing that knowledge, when I know for a fact that Mama asked you that question specifically?'

Aunt Adelaide flushed to the roots of her hair. She raised a hand to her mouth and glanced away. 'I can't remember that question ever being asked.' Adelaide looked away as she spoke.

Emma said nothing; if she did, she would accuse her aunt of being a liar. After a moment, she spoke again. 'Would you be content for either of your daughters to wed someone in their dotage, Aunt Adelaide?'

The woman bristled and brought out the finger again. 'When Gideon Quinn retires you will have a life of contentment, if not one of ease. As the daughter of a clergyman who has passed away, you really had no other decent option. I did you a favour when I recommended Gideon to you. Your future now is as solid as a rock.'

'There is only one rock on which I trust, Aunt Adelaide, only one firm foundation on which I try to build my life.'

'Do you try to sermonise to me, girl?'

'Not at all. I am merely telling you what I hold true for my life. Material wealth should not be the basis on which a marriage is built, but rather esteem and respect, and one would hope, love also.'

'Love doesn't put food on the table,' Adelaide said dismissively and stood. 'Gideon Quinn will be here later this evening. Doubtless he will want to hear from your lips that Euphemie misjudged you and that your marriage plans continue as planned. For if you were to spurn him now, wherever would you live?' With this the woman stood and left the room.

Emma saw her aunt's threat for what it was, and wondered why it was so important to Aunt Adelaide that she should stay true to the agreement, since it would neither benefit nor harm the family, whatever she did. It hurt that her aunt's good graces relied on her compliance alone. More than ever she felt like a castaway, adrift and friendless on a foreign shore.

Emma took up the miniature, which she had worn lovingly around her neck for months. She had not taken it off until she had come to the colony, to Coal River, where she had met her betrothed.

Thereafter, the knowledge of her future kept her from ever putting it back on.

Tears welled in her eyes and she was taken back for moments to the wash of the harbour and the splash of the waves. Emma saw back to the indignity of having allowed the convict Tobias Freeman to divest her of her gown. She had hardly guessed that when he had stripped her of her skirts, he would lay her heart bare besides. He held her still, whether he knew it or not, just as he had when he had ferried her tirelessly through the waves.

She looked down at the likeness in the miniature through her tears. In her mind, it was not the face of Gideon Quinn that she saw, but Tobias Freeman. She did not see him as a convict, outcast, or indentured servant to the crown.

Emma saw him as a man.

He had saved both their lives. She wished that she could share hers with him, that they could be strong together in the uncertain waves of life. As it was, she had hardly more freedom than Tobias himself.

'You may as well be shackled like the rest of us.'

Kevin's words held more truth than Emma could ever have imagined.

Emma turned as Phoebe quietly knocked and entered. When she sat down beside her cousin upon the bed, Phoebe looked at Emma and they shared a sorrowful smile of understanding.

'I am so sorry, Emma,' Phoebe said, 'so sorry that you are trapped in this.'

'I made the choice to give Gideon my consent. I ought to have waited until I knew more of the man, waited before I made the voyage to Newcastle. I can blame no one but myself, when all is said and done.'

'But Gideon, did he say he would think on whether he might yet release you from your engagement?'

Emma shook her head. 'I do not think he has any intention of doing so.'

'Why would he?' Phoebe asked, almost to herself. 'A beautiful, young wife when all hope for any wife at all would have long since faded. Who would not take the opportunity?'

They shared a glance at the knock on the cottage door. Gideon's voice was audible. Emma stood and took a deep breath then smoothed down her skirts. Phoebe quickly clasped her hand.

'I will pray for you Emma. I will pray for you and will continue to do so.'

Emma smiled. 'Thank you cousin; you are a friend indeed.'

Emma met Gideon at the door.

'Emma, will you walk out with me?' Gideon said, and then he took her by the arm and led her down the garden path. She glanced at him as they headed towards the beach in the late afternoon, and his age struck her forcibly yet again. It was not just the grey, receding hair it was the fact that she dreamed of another life, another prospect, another man.

'Emma, last night Euphemie alluded to things concerning the commandant which, I must say, shocked and confused me. I was not a little irritated to hear that my fiancée had been flirting with the commandant—and this in the company of others—and I sought the commandant out to ask him if any of it was in fact true. He denied that anything was between you.'

'He told you the truth,' Emma said. 'Euphemie sees what does not exist. I have no feelings for the commandant save those of a friendly acquaintance.'

'Then I will take you at your word.'

They continued to walk towards the direction of the native camp nestled among the mangrove trees in the distance. Emma took a deep breath and broached the topic they had spoken of in the church.

'After my discussion with you concerning our engagement, I

feel I must ask you if you have since thought about what I asked, and if you have reconsidered your stance concerning our marriage. Will you let me go?'

Gideon looked out to sea and at the setting sun. 'I will not.'

Emma wondered if he saw the sun setting on the years of his own life, whether as Phoebe said, he saw her as his last chance for a wife and family. 'A man's word is his bond. I have given my word, and so, my dear, have you. There will be no release, no second thoughts, no quarter given.'

Emma glanced at him and swallowed. If it were not for his smile, she might have taken him for a tyrant. Yet, of course, that could not be not true.

FOURTEEN

The church bell pealed and the congregation filed inside the cool, dim sanctuary of the sandstone house of God. Emma knew that Tobias would be seated in the gallery but she would not risk a look behind her, no matter how much she longed to look at him. Gideon sat at her side, his face florid above his woollen redcoat, and she thought that though some of the convicts wore their 'slops' in tatters, they would fare the heat a little better than his majesty's soldiers.

The cram of damp, unwashed bodies was an inducement to the blowflies, which made it their business to attend the service and bother one worshipper after another.

'January,' Phoebe said to Emma towards the end of the service, 'is unbearable, but February is every bit as hot.'

'If we open the shutters to let in the breeze, we are like flea-bitten dogs,' Aunt Adelaide complained, 'and if we leave them shut we swelter, sticky as teacakes. Those flies land on us and will not be shooed away, no matter how hard we try.'

The place was also overrun with spiders, Emma knew, and at night they would emerge to hang down, large and round like Christmas baubles, or else look up with shining eyes from tunnels in the dry earth, in wait for a beetle or ant, or even a curious finger.

'Don't put your finger in the hole, Katy!' Emma heard Mary's warning after Sunday school. The little girl looked up with round eyes.

'Why?'

'Because there is a spider in that hole, and if you're not careful it will grab hold of your finger and drag you down there,' Kevin said. This was warning enough for the four-year-old, who quickly stood and backed away to stand beside her mother and hold onto her skirts.

Emma watched as Tobias strode into view and the child danced up to him. He picked her up, and she smiled gleefully. She shared her tale of the spider and told him not to put his finger down the hole.

'He'll eat you up and we'll never see you again,' she said.

'I will be sure to throw that hungry spider a slice of boiled mutton, and that will fill his tummy. What do you think of that idea?'

'I like it.' Katy nodded with a smile, and he knelt down to deposit her on the ground as he reached the girl's mother. He stood up and Katy scampered off after a band of children who marched like soldiers around the biggest tree. As Emma turned back to glance surreptitiously in Tobias's direction, she saw Mary launch herself into his arms and press a kiss full upon his surprised mouth. The convict woman smiled coquettishly into his face as her arms wound around him a little tighter. Emma spun away and narrowly avoided Phoebe's redheaded soldier in her effort not to see the spectacle before her.

'Pardon me, miss,' the youth said as he glanced at Phoebe with a smile and a flush on his cheeks.

'It was my fault. No need for apology. I ought to be more careful.'

Emma hardly knew where to look. Although she steeled herself to avoid Tobias and Mary, her eyes strayed in their direction almost against her will. Mary had released him but she stood close enough that her skirts brushed against his legs, and though she had relinquished him from her embrace, she held his attention, for he smiled down at her as she spoke. Emma couldn't hear what they said, but she remembered earlier words.

'*I'm going to come right out with it and ask him to court me.*'

Perhaps courting among convicts was a far more open affair than she had imagined. She told herself that it was no concern of hers, but it smarted like salt in a wound all the same. She wanted to go back to the cottage, and the excuse of a headache was real enough.

'Do you want company on the way?' Phoebe said, but Emma knew she wanted to stay with her young soldier and merely asked out of her generous spirit. Emma was not going to take the opportunity away from her.

'Stay where you are, cousin. I would be poor company, I can assure you. I intend to lie down with the curtains drawn.' Phoebe smiled her understanding and Emma slipped away unnoticed by anyone, she thought, even Gideon. For this she was heartily glad, and set a brisk pace with a wish only for solitude.

Perhaps, Emma thought, it would indeed be good to be in her own home on Wallis Plains. There she could clean the salt from her wounds. In time she would cease to yearn for Tobias Freeman. Yet she could imagine herself as an old woman. She would remember the love of her youth denied out of duty, and a smile would grace her aged face as she recalled the bittersweet memories from so long ago.

Emma felt the tears that rolled down her cheeks, but there was no one to see her since most people still lingered at the church, and in this knowledge she allowed herself the comfort of weeping. Although she could hide her sorrow from others, she could hide nothing from her Maker.

Emma let herself in at the garden gate and walked around the back of the cottage to stand by the vegetable plot and watch the waves roll in from the sea. In the future, when her memories of longing had gone with the years of her life, the sea would continue to wash against the sandy shore. She wrapped her arms around herself as the breeze caressed her and was consoled. After a while,

Emma let herself out through the gate to walk among the drying sea grass that grew through the white sand.

The clouds veiled the sun so that the sky and sea were pastel grey. Emma had no parasol, and with face upturned she closed her eyes.

'Emma? Emma, what ails you?'

Her breath caught at the sound of his voice, the weight of his shoes upon the waving sea grass. She spun to meet him.

'Tobias, what are you doing here?' He would not be welcome here, of that she was certain.

'Why did you leave so abruptly?' He frowned and stepped up to her. Emma shook her head and turned away. He touched her arm in question.

'My head aches,' she said, but it was not the reason why she had stumbled away. She may as well have lied. Her voice grew thick with emotion. He touched her tears with a finger and she looked up at him, willed her lip not to tremble, and failed miserably. He enfolded her in his arms, and she pushed him gently away.

'You owe me no favour, Tobias,' Emma told him. 'Do not think that you need to comfort me.'

He ignored the dismissal and pressed on. 'No headache can make a woman so heart sore, surely. Will you not look at me, Emma? Can you not give me one moment in the pleasure of your touch?'

And Emma's usually temperate nature cracked as a wave of anger washed over her. 'Tobias, you may take it for granted when women flock like seagulls into your waiting embrace, and women such as Mary will take from you whatever you are inclined to give, but I am not here to quench desire whenever you feel the need for a woman's arms.'

'Ah, so jealousy has its hook in you.' It was a statement of fact rather than a question.

'That is what is known in *polite* company as an insult.'

His head jerked back as though she had slapped him. He tossed a wry smile at the sea breeze. 'Aye, and to a convict, so is what you just said, but then you know that, don't you? You think I wanted you to see Mary gob-smack me with that kiss like some Dublin fishwife? Why would I desire her when all I pray for is you? Aye, even when I ought to be praying for the salvation of my soul! You are like the four-leaved shamrock I've never found, and you think I would slight you to bed Mary?' His voice shook in anger and frustration.

Emma blinked and nodded, then a new tear slipped from her eye. 'Yes. Yes I do.'

'Never.'

He pulled her gently to him then and clasped her within the strength of his arms. He rocked her in his embrace, his head bowed above hers. Then he looked out to the sea as he held her, as though he searched for a miracle.

Emma looked up to meet his gaze. With infinite care he took her face in the breadth of his hands and dipped his head to kiss her lips. In it was a vow more beautiful than any words, which could have been spoken at that moment.

'When I'm working in the parson's garden, I dream of you even though I am awake, and when I lie in bed at night I cannot sleep. I cannot wrench myself free.'

Emma's hand caressed the planes of his face, and she told herself that she would remember all of it.

'Would you be free?' she asked him as she swallowed her emotion. 'I free you to love where you will. I will not see your heart imprisoned because of me.'

'Never release me, Emma,' he whispered fiercely. 'Do not let me go.'

Too late they heard the latch of the gate being shut at the front of the cottage garden, Gideon's voice called for her as he knocked at the door.

'Go. Run down the foreshore!' Emma whispered, frantic in the fear that Tobias should be found.

'I won't insult either one of us by running like some felon who has done wrong.'

'But we *are* doing wrong, Tobias, why won't you see? He will not let me go, and I am bound to him whether I would have it or not.'

Tobias took her by the arms and spoke urgently. 'I might be a government man with no rights of my own, but I have free will, and I will not deny that I love you.' His voice sounded raw as he clasped her to him, and Emma said, 'At least save yourself from harm!'

'I will never give up on us!' His eyes flamed bright and fierce, and as Gideon turned the corner and came upon them, Tobias turned to meet his wrath. Only the picket fence, like bleached bones, separated Tobias from Gideon Quinn.

'Why are you here, Irishman?'

'I am speaking with Miss Colchester.'

Gideon curled his lip. 'That is apparent, and yet what gives you the right to be with my fiancée?' Emma bit her lip and glanced at Tobias.

'The fact that I love her and want her for my wife.' With this Tobias gently took Emma by the hand and placed a kiss on her knuckles. She felt herself groan inwardly. The man had no fear. She had enough for both of them.

Gideon's mouth hung open and the apple of his face puckered as though it had been left too long beneath the tree. Then he laughed at the audacity of the convict. 'Is that so?'

'Aye, it is.'

'Well, there are whores aplenty if you've a mind to look. They are more in your line of life.'

Emma saw Tobias smile, and he stood with feet braced a little more apart, arms folded, while he spoke. 'Jesus said, "I am come that they may have life, and that they might have it more abundantly."

169

So, regardless of what you think, you are not my jailer. What you believe of me has no weight.'

'Oh, it does, believe me, it does, because you will work for me like a slave to finish my house, and there Miss Colchester and I will live, on the sweat of your brow. You will have no time for book learning or Bible reading like you do at the manse, of that I will make very sure.' He smiled, and then held his hand out to Emma, and bid her come.

'Gideon, this fight is not worth the prize,' Emma warned.

'I am beginning to see that, my dear, but still, an officer always prefers to win.'

'*No quarter given.*'

He smiled tightly then took her roughly by the arm. She made her best efforts not to flinch, but Tobias saw it and jumped the fence with a bound.

'Get your hands off her,' he growled. He breathed heavily as he squared up to Gideon.

Gideon sneered at Tobias, looked him up and down as though he reeked of night-soil, and then apparently thought it pertinent to remove his hand from Emma all the same.

'I'll be speaking to the commandant about getting a few more workers to labour on my property at Wallis Plains. You will be one. Enjoy grubbing around in the dirt while you have the chance because it won't last long.'

*

Tobias was left standing in the garden alone. He heard Gideon say pleasantly, 'I will be pleased to stay for luncheon if you have an extra chair at the table.' Tobias heard furniture shift and the conversation buzz inside as he passed the cottage and continued down the foreshore, his Sunday afternoon his own to see out however he wished.

Kevin's toothless smile made him feel better, and he reclined on his cot to read the Bible. He told himself there was nothing better to do, and Kevin was just as eager to listen, as he was to read.

'What does it say, mate?' Kevin wanted to know, as he stretched out and pillowed the back of his neck with his arms.

Tobias began reading and continued well into the afternoon.

'"For God so loved the world that he gave his only begotten Son, that whosoever believeth in him should not perish, but have everlasting life. For God did not send his Son into the world to condemn the world; but that the world through him might be saved." Salvation is for sinners as well as saints, Kevin. No man is beyond redemption.' Kevin looked dubious but hopeful.

The next day, Tobias spoke to the parson when he had finished work. He kneaded his hat between his soil-stained hands.

'What can I do for you, Tobias?' The parson smiled and looked up from the sermon he wrote.

'I want to know if you would baptise me, Parson.'

The man of God put down his quill. 'Why, you may already be baptised, son. Don't you know if you have been brought to Christ or not?'

Tobias shrugged, disappointed. He had wanted to be baptised in the Holy Spirit, but it seemed this was not going to happen. 'Well, if I have, my ma never told me.'

The reverend stood and smiled. 'I don't think the Lord will mind if you get doused twice. I never heard of a man getting too much holy water.'

So he led Tobias to the church, silent and sanctified, and beckoned him to the font where he read from the Good Book. Then he asked Tobias to lean over the sandstone font, and from a jug poured water over Tobias's head. It trickled coolly over his forehead and cheeks and down onto his neck.

'With this chrism I sign you with the cross, to symbolise that you are Christ's own, Tobias.'

Tobias felt as though he rose as high as the roseate windows in a way he had hardly known, and he stood in wonder as the parson said a prayer of blessing over his life.

'I am told to expect to go and work at Wallis Plains any day now,' said as he prepared to walk back to the cottage he shared with Kevin.

'I am sorry to hear that.' The parson frowned, and Tobias saw that the man was being sincere.

He nodded, 'And so am I. I want to thank you for the kindness you have shown me, and for baptising me, above all.'

'We are all his servants. Whether we do the work he sets us is up to the individual.' He shook Tobias's hand, unwashed as it was, and the parson's unassuming ways humbled Tobias.

'Walk with God, Tobias.' He smiled.

Tobias pulled his hat on his head and let himself out of the garden in the late afternoon with the full knowledge that if Gideon Quinn wanted him gone, then he would make sure he achieved that end. Tobias's heart felt heavy that he would most probably leave, and yet at the same time he felt strangely elated. He reached a tentative finger up to the chrism on his forehead. He turned back for one last look at the church on Prospect Hill and saw that the parson still stood there. They waved in turn.

*

A few days later Tobias bid his Cockney friend goodbye. It was a sombre farewell between the two men, and Tobias knew he would miss his companionship.

'He's going to try to work you to death, Toby mate.'

'Let him try.' Tobias winked, all bravado. 'I'm made of tougher stuff.'

'Mary will be sorry you're gone.'

'There'll be someone for her. Hopefully, she'll pick the right one.'

'I'll keep an eye on her,' Kevin said, and Tobias clapped him on the back in brotherly affection.

'I've been writing out verses from the Good Book for you to think on.'

Kevin appeared disappointed and stared at the words before him as though they were in a foreign language.

Tobias smiled gently and with understanding. 'Go to the parson and ask him to read a verse over a couple of times. In time, you can learn them by heart. It will be like you can read and write. It will give you strength and hope.'

'Hope for freedom before I die of hard labour?' Kevin asked with a chuckle.

'Hope for everlasting life, and there's no one that can take that away.'

Kevin took hold of Tobias hand then and clapped his arms around him.

'Farewell, Toby mate.'

'I believe we'll meet again.'

FIFTEEN

There was only so much sewing, crocheting, and embroidery that Emma could do. She would sit by the window after breakfast, ply her needle to the linen, and remain there until midday. Day after day she continued the same routine, her hands occupied, and her mind free to wander where it would, for she found it nearly impossible to tame her thoughts. They took her back time and again to Tobias, for although duty imprisoned her, she was nevertheless torn by love.

She was glad to be free of Gideon's presence for the time. He had travelled down river to check on the building of their house. The boat had been stocked with provisions, she supposed, for the containers were well covered with an oilcloth and left little room for Gideon to stretch his legs.

While at the riverside she had also watched a free settler and his family who had come recently from the Isle of Skye. She had heard them talking to one another at the pier; they spoke in Gaelic as they boarded an open boat. She smiled and waved at the children as they pushed off, with hope for their safety. They had come far and she wished the broad cheek-boned crofter well. Emma had already heard of one family who had piled the barge with a cargo of bricks to start the building of their house, only to have it sink with the load. That family perished in the event.

'I must do something for someone, Phoebe,' Emma said later

when her thoughts returned to the present, 'not just sit here day after day in this thoroughly boring occupation.'

'You are not permitted to work in the convict hospital,' Phoebe reminded her gently. Emma tried not to be piqued. After all, Phoebe only spoke the truth.

'I know, and I will not do it, but I will go and see the parson to ask if I may help with the children at Sunday school.' Emma stood and stretched her cramped muscles then put away her needlework gratefully.

'Where do you go, Emma?' Aunt Adelaide asked as Emma opened the cottage door.

'I am going to the parsonage to ask the parson if I can be of assistance with the children on Sundays at Sunday school.'

Aunt Adelaide showed her concern. 'Emma, those children could well be crawling with lice.'

'Then I will go to Mr Tucker's general store to buy spirits to treat their heads.'

'You have no money,' her aunt reminded her rather caustically.

'I could use a little of what Gideon gave you for my trousseau,' Emma said reasonably, daunted only for a moment.

'Gideon Quinn did not give me the money to spend on the children of convicts, I am sure. He did not want you to work at the hospital, and this is no different.' Her aunt turned away, signifying the end to their conversation.

'You do not need to give me any of the money Gideon left in your keeping, but I will help with the children regardless of whether you help me or not. If I come back infested, it is not because I have wanted to.'

Aunt Adelaide spun around angrily to confront her niece. 'All right, I will get the money. But your disobedience does you no credit.'

'I mean you no ill will, Aunt Adelaide.' Emma saw her words

175

fell on deaf ears. Her aunt passed her the coins and turned away.

'Thank you.'

The woman made no reply.

Phoebe stood in the open door, a hopeful expression on her face.

'Don't entertain the thought that you might go with her, Phoebe, for you will not,' Her mother warned. But here, Aunt Adelaide's voice was tempered with love, and Emma would have liked to have her own mother with her, for she missed her and would have given much to share her confidences.

Emma and Phoebe exchanged understanding looks, and then Emma left the cottage and walked in the direction of the parsonage, as she pondered her aunt's change of attitude towards her of late. Ever since the intelligence of her supposed dalliance with the commandant had come to her attention, Aunt Adelaide had kept a sharp eye on her, as if afraid that she would not wed Gideon after all. Emma wondered at this, since her aunt did not seem to like Gideon any more than she now liked Emma herself, and the shift in her aunt's affections saddened her.

'*For if you were to spurn him now, wherever would you live?*'

It was a question she could not answer, and well her aunt had known it, for she seemed to rely on this warning. When Emma arrived at the manse, she came upon the parson's wife as she pottered about the garden and warbled some hymn.

'Good day.' Emma said.

Mrs Brown looked up. 'Emma dear, come in, come in. It's time I stopped and made a cup of tea. It's far too hot to be out here in this heat; the parson called out of the window to tell me so just now.'

'Your flowers are feeling the heat,' Emma observed as she let herself in through the gate.

'They certainly are, although I think it has more to do with the lack of Tobias's care. I suppose I will have to find myself another gardener, but Tobias was trustworthy and nothing was ever too much trouble. Not all the convicts are like that.'

Emma sat down where she was bid and gladly accepted a cup of tea.

It had been stewed for some time – it was tepid and very black – but it still managed to refresh her. Emma thought it probably had more to do with the fact that she was away from her aunt's hostility, and she gave the parson's wife a listening ear.

'Did you hear about the theft from the store?'

'I believe I heard my uncle mentioning something to Aunt Adelaide. What was stolen?'

'Some kegs of rum. They have disappeared and no one has seen hide or hair of them. The commandant had a search carried out, but no one is any the wiser. He believes that they are long gone by now. I imagine he is correct, because they would not be easy to hide in a convict's cottage.'

'The commandant believes convicts were behind it?'

'Who else would be behind it?'

'Yet surely, if it was a convict, they would find it hard to leave the colony unseen. There is roll call so many times a day, and it would seem difficult indeed to go unreported for any great length of time.'

The parson's wife shrugged. 'They are not all as trustworthy as Tobias Freeman. Who knows what some of them could achieve? Did Tobias ever tell you why he was convicted? Any man would have protected his young sister like he did. The farmer got his comeuppance when he fell and hit his head. It's a pity that Tobias was transported because of it.'

Emma nodded in agreement, but then, she supposed, if he hadn't been sent away she never would have met him. This she knew was selfish, for he had a family in Ireland who would mourn his loss almost as much as if he were dead.

'I was hoping to help with the children at Sunday school,' Emma said before long. 'That's if you think I could be of assistance.'

'Certainly you may.' Mrs Brown leaned over and touched her hand. 'There is another convict who has been attending and every time he does he brings a tattered piece of paper with Bible verses written on it, and he asks the parson to read them to him. My husband is so encouraged by this that he sits the man down at one of the children's chairs, and the man joins in at the lesson as though he were one of the infants.'

'That is heartening, indeed. Perhaps he might have a green thumb like your last garden help.'

'That is an excellent notion. I believe I will put it to my husband. Although the man is rather a bantam, if he is keen to do the job, then I am happy for him to dig onions and potatoes.' The woman fanned herself. 'No one in England would believe how hot the colonies can get. Oh, and that reminds me, my husband received a letter from Tobias just yesterday.'

'Oh, how wonderful,' Emma whispered.

'Yes, it is. One of the vegetable growers near Wallis Plains brought back the note. I don't know how Tobias managed to give it to him but the parson was over the moon to receive it. I think he looked upon Tobias in some ways as the son he would have liked to have, had God thought fit to bless us with children. Would you like me to read it to you?'

'Certainly, if you don't mind,' Emma said as she sat forward on her seat.

'Now, where did that man put it? Oh, here it is. You may as well read it yourself, dear. My eyes aren't what they once were.'

Emma took the letter and pored over the carefully written copperplate wording. It looked like the writing of a painstakingly careful schoolboy uneasy with the quill and with spelling. Emma smiled. She touched the words that he had written as though she touched the man, and as she read the words, Emma found in it a bittersweet pleasure.

The eighth day of January 1822

I hope this note finds you and your family well, as it does me. I have found the work here to be much harder and longer than when I worked for you, Parson, and I am always glad when dusk falls and the bell calls us to supper. We sleep beneath the house in the cellar at night, and though the mosquitoes beside Hunter's River are ferocious at night, it is not as bad as they were when I was with the lime-burners, where a body was almost carried away by their thirst for warm blood. The house we work on for Officer Quinn is a grand affair and is made of yellow sandstone. It will be a fitting place for his bride when he brings her home to live in it, and Miss Colchester will do it justice. Please tell her, when you see her, that I am still waiting. She will know what that means.

Yours sincerely,

Tobias Freeman

'Thank you for allowing me to read that.' Emma smiled, her throat tight. She willed herself to show no emotion. The parson's wife didn't seem to notice, and for this she was grateful. Nor did the woman ask about the reference to her, and how would she have answered even if she had? Emma handed the letter back, glad for the woman's discretion.

'Will you have another cup of tea, Emma dear?' Mrs Brown asked.

'No, thank you, Mrs Brown. I did not mean to take up so much of your time.'

'Nonsense.' The woman patted her arm. 'What is a doddering old woman going to do with her days anyway?'

Emma smiled. 'You are hardly doddering, and well you know it.'

That brought a chuckle. 'We will see you at Sunday school then?' 'With pleasure.'

The fragrance of lavender brushed her skirts as Emma clicked the gate shut behind her, and the memory of another day not so far distant, brought a moment keen and sweet.

'They are the colour of your gown, Miss Colchester.'

Emma made her way back to her uncle's house, slowly and thoughtfully, as she recalled moments with Tobias. She knew that some, if they had an inkling of her thoughts concerning the convict reprobate, would brand her a pariah, no higher than the convicts themselves.

As she recalled Euphemie's acidic innuendo at the commandant's dinner party, Emma could hardly bear to think of what her cousin would say if she knew the true identity of the man with her that night. She would make it her business to vilify Emma from Macquarie Pier to Prospect Hill, from the Broad meadow to the Sugarloaf Mountain that rose smoky violet in the far distance. Yes, indeed, Euphemie would be sure to spread the word.

Euphemie had acted oddly of late. She was taciturn towards her mother but was otherwise unusually silent. Yet she did not seem to be unhappy. On the contrary, it seemed as though she waited and bid her time, though for what, Emma hardly knew. She and Euphemie did not share confidences regarding anything. Her cousin would smile into the distance when she thought no one watched, but the quirk of her lips quickly stilled when she was perceived. Yet it was not Emma's business, and Euphemie did not seem to want her as a friend unless it met her own needs.

'I will be back shortly,' Emma heard Euphemie tell her mother, as the girl briefly checked her reflection in the looking glass.

'Where do you go?'

'Out for a walk, Mother, that's all,' Euphemie replied airily at the entrance to the cottage, as the sun spilled through the door. A breeze caught the hem of her muslin gown and she went with its pull into the garden, and then shut the gate behind her.

'Whatever is wrong with that girl lately?' Aunt Adelaide asked Phoebe. Her daughter shrugged.

'I am going to go and rest before thinking about supper,' Aunt Adelaide said. 'It's too hot for any occupation whatsoever. Only don't let me sleep the whole afternoon, Phoebe dear, or else I will do nothing but toss and turn all night.'

A short while later there came a peremptory knock at the. Emma and Phoebe looked at one another askance before Emma got up to answer it.

'Good afternoon, Miss Colchester.' The commandant offered her a quick military bow. 'I would speak with your aunt if I may?'

'Certainly.' Emma nodded. She stepped aside to allow not just the commandant, but two other officers, and with them, Euphemie, her smile of triumph malicious as she gloated at the commandant's side.

'I will just wake her, Commandant, if you will wait here in the parlour a moment,' Emma said.

'No need, Emma, I am wide-awake,' her aunt said as she entered the room. She appeared more than a little worried, though she smiled and offered the commandant a seat, which he graciously declined.

'Madam, I pray you will forgive this interruption, but I have just been given intelligence of stolen goods.'

'Really, Commandant?' Aunt Adelaide asked. Her voice held none of the strident tone that was normally her style. The woman glanced at Euphemie, but her daughter looked away. Emma's stomach rolled and she wondered what one earth was going on. The only thing she did understand was that Euphemie was the instigator, and her mother the party under suspicion.

'Kegs of rum belonging to the Crown have lately gone missing from the government stores, and Miss Euphemie believes they are in your cellar.'

181

Emma realised then what was happening and was shocked to her very core.

Another look passed between mother and daughter, and Emma would remember it for years to come. Aunt Adelaide began to fan herself furiously as her neck, flushed as red as the wattles on a fowl. She clucked nervously as she made her way to the cellar entrance followed by the commandant, the officers and Euphemie. Only Emma and Phoebe stood to attention, hardly able to breathe. And Emma asked herself why on earth her aunt and uncle would keep stolen goods. The very idea seemed ludicrous.

'We must have a candle, madam,' the commandant said courteously, and Aunt Adelaide hastened with trembling fingers to do his bidding. Emma had never seen her aunt so nervous, and she went to pick up the candle off the floor for the woman when it fell from her hands.

'Let me help you,' Emma said, and she looked into her aunt's eyes to see both fear and gratitude on her face.

'Thank you, Emma dear.'

The commandant descended the stairs and swept the light in a wide arc over the cellar. The women, all except Euphemie, stayed upstairs. They joined hands in their distress as they waited for the commandant and his officers to finish their search, but Euphemie stood apart.

'There is nothing here, miss,' one officer said.

'There was,' she assured them, though her self-importance appeared to give way to frustration. 'I came down only a few days ago and saw the kegs here. There must have been three or four. Perhaps more.'

'Well, they aren't here now,' the commandant told her patiently.

She stepped closer to him, softened her tone, and held out her hands as she implored him. He seemed uncomfortable at her fawning manner, and Emma saw from her vantage point that he took an almost imperceptible step back. 'I am sorry to have troubled you, madam. Please give my regards to your husband.'

Again the polite military bow. But this time his address was not apologetic, but rather, irritated, as though he had been given a red herring.

An expression flashed over his face, and Emma wondered if the commandant was repelled by the disloyal behaviour the girl had shown to her parents.

After the officers had gone, Emma, Phoebe, and Aunt Adelaide turned to Euphemie. Her face was flushed. She might have been humiliated at her mistake, but she was defiant nonetheless.

'How could you do this to me, Euphemie?' her mother asked.

'How could I do this to you? I might well ask you the same question, Mother, for because of you I was made to look a fool in front of the commandant. I may as well be a liar, for all he knows or cares.'

'So that's it, is it?' Aunt Adelaide said sadly. 'You would give away your mother's good name for a chance to have the commandant look in your direction?'

'And why not?' Euphemie said, 'I have done nothing against the law!'

'You know naught of what you speak! Why did you not come to me?'

'Because you would not have told me the truth,' she said with scorn.

Adelaide shook her head. Emma and Phoebe looked at one another in silence.

'In all I have done I have had your welfare in mind,' her mother told her, her voice little more than a whisper.

'Well, Mother, now I am looking out for myself.'

'And what have you achieved? You have shown yourself as a young woman without love or loyalty; a conniving chit who cares only to feather her own nest, yet who hasn't the sense to realise what she has, so keen is she to have something else.' Aunt Adelaide spoke in a heartbroken whisper. 'That you would play the part of Judas ... it is more than I can bear.' She swallowed hard and turned her back to her daughter. 'That you would sell our love for a come hither smile and a pair of buff breeches ... you are naive.' Then she wept. Emma knew she wept not just for herself, but for Euphemie, who for all her intelligence, understood nothing at all.

Emma looked at her aunt, whose tears fell in silence. At that moment she felt sorrier for her uncle's wife than she had ever felt for anyone and passed her a handkerchief. Aunt Adelaide, blinded by tears, did not see it, and Emma pressed it gently into her hand. She looked down at it for a moment as if wondering what it was for, and then dabbed at her face absently.

'I was right,' Euphemie continued, pointing at the cellar. 'I know there was rum in there.' With that, she spun on her heel and strode away.

Aunt Adelaide sunk onto a chair. Sometime later, she took out her handiwork and sat in silence with Phoebe.

'Would you mind if I walk to Mr Tucker's store now to buy the spirit, Aunt Adelaide?' Emma asked in a gentle tone. Her aunt glanced up and nodded; the fight had left her for the moment.

'Do as you must,' Phoebe said. 'I will stay here with Mother.'

'Of course.' Emma walked out of the cottage.

It would seem that Euphemie had more than one grievance, but Emma didn't know the reason for her actions and whether it had anything to do with the commandant. Yet it seemed unlikely that her ship would come in because she had given the commandant information at the expense of her parents. In fact, she had probably done her interests more harm than good, as she humiliated and grieved her mother in the process. And surely her aunt and uncle were not the people to harbour stolen goods? Emma did not believe it, and yet, what other reason was there?

'Good afternoon, Miss Colchester,' she heard as she left the store a short time later.

Emma turned at the commandant's voice. She dipped a curtsey.

'It has not been a good afternoon, Commandant Morisset, but I do not blame that on you.'

'I was sorry to have to do it.' He shrugged, palms upward. 'Yet what else could I do? The law must be upheld.'

'I understand that, I assure you.'

'Would you mind me asking you if you have any inkling whether your cousin did in fact speak the truth? Have you heard anything untoward at any time or seen anything suspicious?'

'In all truth, I have not.'

The commandant nodded and after they spoke on more amicable subjects, they went their separate ways.

When Emma returned to the cottage, she went around to the back of the house where the cellar door exited. She was curious now, especially in light of Euphemie's certainty.

Emma looked down at the gravel by her feet.

She saw recent marks where the doors had brushed the ground as they had been swung wide. But it was the semi-circular indentation, the bruised sea grass that had been dislodged here and there from its roots that arrested her attention. Emma's heart beat fast and she wondered how much of what Euphemie said was correct.

SIXTEEN

Tobias gazed as he worked at the yellow sandstone of the house, a colour between butter and buff breeches. Generous blocks were joined with as much perfection at the top as at the bottom and the windows rose tall enough to let in the sun, yet remained as private as any lady could require, with shutters at every sash, both back and front. There were servants' quarters as well as a kitchen on the left of the family building. Even these, Tobias decided as he wiped his brow in the sun, were grand, visible from the new road that wound around the river.

Although dark like a glossy Eastern Brown snake after a rainfall, the river rippled cool grey when the sky was its dazzling blue. Tobias stared at the river and daydreamed of Emma.

At midday when they had eaten, he stared up at the vivid heavens and wondered how the sky in this place could be as blue as Irish grass was green, and decided that perhaps it was a good thing that the pasture in parts was dull like the unbleached flax his mother would sit and spin. Otherwise there would be no rest for the eyes.

He heard a screech and looked up to see a few black cockatoos harvesting she-oak nuts which they cracked with sharply curved beaks, only to take off in slow flight, their primitive screeching wild and empty as the brown southern land.

'Three days' rain,' Tobias heard, and turned to see the young stonemason sit down beside him. 'That's what they say.'

'Who says what?' Tobias asked as he pillowed his head more comfortably on his arms.

The young convict shrugged. 'Anyone who's been in this country long enough to take notice of them. Black Cockatoos are always around when it's about to rain. There were three of them then, so that will mean three days' rain. Don't know if it's true, but I reckon that the nuts on them there trees, for example, would be softer after a downpour.'

The young convict got comfortable and began to pick his teeth with a blade of grass as he talked. 'Did you leave a lass at home?'

Tobias smiled at the forthright young Scotsman. 'No, I didn't. My ma and sister are still in Ireland. I miss them sore.'

'Aye, I ken how that feels.' His voice spoke of memories far behind him. Then he bucked up and said, 'I thought you must have had some bonny lass you were dreaming about, judging by the smile you had on your face.'

Tobias chuckled. 'Sure, I won't deny it, but she's not my girl, though I hope and pray for a miracle from the Holy Trinity all the same.'

The Scot nodded. 'I wish I had listened to the Holy Trinity before I thought to commit arson. But the farmer owed me money, the old soak, and he couldn't play cards for nuts, especially when he was drunk. Called me a liar one too many times, so I struck a light and let the hay have it.' He shrugged. 'Old man saw me, and now here I am.'

'Aye, well you're not the only one to have lost his temper before now,' Tobias admitted with a smile.

The Scotsman grinned and put out his hand. 'Alan Campbell.'

'Tobias Freeman.' The two shook hands.

The bell rang for the men to continue work. The sun had hidden behind the clouds, and Tobias was glad of the respite. The day was humid nonetheless, and sweat ran in rivulets down his temples, chest and back, so that before too long his shirt dripped wet with his toil.

He squinted into the distance and saw Quinn, who strutted around with more importance than a bantam rooster, his red coat just about as gaudy. The man saw Tobias and headed in his direction. Tobias continued to hoe the ground, stooping every now and then to pick up stones, which he tossed on the barrow.

Quinn stood with arms folded as he watched Tobias work. He unstopped a flask and took a long swig. Tobias needed a draught of water too; his throat was parched. He glanced up and wiped his brow. Quinn said nothing but offered him a smile that was no more than a sneer and continued to look on. Tobias set his jaw and put his back into the task.

If Quinn thought that he could goad him into saying or doing something he would regret then he would be proven wrong. He would not lose his temper on the man, for that was all Quinn wanted.

'Your work has slowed. Increase your pace.'

'If I go any faster, I may miss the stones,' Tobias pointed out reasonably.

'You've slackened off. The hoe is hardly scratching the surface.' This wasn't the case, and both of them knew it. Tobias wiped his forehead with his arm again and continued his labour without comment.

'If I didn't know better, I'd say there was a pig rooting around, but it's only a sweating Irishman. Still, there's very little difference. The stink is just as strong.'

'Fair crack of the whip, Governor,' Alan Campbell said then leaned on his shovel as he defended Tobias. 'Ye can't say that, for all that you're the boss.'

'You're not using much elbow grease either,' Quinn said. 'Let me show you how to do it properly.' The officer took off his coat and placed it carefully on the ground.

'I ken very well how to do the job. I don't need to be educated on the finer points of hoeing the sod, for I've been doing it since I was little more than a bairn.'

'I disagree,' Quinn argued. 'Pass the shovel to me.'

'There's naught to it,' Campbell argued. Quinn's eyes flickered stonily. Campbell pushed the shovel Quinn's way with a truculent sigh and waited. Quinn smiled.

'Pay attention and let me show you how it's done.'

Yet Quinn didn't put the shovel to the earth. Instead he swung it like a mighty claymore on the battlefield, and with a wallop that Tobias would have thought could not have come from such a lightweight man, Quinn levelled the Scotsman with the flat of the shovel so that he fell, face first, onto the black soil of the river bank.

Apparently not content unless the job was well done, Quinn delivered another ringing blow for good measure.

He held out the shovel to Tobias. Tobias stepped back and almost fell over his own feet in shock. He would not take it.

'I won't have his blood on my hands,' Tobias told him as he pointed to the bright trickle that pooled around the Scotsman's head.

'I advise you to dig his grave, otherwise you will be the one on whom I will lay the blame.' Tobias looked at him, appalled. Quinn went on, 'He scampered off into the scrub without a trace, that's what they'll think, unless of course, you want to end your day on a very sour note?' He waited. 'No? I didn't think so. Dig the hole and throw the body in it.'

With that he stooped to pick up his coat and brushed it free of any specs of soil. Then he shrugged it on, buttoned it to the neck and sauntered away.

Tobias dug for all he was worth. He shovelled the soil because his life depended on it. Of this he had no doubt. He heard his ragged breath catch hotly in his throat and felt the sweat drip from his face and fall to the earth like tears. Yet he did not stop until the grave was dug and filled with the limp body, and then covered over with shaking hands.

He thought that at any minute someone would come, someone would see what he was doing, and he would be blamed; he knew that with deadly certainty. Yet not one person asked him his business. He was the only one at work in the field, and as the storm clouds hung low and purple above him, Tobias called out to God.

Father, put your angels around me and save me from the wickedness of men. Do not let their evil deeds go unpunished Lord, but protect me from their foul intent.

The rain fell heavily and stung his back with the onslaught. He held his face up to the sweetness of the droplets then opened his mouth with thirst. Then as he dropped to his knees, Tobias wept under the heavens, and he was washed clean.

Tobias turned his thoughts towards Emma. How would she fare with a murderous villain like Quinn? With cool glee the man had stoved in Campbell's head as though it were of no more worth than a field potato. When Emma became his wife, he could do with her as he pleased, and she, without kith or kin near enough to this solitary house to protect her, would be beyond help.

He would write to her. He would warn her about the fiend who wore the king's colours and professed himself a model citizen but who in reality was blacker than any convict he had ever met.

Tobias threw the shovel over his shoulder at the sound of the bell and strode towards the big house. He would find someone who was headed to the colony of Newcastle, eventually he would; no matter how long it took. He would make her see that Gideon Quinn was fit for no woman, let alone the woman he loved.

He turned the corner to where the other men cleaned and put away their tools for the day under the overseer's eye. Tobias felt guilty when the man looked his way, as though when he covered the body of the poor young Scotsman he became guilty of the murder. But the overseer looked away and marked his name off the role, unaware that Tobias sweated like a man freshly condemned, that his whole frame shook with the knowledge of what lay buried in the paddock beyond the house.

'The master has started the trip back to the Coal River,' the overseer told them. 'It won't be long before he brings back a bride, so work needs to continue at a good rate to finish everything off.'

'Bet he copped a soaking in the downpour,' one of the convicts said. The overseer nodded and looked up at the sky, which had cleared to a wash of blue. Then he continued his task and looked down at the roll ledger in his hands.

'Where's Campbell?' he asked them. Tobias glanced around. A few shrugged. No one answered at first.

'He was working with Freeman,' someone then said. Tobias felt his stomach churn.

'Was he with you?' the overseer wanted to know. Tobias nodded.

'Aye, he was.'

'Where is he now? Do you know?'

'I'm not his da',' Tobias told the overseer. 'He didn't tell me his business.' He heard a snicker.

The supervisor scowled. 'I am aware of that fact. I am merely trying to learn his whereabouts.'

'He will have gone bush,' one man said. 'Probably learn he's turned bushranger sooner or later and is making a quid and living in some humpy like a native in the scrub.'

The overseer grunted noncommittally.

'I wouldn't take his lead if I were you,' someone said, 'because they all get found by the black trackers sooner or later. That's if they don't thirst or starve to death. It's not easy to box with a kangaroo. If you'd seen the claws on them, you'd know what I mean. I'd rather raid a badger set than go near one of them things.'

'There's something to be said for salt beef and pork. We don't have to hunt it down or forage for it; there's something to be said for that. Oh, but what I wouldn't give for a bowl of plum duff,' another man said.

The overseer held up a hand. 'Well, guess what's on the menu for tonight's supper?'

'Plum duff?'

'Fat chance of that I'm afraid. How does salt beef and damper sound?'

'Better than a feisty kangaroo.'

Tobias washed at the river with the others. He could swim, unlike some, and spent a few precious moments as the tepid river water washed over his skin. It was a simple pleasure, a rare one, and he floated on his back and looked up to the heavens.

'*My life might be counted as worthless, but it's the only one I've got,*' he had told her. If he wasn't careful, Quinn would make sure it was short-lived at that. Just as young Alan Campbell's had been.

By rights, he told himself, he should have been sick to the stomach with no appetite for food at all, yet he fell to it like the others with eager hands and a watering mouth.

'Will you give me paper?' Tobias asked the overseer later. But the man apparently hadn't forgotten the convict's earlier smart quip and was disinclined to accommodate his request.

'What, wanting to practice your copperplate again?' Tobias knew he had small chance in getting what he wanted, and he feared he wouldn't get the message to her at all. The overseer walked away and tucked the ledger firmly under his arm. Then he seemed to remember something that had momentarily slipped his mind, and he turned back to address the men.

'A couple of you will be required to go to the market tomorrow to get seed potatoes to plant in the garden.'

'Aye, I'm willing.' Tobias walked forward.

The overseer frowned at him. 'Why would I choose you?'

'Haven't you noticed my shoulders hardly fit the doorframe? I can heft as many potatoes as needs be.' A few of the convicts laughed.

'You'll be better employed using your strength here.'

'The work is mostly done,' Tobias argued.

'Have you removed every single stone from the garden bed?' Tobias nodded his head and swallowed. Just the thought of what was veiled by the soil made him sweat. Maybe it was better that it was him who raked through the paddock and not someone else after all.

That night he dreamed of Alan Campbell. In the dream Campbell walked in the moonlight and Tobias saw him like a blue wraith as the dead man proceeded over the black soil. His white toes dug into the earth like maggots. Alan pointed his finger at Tobias and Tobias tried to hide, but at every corner he turned Alan would be there to meet him. But in the end it was no longer Alan, but Quinn who strutted in the moonlight like a blood-red bantam, his grin more frightening than any cadaver that Tobias could conjure in his dreams.

The next morning after they had breakfasted, two of the convicts prepared for the walk to the market where farmers met to buy and sell produce. Tobias wished there were some way he could tell Emma to be wary of the man she would soon wed. He stood irresolutely by and twisted his woollen cap, when a cry went up from behind the kitchen.

'Snake! Jack's been bitten by a snake.'

Every man rushed around the building to see that Jack had indeed been bitten by the big brown snake and would be going nowhere at all, ever. Jack was stunned as much by fear and trembling as anything else at that point, and Tobias knew that the overseer would need to choose someone else to take his place at the market. Yet

Tobias didn't even voice the question because the overseer asked him before he could.

'Do you want to go to market?'

'Aye,' Tobias answered, sorry for Jack, as there was naught anyone could do. He could, however, help Emma, and that was what he would do, as if his last breath depended on it.

'Make sure you come back,' the overseer warned.

'As if we'd want to leave three square meals a day and a mansion like this,' Tobias quipped. The overseer almost allowed himself a smile.

'Be back by sunset.'

'If not before.'

They walked over to where Jack had dropped, and Tobias shook the man's hand in solemn farewell.

'God bless you, Jack,' he said.

'You too, mate,' quavered Jack.

'Ah, the devil always looks after his own, Jackie lad,' another of the convicts joked. Jack tried to chuckle at the quip. As Tobias and his companion made their way, he only hoped that poor Alan Campbell's body was not dredged up with the stones in the wide brown field. Guilt was a spectre that followed him, and although he told himself that he had not killed the likeable Scot, it felt as though he had taken a life all over again.

He was afraid of snakes and fearful of what his future held, but to be hanged by the neck until he was dead haunted him most of all. To make it worse, Emma might never know the truth, never be told the whole story concerning the lonely paddock where Alan Campbell had met his maker.

Tobias wondered how on earth he would be fortunate enough to meet someone willing to take Emma a message through word of mouth. The last person Tobias expected to see was the red-haired soldier who had danced with Emma's cousin on the green above the beach. They nodded at one another in greeting, and Tobias knew that this opportunity must have been heaven sent. All he had to do was get close enough without anyone else hearing what he had to say. The warning was for Emma's ears alone. If the heavenly Father wanted to see Gideon punished for his crime, then he needed no help from him to accomplish it.

'I'm going over to look at the oranges,' Tobias told his companion. 'Least I think that's what they are.'

'We weren't told to get citrus fruit,' Mick said. Then he recalled something, which made him smile. 'I was given an orange for Christmas when I was a lad.'

'What did it taste like?'

'Like the sun I'd reckon.'

Tobias thought about this but couldn't conjure the flavour any better for the description.

Mick went on, 'Look at the size of them. Some of them are the width of my hand. I've never seen the like. The one I had was more the size of a billiard ball. Still, I'm going to see about those seed potatoes, are you coming?'

'Aye, but first I'm going to pay my respects to that redcoat over yonder. I know him.'

The other convict shook his head. 'The likes of us don't mingle with them.'

'Are you going to live the life of a condemned man for the rest of your years? Why punish yourself when there are plenty of others at the task as it is?'

His friend gestured to his clothing. 'Even if I forget the slops I've got on, every man, woman and child sees me for what I am.'

'No, they don't. Man looks at appearances, but God sees the heart. We are more than the sum of our past mistakes.'

Mick seemed to consider what he said as a slow grin split his countenance. 'Watch out, else they'll be getting you to take us for evening prayers.'

Tobias smiled and walked away. He gazed at the baskets of oranges. They smelled sweet like flowers. His mouth watered.

'Tried oranges before?' It was the soldier Phoebe was sweet on.

Tobias shook his head. 'Never.'

'They grew these on the Hawkesbury River, but there are orchards begun on the flats for oranges and cider apples that will start producing soon. The soil above the river bank would grow hairs on a wooden leg so they say.'

Tobias smiled until he remembered the limbs beneath the black soil at Quinn's Folly, then he felt the cold sweat break out on his body just as fear clamped a hand around his heart. What the young soldier said held more truth than he realised. Tobias wiped the perspiration from his brow and put the hat back on his head.

'Tell you what,' the other man said, 'I'll buy us a couple.'

'Wooden legs?' Tobias asked, trying for light-heartedness. The younger man chuckled and put out his hand.

'The name's Rory.'

'Tobias,' he said and grasped the soldier's hand. The soldier paid for two of the bright orange globes and passed one to Tobias. Tobias brought it to his nose and inhaled the perfume of the glossy fruit, then bit hungrily into the tough skin and made a face as he chewed then swallowed, not nearly as impressed as he thought he would have been.

Rory laughed. 'Peel the skin off man, and you'll find it more to your liking.'

Tobias grinned and peeled away at the orange as if he were a gleeful child unwrapping a gift. He saw that it had segments and tore off a lift and put it into his mouth. Juice ran down his hands and into his sleeves.

'What did you think?' Rory asked. He made as much noise as Tobias had.

'It was grand,' Tobias breathed as he wiped his mouth on his sleeve.

The orange finished, Tobias recalled his mission and considered his words. 'Are you going back to the Coal River?'

'Aye, I am. Tonight's high tide.'

Tobias cleared his throat then looked down as he chose his words. 'Would you take a message back to someone for me?'

Rory grinned then. 'Is it for the colleen who has almost all the men in the colony vying for her smile?'

Tobias nodded. 'Sure, and what business does a man like me want with a girl like her, is that what you're thinking?'

Rory shrugged his shoulders.

'Will you do it?' Tobias asked.

'Aye, I will,' his fellow countryman told him.

'Tell her this from me: he has broken the sixth commandment.'

Rory nodded. Tobias wondered if Rory knew what the sixth commandment was.

'You have broken the sixth commandment,' Rory repeated.

'*I've* done no such thing,' Tobias said. 'I said *he* has broken it, not me. Tell her that. She'll understand.'

Ferguson nodded. 'I'll be sure to.' The two men shook hands.

'God bless you for an angel, Rory Ferguson,' Tobias told him, and went to join Mick, with half a wish that he had saved some of his orange for his companion. Mick grinned and asked, 'So what did you think?'

Tobias nodded in agreement. 'You were right. It tasted like the sun.'

SEVENTEEN

The heat was intense. A hot wind licked over Prospect Hill and sent up a tongue of dust. Emma shaded her eyes with one hand as she walked, the other hand held the parasol in a firm grip so it wouldn't be snatched from her hand and blown over the cliff and into the sea below.

She watched white horses race to the yellow sand, sand made dazzling by the sun and hot as molten glass. The heat had been unrelenting as the mercury rose higher with every succeeding day.

There had been no respite, no quenching rain or fanning breeze. A glimpse of Tobias had not been there to lighten the load of the passing hours, yet he occupied her thoughts all the same. The calendar marched ahead to Emma's wedding day, and still she was no more used to the idea than she had been at the start.

Her muslin gown flapped around her like the wings of a caged bird, her parasol dared her to fly, but she felt trapped just as surely as if there were bars on her cage.

'*Gideon, this fight is not worth the prize.*'

It was clear to her that he did not care for her, and she most certainly didn't care for him. She couldn't understand why he wanted her, regardless of the fact that he knew her heart had been given to another. Then it occurred to her that it wasn't about affection, but rather it was to win the battle. Gideon would rather have her unwilling than not have her at all.

It was about position, it was about pride; it had nothing to do with love.

Emma brushed tears from her eyes. There was no point in sorrowful feelings for herself. She was betrothed to Gideon Quinn. She had told him truthfully how things stood with her but it had not made a jot of difference; he would wed her, and she was honour bound to see it through.

Your will be done in my life. If it is what you want, Father God, help me to be a willing servant. If it is not fitting in your eyes that I should wed Gideon, then bar the way. You know my thoughts, my wishes, my dreams. Let that be enough Lord, to do with as you will.

The smiles of the children at Sunday school later that morning cheered her spirits. Many were dirty, ragged and just as she had expected, infested with lice, but they all wore smiles of welcome as Emma entered, closed the door behind her and left the heat and swirling dust behind her.

'This is Miss Colchester, children,' the reverend said.

'Good morning, Miss Colchester,' the children sang, and Emma knew that her decision to help in the Sunday school would be as good for her as for the children. How could she not be merry in the company of so many openly cheerful faces? It would not be a chore, she decided, and set down the crock of spirits with which she intended to douse their crawling heads. The comb too, she would put to good use. It was *her* comb, that was true, but boiling water killed all manner of unwanted stuff, including lice, she supposed.

'What are you going to do with the spirits, miss?' one lad asked as he scratched his thatch of hair.

'I am going to pour it over your heads and kill the lice,' Emma informed them all. They all looked at her as though she was an ignoramus.

'Father will squeeze my plaits into his tumbler for a sip of spirits,' one girl said with a laugh.

'Aye, Da' says a tipple a day keeps the doctor away,' another announced. Emma was not sure whether this was so but decided to keep it to herself. The child seemed to think it was gospel.

'This is all very altruistic of you, Miss Colchester,' the parson began as he pushed his spectacles further up on his nose, 'but the children came here to learn about Jesus.'

'And how much better will they absorb the idea of Christ's love, Parson, when they are comfortable and not scratching at their heads as they try to listen. So who is first?'

'Jimmy, miss,' someone said. When Emma saw how bug-ridden Jimmy was, she understood why.

'My da' will say it's a waste of good rum,' Jimmy warned her.

Emma merely smiled. 'I am sure he will, but it is important to me that you are content when you sit at Sunday school with Parson.'

'Well, the Admiral's Blood is stinging my head like the devil, miss.'

'That's because of the scratches you have inflicted on your poor head, and I can safely tell you that the only blood you have on you is your own. Yes, the rum will sting, but it will kill the lice, and every Sunday we are going to take turns combing the eggs out of one another's heads.'

'Will you give me another boiled sweet if I sit still?' a fair-haired little girl asked, and Emma realised that this girl was Katy, Mary's daughter.

'Perhaps I may. We shall see,' Emma said, and determined to buy sugar to make toffee with the remainder of the money her aunt Adelaide had given her.

'My ma's getting married,' Katy told Emma. Emma's hands stilled and she looked at the child with a frown.

'Your mother is to be married?' Emma was nauseated.

Katy nodded. 'Aye, I'm to have a da',' she told her proudly as she nodded her head.

'Who is she to wed, Katy dear?' Emma asked, her voice more light-hearted than she felt.

'One of the government men,' Katy told her, shrugging her shoulders. It did not matter who her da' would be, it seemed, only that she was going to have one.

Though she told herself that it would not be Tobias, she hardly knew who else it could be, for Mary had fished for Tobias from the start. Tobias knew how hopeless it was for them, so perhaps he had succumbed to Mary after all. The pretty, buxom young woman was both willing and available, whereas Emma could give him nothing.

She heard the children's chatter as though from afar as she worked on their heads. They compared the size of head lice from one head to another as they dropped onto the table, but all Emma could think of was Tobias.

'You think I wanted you to see Mary gob-smack me with that kiss like some Dublin fishwife? Why would I desire her when all I pray for is you? Aye, even when I ought to be praying for the salvation of my soul! You are like the four-leaved shamrock I've never found, and you think I would slight you to bed Mary?'

He deserved to be happy and all he would have of her was a daydream. Mary was flesh and blood, was needy and wanted a man's love. Her brazen bust and her come hither stare were enough for many a man. Tobias, it seemed, had been no different, and she would not blame him at all if he had changed his mind.

Sunday school finished, unorthodox though it had been, and the children scattered, wet headed and reeking of spirits, heady in the afternoon heat. Emma collected her things and bid the parson goodbye.

'My dear wife and I would appreciate if you would give us your company over supper one evening before you are married, Miss Colchester,' the parson told her.

'We will miss having you in the colony once you move to Wallis Plains.'

'I will be sure to.' Emma smiled.

'Wonderful. Don't forget, will you? My wife gets lonely at times in this place. She appreciated having Tobias work for us because she enjoyed his company. They would often chat, and she would feed him like some stray dog in need of a good meal.' They both laughed.

'I will see you next Sunday, Parson, and I will be sure to speak with your wife about that supper date.'

Emma listened to the laughter of children giddy with merry hearts as she walked back down Prospect Hill.

'Miss Colchester!'

Emma turned. A soldier strode towards her from the direction of the barracks. She waited as he came closer. It was Rory Ferguson, Phoebe's young man. Emma put up her parasol and lingered, a smile on her face.

'I was asked to give you a message, miss,' Ferguson told her as he reached her.

'A message from whom?' Gideon perhaps? She wondered. Not …

'Tobias Freeman gave it to me just two days ago, miss, and charged me to give it to you just as soon as I could.'

Emma's concern showed on her furrowed brow. 'What is it?' she asked as she tried to hold impatience at bay.

'He told me to tell you that he has broken the sixth commandment.'

Emma put a hand out to steady herself.

'Are you all right, miss?' Ferguson asked. He steadied her for a moment.

'Quite all right, thank you,' Emma whispered hoarsely. 'Just repeat if you would, what Mr Freeman said.'

'He told me that *he* had broken the sixth commandment, and Tobias was concerned that you should be warned.'

'*Can you not see the blood on my hands?*'

'Are you sure of this?'

Ferguson shook his head. 'I'm not sure of anything, miss. I'm just passing on a message.'

Emma nodded. 'Thank you, I appreciate your efforts to make me aware of it.'

'How is Miss Phoebe?' he asked with a shy smile and a fierce blush.

'She is well.'

'Perhaps I ought to call on her.'

'Perhaps you should.' She smiled and tried not to seem preoccupied.

Emma continued her walk back to the cottage and thought about what he had said. Tobias spoke of murder and wanted only that she should be warned. A sick feeling spread through her as she pondered it. What had he done?

Emma entered the cottage, and her aunt confronted her the moment she stepped over the threshold.

'You must wash, Emma,' Aunt Adelaide said. 'I will get out the tub and put the kettle on to boil. Not that you will need much hot water, it is like an oven outside and not much better within. You can strip off in the kitchen and bathe in there. Goodness knows you won't catch a chill from the draught.'

'I should like nothing better,' Emma admitted, suddenly aware of the perspiration that slowly trailed down her back.

'Take off every stitch of clothing, mind, even your chemise and drawers. The thought of lice makes my skin crawl.'

Emma followed her aunt to the kitchen adjoining the cottage. The stove was a mere spark of life, only lighted enough to keep it going throughout the day. Emma unhooked her boots and set them on the chair as her aunt lifted the black kettle from the heat.

'How luxurious to have a bath,' Emma said. Aunt Adelaide huffed.

'Well, you would not have needed to bathe at all had you stayed away from those infested children.'

'They need help.'

'Well, can't someone else help them?' Aunt Adelaide shook her head. 'By the way, you must hurry along on your needlework, Emma dear. The time fast approaches when you will be wed.'

Emma sat on the chair and slowly removed her stockings.

'I don't want to wed Gideon Quinn,' she whispered. She looked up, and tears welled in her eyes. Her aunt looked at her for a moment, compassion evident in her expression, then blinked.

'I know this already, Emma, but there is nothing you can do. You could do worse than wed an officer of the Crown.' Coldly she turned away and closed the door behind her.

Emma undressed and sank into the embrace of the tepid water. She was angry and frustrated at her aunt's lack of compassion, and disappointed at the lot that only Emma herself had chosen. Her tears fell freely as she allowed herself to weep.

Her uncle had arrived home, for she heard his cheerful whistle as he came through the garden gate. He was met by Euphemie. Emma recognised the voice. As she began to dress, she heard their conversation, unavoidable as Euphemie's voice rose.

'Daughter, I have no idea of what you speak,' her father said for a second time.

'Of course you do. You and mother were holding stolen rum and I found it in the cellar. Are you going to tell me that I am blind now? I will not be made a fool of a second time in front of the commandant.'

'Come inside that we may speak to your mother of this, for I am in the dark about it all. But I am sure that you arc in some way mistaken, dear, for if I know nothing of the stolen rum then neither does she.'

'Don't be so certain. Mother knows of it, you may be sure. She is guilty as charged.'

'Hush, Euphemie! You speak out of turn.'

'No, Father, I do not, as you will soon find.'

Their voices faded as they entered the cottage and Emma slipped on her stockings and boots. There was trouble afoot, and Euphemie, it seemed, scorned by her would-be suitor, was not about to forget her disappointment anytime soon. Emma knew her cousin had an axe to grind and was not above sharpening it on her family if it suited her.

Emma opened the kitchen door then made her way back into the house. She took a deep breath and hoped that she would avoid hearing the confrontation that was bound to begin. She heard her uncle's questions as she slipped to the room she shared, and he was becoming irate as his wife's apparently insufficient answers frustrated him.

'Is Euphemie right in what she says?'

'I don't want to talk about this now.'

'The commandant has been knocking on our door looking for contraband, and you tell me you aren't up to conversation? My dear Adelaide, that will not wash with me. Did you or did you not harbour stolen goods?' His usually composed manner had been traded for another Emma had never before witnessed, and she only wished that she go out for a while. As she left to go walk on the shore, Emma stopped in her tracks at the door of her room and looked round wide-eyed at Phoebe as they heard the next words.

'What did you say?'

'Do not make me say it again,' Aunt Adelaide sighed tiredly.

'You will say it again, madam, until I have heard you right. So repeat to me what you just mumbled, for I am sure I must have misheard you the first time.'

'I was asked to hold the rum for Gideon Quinn.'

'Gideon Quinn?' Emma's uncle cried still without comprehension.

Aunt Adelaide snapped. 'Yes, Gideon Quinn. Are you deaf?'

'No, just stupid, it would appear, for I cannot, for the life of me, understand why he had rum in our cellar, and why you had to keep it here for him in the first place.'

'That I will not tell you.' There was a short silence, broken only by the loud tick of the mantle clock.

'I am your husband, Adelaide. We ought to have no secrets from one another.' There was disappointment in his tone.

'I have no secrets from you, husband, save for this one alone, which I have kept these many years until now, and I will not relinquish it to you.'

Her uncle gasped, clearly flabbergasted. 'I cannot understand why you would have stooped to such an underhanded deed, wife. Why, it makes no sense at all. And too, I would have thought Gideon Quinn above such skull-duggery as thievery.'

Aunt Adelaide made a scornful sound. 'Then you do not know the man.'

'Nor do I know the woman to whom I have been wed, it would seem,' he said and strode from the room.

'Where do you go?' she called to her husband from their bedroom.

'Why, to see the man who would use my wife in a bid of cunning and deceit, for I will get to the bottom of this puzzle, you may be sure.'

Emma could hear her aunt as the woman sobbed inside her room. She sat back down upon her own bed.

Eighteen

A storm brewed and hung low and ominous over the port as George strode along. The late afternoon, though still hot, would soon give way under the burden of the rain clouds that roiled and rumbled above. He did not care if he got soaked.

George despised this feeling. He was not a violent man. He had never used his hands for anything save helping the sick and injured. He could not remember ever scrapping with raised fists, but he was irate. That Adelaide had harboured stolen rum under his very nose shocked him; that Gideon Quinn was the instigator of such a deed infuriated him. Yet he had not been privy to their deceit and was impatient to know the reason for it. Why the man saw fit to threaten the good name of his family—a family who knew nothing but respect and high standing in the colony of Newcastle—he did not know, but he determined to find out before the day was through why Quinn had seen fit to jeopardise his family.

It had been a day of disappointments. A young man of perhaps seventeen had come in from Lime-burners' Creek. He was suffering extreme mental unrest. He had tried to hang himself from a gum tree, but the branch had snapped and saved him. Once he had the young man settled in the ward, George had hoped that he could help him. It always made him glad when he was instrumental to a cure, but this time he was devastated. The young man had succeeded in his endeavour the second time, and had ended his struggle alone in the wee hours at the end of knotted, threadbare sheets. George shook his head. The boy had been little more than a child, and it had all begun when he had stolen a handkerchief for his mother. Convicted for a square of linen. Condemned for life.

Newcastle was for the hearty and hard-hearted. Sometimes he wished he were either one of those things. As he came upon the barracks his mind settled on Quinn once more, and George set his jaw.

The barracks smelled of horseflesh, hempen rope, straw, dung and dust, all bright with the smell of imminent rain. He pulled at the neck of his shirt, sticky with perspiration. A few of the horses nickered and snorted, just as eager for the relief of rain as he, then clearing their nostrils of dust.

'Just the man I wanted to see!' someone called out. George spun around as Quinn emerged from one of the far buildings, his parade boots buffed to a high gloss and just as immaculate as they would have been since the morning. George always wondered how the man accomplished it. George blinked and felt his spectacles begin to slide down the bridge of his nose. He removed them and began to rub the lenses as he did whenever he was preoccupied.

'That's why I am here,' the surgeon told Gideon as he approached. 'I wanted to talk to you.'

'Ah, so you were going to invite me to supper?'

'That's not the reason I came, no,' George admitted. He took a deep breath and soldiered on; he never liked conflict. 'I want to talk to you about stolen kegs of rum.'

Quinn glanced around them so quickly that George knew he was not far from the truth. 'Why don't we go for a walk and talk about this?'

'That's a good idea, because I am under the impression that my family has been used under my very nose. Help me to understand what is happening.'

Quinn cleared his throat and considered his words. 'Your family are my own, George, and they have not been ill used, I assure you.'

'Then you refute having anything to do with contraband in our cellar?'

Quinn chuckled and scratched the back of his neck thoughtfully. 'There are not many men who have not made use of their circumstances to feather their nests, George. I was merely increasing the size of my nest egg.'

'At the expense of the good name of my family?' He glanced at Quinn and saw him smirk. His annoyance flared. 'You seem to find the idea of damaging our house humorous.'

'We all of us have things for which we are guilty. You are justified in your displeasure, it is true, but …'

'But my wife, my daughters are guilty of nothing.'

Again the chuckle as Quinn glanced out to sea. George's fingers twitched at his sides. The thunder rumbled, and slow drops patterned the road. 'Adelaide is a model of propriety in the colony and teaches our daughters to conduct themselves in a like manner.'

So loud and long did Quinn laugh that the thunder seemed to join in his hilarity as his throat crackled with the sound. Quinn turned to him. 'George, for a temperate man, you really are quite the wag.' He made no attempt to control the laughter that bubbled up from his chest.

'What are you talking about, sir?' George demanded. 'I do not jest, I assure you.'

'I am talking of your *lady* wife, George. The woman is a whore.'

George blinked in shock.

'You think your wife was a model of purity before you walked her down the aisle? I tell you man, the woman was a strumpet and painted London red many a night before you came along. I knew her before you did. She lost her appeal long ago for me.'

George fumed. His face purpled under the dark sky as the heavy drops of rain fell closer together. 'You lie!' His glasses spotted with rain so that he could barely see, but he didn't need to. He grabbed

Quinn's sleeve as though he could throttle the man with mere intent.

'Why do you think she would not tell you? Why do you think she hid the rum for me? I doubt it was for old time's sake, though it would be a flattering notion. No, George, she did it because she didn't want her husband to find out who she really is. I threatened to tell you if she could not find it in her heart to help me, but I've done it anyway. I never could keep a secret.'

With a gurgle of fury, George leapt at Quinn, who tried to disengage him as though he were nothing more dangerous than a fox terrier, but George would not let go.

'I am soon to be your in-law, George,' Quinn said. 'This is no way for family to treat one another.'

'You will never be part of my household, sir!'

'I beg to differ. I distinctly remember plighting my troth to Emma inside the church in the presence of the parson, who even now holds both mine and Emma's names on a betrothal contract. In short, I am her fiancé.'

'I will tell Emma what you are!' George yelled above the thunder.

'A man who is keen to wed and bed a young wife?'

'No, a thief and a liar! You will be brought to justice.'

Quinn threw George away from him, and he staggered back. His glasses fogged, his gaze grew bleary, but he saw the red coat of Quinn well enough and righted himself enough to charge again.

*

Quinn saw the cart approach at a brisk pace. The horses' mouths and chests foamed with sweat as the driver cracked the whip to get them into the colony before the storm hit.

As the animals turned the corner and came towards them at the point of a canter, Quinn pushed George into the path of the vehicle, and then watched passively as George rolled into the road and beneath the hooves, his face and glasses dusted with the grime of the road.

'Whoa, steady on!' The driver wrestled the horses to a stop, and then jumped from the cart. 'I don't know how he didn't see me coming,' he told Quinn over and over again, as though pleading for him to understand.

'Don't blame yourself. It could have happened to anyone,' Quinn assured him with a glance down at George, who looked for all the world as though he had been rolled in a bowl and smothered in cocoa.

'Do you think he's dead?' Quinn asked as he warmed to the role of concerned friend. He looked at the man with feigned distress.

'Oh, no, don't say it,' the driver begged, wringing his cap ever tighter. 'We need a doctor!' The driver cried out into the street as the rain began to fall in earnest. The driver worried his hat in hands that trembled.

'This *is* the doctor,' Gideon said quietly. His voice spoke as ominous as the iron tongues of the tolling bells and sounded more like a death knell, as the driver tore off his coat and threw it on the rig then made to pick up the surgeon.

The rain fell hard and heavy on Gideon, torrential as the slowly forming crowd dispersed for cover.

'Will you help me get him onto the cart?' the driver yelled above the noise. Quinn bent to help the trembling man who fumbled with the recumbent form of the surgeon.

A trickle of blood reddened the road immediately where George lay, and Quinn thought that if the man didn't calm down, he would have to get both the driver as well as George on the cart himself.

Between them they managed to pick the injured man up and lay him in the back of the cart. The driver shook like calf's foot jelly and Gideon heard his teeth chatter. He was a bundle of nerves, and Gideon smiled at the fervour of the man's frantic prayers for deliverance.

'One minute the road was clear, and then before I knew it he was under the cart,' the driver voiced aloud, cutting off a prayer mid appeal. 'How on earth did he stumble into the road like that?

He came at the cart like cannon fire.'

'I don't think he can see too well,' Gideon said. The driver raised his brows askance.

'I thought you said he is the surgeon?' The driver was clearly confused.

Quinn nodded. 'Better hope he doesn't get the chance to operate on either of us, eh?' The driver glanced over at him. Gideon winked, and saw the man's look of horror.

He turned back to the road ahead of him and fumbled with the reins before he cracked them in the air like a whip. The cart lurched forward.

By the time they reached the hospital they were soaked to the skin. The driver couldn't stop himself from talking as he tried to account for the accident and felt he was solely to blame.

Just as well this ignoramus was too busy quaffing ale from his jug to see anything except the dregs in the bottom when I pushed George, Quinn scoffed to himself. His smile faded, however, when the driver seemed intent on beating down the hospital door to gain entry.

'We need help! Can someone open the door? This is an emergency!' They stood beneath the porch as the torrents continued to fall over the landscape, over the sea, over George curled in the back of the cart. 'I'll go around the back and see if I can get anyone's attention!' the driver yelled over the downpour.

'No need to bother,' Quinn told him, lackadaisical. 'The door is being opened now.' The driver ran back around the porch.

'There's been a slight mishap,' Quinn explained. The driver looked at Quinn as though he were mad.

'I think I've killed him!' the driver spluttered. 'He fell into the path, and I couldn't stop in time!' The orderly nodded calmly but moved quickly. 'Let's get him inside.'

The three men carried George. The blood around the doctor's head was caked with dirt and rain, and his spectacles were perched askew on the bridge of his nose, one lens cracked like a lightning bolt.

'He lives,' the assistant surgeon asserted.

'I haven't done him in?' the driver asked, and started to blubber with relief. Quinn looked at the man dispassionately and wished he would shut his trap.

'Not this day, I am happy to say. Still, I don't know until he wakes what damage, if any, has been done to his brain. He's sustained quite a blow. But he lives, and over the next few days I'll know more. He could die, that's true, but time will tell.'

'So I am free to go?'

'Are you a *convict*?' Quinn lifted a brow askance and wondered if the driver was not the one with the head injury.

'No, I'm not, I'm a free settler,'

'Then you are free to go.'

'I'll go and tell the family he won't be home tonight,' Gideon told the surgeon's assistant, but probably out of guilt, the driver turned back around.

'I'll come and explain what happened. It's the least I can do,' he said.

Gideon brushed the suggestion aside. 'I am to wed their niece by week's end and was going there myself in any case, so you really needn't bother. I'm sure you're shaken; better to get yourself home.'

The sulky driver nodded and doffed his cap with a look of relief.

*

The rain had eased to a drizzle but the driver kept the horses to a slow walk. He remained nervous in case anything or anyone else was hurled into the gutter. He glanced to the side at the redcoat who strolled down the street with a bounce in his step and a whistle on his lips. It was as he did this that he recalled something that had happened in the moments before the surgeon rolled under the cart, and it was the swinging arms of the king's officer that reminded him of it.

There had been some kind of a kerfuffle. Someone had given the

213

surgeon a violent push into the road, and the driver was positive in that moment that it had been the redcoat who had done it.

He glanced at the whistling profile of the man on the street and felt distinctly uneasy, and then he lifted the whip and brought it down on the horse's rump and rolled quickly out of town.

*

Adelaide glanced up when a driver called out to his team and craned as if to peer through the small window.

'Someone is in a hurry this evening,' she noted conversationally.

The four women sat around the dining table. Napkins spread over their knees, they had waited. Emma looked at the clock when it struck seven and then watched intermittently as it continued its journey to the next quarter hour. Still the women waited. The mutton had begun to go cold, and still Emma's aunt hesitated to carve it before her husband returned.

'I cannot think why your father is so late in coming home,' she said for the umpteenth time.

Euphemie sighed heavily. 'Doubtless something has kept him back, Mama. It does not mean that we should be kept back from supper.'

'I'm famished,' Phoebe said.

Emma's stomach chose that moment to voice the same sentiment. Phoebe glanced at her and the two girls smiled in unison.

'Emma is hungry, too,' Phoebe giggled.

'Oh, here is your father now,' Adelaide exclaimed then put her napkin on the table as she got up to greet him, to ask him why he had been so long.

'Oh, it's you, Gideon,' Emma heard her aunt say wearily, and there seemed to be no pleasure in her voice. Nor was there any for Emma as her appetite plummeted with her spirits. 'I thought it was my husband returned for the day.'

'I am afraid I am the bearer of grim news,' he said.

Aunt Adelaide stilled, her full attention on him.

'There was an accident and George has been injured. The assistant surgeon believes he will make it but doesn't yet know the extent of the injury to his head.'

Emma's aunt tottered to the table and sat down with a soft plop.

'We were talking. We had just said our goodbyes. The rain had begun and the wind was whipping across the street. He can't have seen the cart because he went straight into its path. There was nothing I could have done. It happened so fast.'

Gideon's words were plausible, but somehow his tone was not, Emma thought.

*

Adelaide looked up then slowly blinked as she studied Gideon's face. *He* assumed that she knew nothing of why George had gone to see him that day, but he was wrong. Adelaide looked at Gideon with a new awareness. She stood slowly and met his gaze. Her words were measured so that only he could hear her.

'You are a liar and a thief. One day you will be judged according to your deeds in this life, but it is not for me to weigh the scales.' With this she sailed past him and walked into the night towards the hospital without another word.

*

Gideon noted that Adelaide had become upright in the years since her marriage to the surgeon. Still, her scorn embarrassed him to the extreme, and he pulled at his clothing, hot about his neck.

'I see you were about to have supper,' he noted as he walked through the door, mustering a chuckle. 'There is no point seeing good mutton congeal on the plate when we all have earned a hearty appetite.' He walked over to the dining table and pulled out the surgeon's chair. 'Shall I carve?'

Nineteen

The day after the accident, Adelaide wiped her husband's mouth with a linen cloth and tried to smile, as well she ought, she reminded herself for the umpteenth time, for she had not lost him after all.

'You are as weak as a babe, my dear, and you must eat,' she scolded gently.

His face was wreathed in bruises and lacerations, his leg broken, his frame weak and sickly, but he was her George even though he looked nothing like the man she had married not so many years ago.

'I am not hungry,' he said. 'We need to talk.'

Adelaide ignored him and tried for a while to spoon soup between his unwilling lips. She avoided his look and he slowly lifted a hand to caress her cheek. She met his gaze. A look of satisfaction as he touched her gave way to an expression of urgency. He struggled to talk.

'Adelaide,' he whispered. She looked away. He said her name again. Her mouth trembled and she hung her head.

'He told me,' her husband said.

She nodded and dipped her head still further. She knew he wanted her to look at him, but she would not.

'There is nothing to hide anymore. It is no secret.'

'I know,' she quavered, 'and you must be so ashamed.'

George frowned sorrowfully, lovingly at his wife. 'Look at me,' he commanded her gently.

She shook her head.

He tried again. 'Look at me, Adelaide.'

She glanced up, and her eyes were so full of tears she could not see. 'I do not judge you.'

'I judge myself.'

'Then it is time you forgave.' He smiled and stroked her cheek with the back of his hand. She closed her eyes at the sensation as tears continued to fall.

'He cannot hold it over you any longer, this guilt, this shame you have harboured, this fear that you will be found out. Because I have found out, and I love you just as much. Yes, I have questions, and yes, it was a shock, but that was part of your past. I love you, and I will cherish you, until death us do part.

'We have gone through life's joys and sorrows together thus far; we have survived the journey to this foreign place, and we will pull together with God's help and overcome this as well. Come, lie beside me, Adelaide.'

He cradled her in his arms as she wept in gratitude for the grace he showed to her.

'What happened, George?' Adelaide asked after a time. 'How came you to be injured so?'

George frowned, looking into the distance, as he delved into his memory, thinking of the late afternoon in the rain.

'I'm not certain. I wondered if Gideon wrestled with me, and yet I know it can't be so, because I have no recollection of anything save slipping because of the rain. There was no hand upon me that I recall. I want to tell the authorities that if nothing else he is a thief and a cur, but in doing that, my love, I open you to his cruel slander. But more importantly than that, I implicate you as an accessory to his evil.' He reached for her hand and squeezed it. She saw then that tears of frustration and indecision welled in his eyes.

'I do not want my niece to marry that man. I am certain when I tell you that.'

Adelaide pulled her hand away, once more the woman with a past to hide, a fear to squelch.

'But she must wed him, George. Don't you see? If we forbid it then he holds me captive just as he always has. He will spread my sin from near and far. Neither of us like the thought of it, husband, so marry him she must.'

*

Emma sat in the parlour and sewed the final adjustments to her wedding gown, as she hummed the tune of *Amazing Grace*. She hoped her aunt, who was at the hospital with Uncle George, would come to feel its truth as she did, for God worked in all of them whether they knew it or not. She thought of how God had been shaping her for a life such as this, a life with Gideon, and how over the past days she had come to accept, if not yet to relish the prospect.

Tobias was in her thoughts, as always, but whenever she dreamed of him now, she asked her heavenly Father to bless him, and there she had left him, in the Lord's hands. Her longing was tempered with enough wisdom to know that yearning for something she could not have would serve no good purpose. She pricked her finger and bright blood beaded her flesh.

'*You're bleeding.*'

'*Aye, but I'm alive.*'

She would never be his, but he lived, and that would be enough for her.

'*The Lord has promised good to me. His word my hope secures. He will my shield and portion be, as long as life endures.*'

'Will you come back from Wallis Plains for my wedding, Emma?' Phoebe asked breathlessly as she entered the cottage. The heat of the day made her cheeks glow, but her eyes were lit by love alone. Emma looked up from her needlework and smiled.

'You know I will if I am able.' Emma put her work aside as Phoebe plumped down on the settle. The two girls embraced.

'He is going to ask Father,' Phoebe whispered. 'Do you think he will give his permission?' Phoebe frowned, and Emma touched her arm as she reassured her.

'Your father is a reasonable man, cousin. I have no doubt that he will say yes.'

'Rory is an Irishman. I hope this doesn't sway Father against him. Although I don't know why it should. If you could stay, if you could wed the man of your choice, Emma, then my joy would be complete.' Phoebe took Emma's hands and squeezed them.

'We make the best of what we have been given,' Emma said, 'and that is what I intend to do.'

'Did Gideon have any idea how well he had done, I wonder, when you stepped from the water like Venus?' Phoebe asked. 'I think perhaps he knows. He is no fool. Does he dine with us this evening?'

'No, daughter,' her mother told her as she entered the room. 'I am afraid to say that he does not.' The girls waited for further explanation but none was given.

Emma saw that her aunt had been crying, but there was a peaceful smile on her face, and she turned now and bestowed it upon Emma.

'My dear, if I had known before what I do this day, my consideration of your future would have taken a different course. Still, your time here with us is something which I cannot be sorry for, and our only loss is that you will shortly leave us. I can only wish you the best, and I do this wholeheartedly.' At this Aunt Adelaide bent and kissed her forehead and Phoebe had a look of wonder at the change in her mother, at the lift of her spirits and her words to Emma.

'Thank you, Aunt Adelaide. Your sentiment means much to me.'

Something in Aunt Adelaide's eyes seemed to want to apologise to Emma. But when the older woman opened her mouth then closed it again, Emma sensed that she could not speak the words just yet. Instead, her aunt had a look that simply longed for forgiveness, though whether from God, Emma, herself, or all three, she did not know.

A knock sounded on the cottage door and Phoebe jumped up, one plump hand on either cheek in an expression of excitement and fear at once.

'Mother I wonder if I might set the table for tea? You see ...'

Her mother smiled and raised a brow askance. 'Your beau is coming to call?'

Phoebe flushed deeply and pursed her lips. She looked unsure how to answer the question.

'We have been expecting this, your father and I, so now is not the time to leave the young man standing there rapping at the door, is it? Let him in, Phoebe,' her mother told her affectionately, 'before he thinks to walk away.'

*

Emma did not see that same warm welcome when Gideon strolled down the path later that evening. Aunt Adelaide walked to the door in full sail, proud as the prow of a ship.

'Gideon, it has been a tiring day nursing George at the hospital. I hope you understand?' Her aunt's words were apologetic, but her tone was brittle.

'Why of course, Adelaide. I would expect nothing less,' came Gideon's soothing words. 'Please give him my regards.'

'You can be sure I will.'

Emma went outside to greet him. She took a deep steadying breath. They had to clear the air concerning the issue of the rum.

'Were you aware that Euphemie had the authorities check this house for stolen rum?'

Gideon was wide eyed. 'I was not. That kind of slight made against decent people can stick.'

'Euphemie told them she found it in the cellar, but when the commandant came, there was nothing to be seen. Aunt Adelaide was devastated that Euphemie could have implicated her as a thief.'

'As well she might!' Gideon sounded shocked.

'After the officers left, I overheard Aunt Adelaide admit to my uncle that she had merely held it as a favour to you.' Emma looked at him then, biting her lip.

'And so she had, Emma my dear,' Gideon told her gently, 'but I can assure you that none of that was contraband. On that I stake my life.' He looked down at her earnestly in the half-light. Emma's mouth was a circle of surprise. 'Please tell me my darling girl, that you never thought for a moment that it was otherwise?' Emma's face was apologetic.

'Aren't you aware that when an officer farewells His Majesty's service, he is thanked with the gift of rum?'

Emma slowly shook her head. 'No, I was not.'

Gideon was for a moment crestfallen. 'Poor, dear Adelaide. No wonder she didn't seem her hospitable self. I cannot blame her, nor yet Euphemie. The child probably only thought to do what was right.'

Emma wasn't sure that this was so but kept it to herself.

'I will speak to Adelaide, you can be sure, and I will apologise that your aunt has had to suffer such a slur. All because she minded the stuff for me. Now here everyone in the household takes me for a thief.' Gideon shook his head sadly. Emma opened her mouth to speak.

'Hush, dear one. I will put the whole sordid mistake to rest, never fear. This matter has been spoken of between us, and I am only glad that you didn't keep it to yourself to worry over. As we grow as one we will both of us learn to trust.'

Emma nodded, feeling foolish.

'Emma, I leave in the morning to go to Wallis Plains one last time to ensure that the finishing touches have been made on the house. As soon as I get back we'll marry, so kiss me now before I go.' He took her around the waist and planted a soft, wet kiss on her mouth. Did she smell liquor?

'Gideon, there will be time enough for that when we are married,' Emma said as she pushed away from his ardour in confusion.

His head came up. 'I wager you didn't say that to that greasy headed lump of a convict I caught you in the garden with some weeks back.' His truculent tone was so different from moments before.

Emma's silence said enough. Yes, she had invited Tobias with all that she was, and Gideon's sneering remark was enough to remind her that her heart was not her own, that she loved Tobias Freeman regardless of circumstance, of social standing.

'Never mind, I will make you forget his animal fumbling. He is no gentleman.'

'Not in the usual sense of the word.'

'Not in any sense of the word, my love. It doesn't matter how cocky they act, everyone knows them for what they are.'

'All men are redeemable,' Emma said. 'Why, there are convicts even now who have *served* their terms and have been given not only freedom but land grants, and have gone on to begin new lives, Quinn. Their past sins have been paid for, and they have been set free to change what they did and learn from their mistakes.'

'*We are not the sum of our past mistakes.*'

Yet Rory Ferguson had told her from Tobias's own lips that he had broken the sixth commandment. What did he mean? Did he refer to himself? It was something Emma dwelled on at night, sleepless as she tried to make sense of the message.

'*Can you not see the blood on my hands?*'

She was at a loss, and heaven help her, she loved him yet, whatever he may have done. Still, she feared for him, and it broke through from her dreams and into her waking moments, and yet she was none the wiser.

Just then a jovial laugh broke through the sunset evening and into her musings. Gideon turned and aimed a curse at noisy convicts making merry somewhere down the road.

'What are they celebrating?' Emma wondered.

'A *wedding*,' he scoffed. 'Though why they bother joining to procreate and breed more reprobates into the colony, I don't know. Why they are given permission to wed at all is beyond me. The commandant is growing too soft in his rule of this colony.'

'I wonder who got married.' Emma smiled tightly and tried to ignore Gideon's ill temper and unjust attitude.

He shrugged. 'Does it matter, dear?'

'I suppose not.'

'Still, they might tap the admiral and share a dram with us before the night is out.' He took her by the hand and paid no mind to her reticence.

'I don't think we ought to,' she said as she bit her lip worriedly.

'It will give me the opportunity to see that all is as it should be and you the opportunity to see who was wed,' he reasoned with jollity that probably had more to do with the prospect of quaffing more of the Admiral's Blood than it did natural high spirits.

In the distance, the lilt of a tin whistle soared high in the evening air. Emma followed, albeit unwillingly, almost dragged along by Gideon as he strode out with purpose and went in the direction of the strains of music: bodhran, fiddle, and flute.

Sunset over the water glowed as deep as a blood orange and Emma wondered if Tobias too had chanced to glance up and see the beauty of the lurid sky.

'You can dance with me, Emma dear,' Gideon said, 'for I know you like to do so.'

She knew he referred to Christmas Day on the foreshore, the evening on Prospect Hill, and although his voice held a smile, Emma had enough sense to realise that his good humour would slip if she denied him her hand in the dance.

'After all, you danced with the convict, did you not?' he asked slyly.

Emma glanced at him, and he grinned like a fox. She said nothing. He goaded her as though he wanted to see her respond, to refute the truth, but she would not. She glanced away to her right and back into the sunset and thought of sweeter times.

Just then the curfew bell sounded, and Gideon pulled her to a stop outside the convict residence where the music still rang and voices laughed within.

'*Whenever you hear the bells pealing, they'll remind you that I am waiting.*'

Did he wait still, even now, even yet? Had his words been true? Yes, she knew they had, but perhaps he had given up hope, as she had. Maybe he finally realised that to wait was in vain. Knowing that he thought of her was enough to help her keep up her strength at times, that, and trust in God.

'A drink for the lady!' Gideon called out as he pulled her inside the abode. The place smelled of hemp rope and old sweat and rum.

'I don't want any, Gideon,' Emma said firmly.

'Nonsense,' he told her as he grabbed a tin cup and held it to her lips. 'You cannot live in the colonies without trying a shot of rum.'

He tipped it up and she swallowed and spluttered. He laughed and tilted the cup against her mouth once more. It dribbled down either side of her face and chin. Gideon took out a snowy pocket-handkerchief and vigorously wiped her mouth. Then he grabbed hold of her hands and began to dance her around like a wooden doll that refused to move.

'Miss Colchester!' It was Kevin. He smiled toothlessly as he walked over to where Gideon continued to twirl her against her wishes.

'Kevin, how do you do?' When she saw Kevin, she thought of his strapping Irish friend, and her smile was very glad indeed. 'Who has been wed?' Emma asked, glad that Gideon had released her to quaff another draught of rum.

'Why, me, miss. Aren't I the lucky one?' He chuckled.

'Oh Kevin, that's wonderful. Whom did you marry?'

'Mary.' He winked. His expression showed he was more than a little pleased with himself. 'Katy is a real little cracker of a kid. I'm thinking that if I behave myself like I have been, why, I might even get a pardon.'

Emma was happy for Kevin, and deliriously pleased for herself that she did not need to relinquish the love of her heart so soon. 'I only wish I could tell Toby that me and Mary have decided on the horse and carriage.'

Emma blinked. She hadn't seen any horse tied up outside. Perhaps it was around the back. Perhaps it was another one of his nonsensical rhymes.

Kevin pulled a folded piece of paper, much used, from his jacket pocket.

'Toby said to ask the parson to read bits and pieces of the Bible so I could learn how to commit them to memory, but since you're here, miss, I wonder if you might do the honours?'

Emma opened her mouth to tell him she would but Gideon spoke first.

'And who is Toby?' Gideon wanted to know, his head thrust forward.

'Toby's my mate,' Kevin explained above the noise of the instruments. Gideon hadn't heard him and didn't bother to ask again. Instead he drew Emma into his arms to begin to dance again, and ignored the outthrust paper.

'I don't want to dance, Gideon,' Emma tried to tell him.

'You danced for him,' he grunted then pulled her against him roughly, 'so now you can do it for me.'

Gideon was too liberal with his touch. His hands snaked around her, persistent, without thought for anything save his own pleasure. Emma tried to disengage herself from his attentions. He merely laughed. It was a lewd sound and it was careless. Emma flushed deeply and wondered what to do. Gideon had imbibed way too much.

*

'I don't think the lady is interested to dance.' Kevin frowned, folded the paper, and put it back where he kept it.

'Women always say no when they mean yes,' Quinn grinned obscenely. As he watched the coarse officer, overbearing and crude, Kevin saw that the young Miss Colchester was not enjoying herself in the least. In fact, she seemed close to tears. Toby wouldn't have stood for it, the way the man treated her, he knew, so neither would he.

'Well, to my way of thinking, this young lady seems to know her own mind, and I'm telling you to release her. It's curfew now anyway and the fiddler has just left.'

But Quinn did not seem to need music—certainly not more rum— and continued to twirl Miss Colchester without regard for her or Kevin. Kevin took hold of Quinn, who stopped then and looked down at Kevin with disdain.

'I think you are forgetting that I am an officer of the crown,' Quinn slurred arrogantly.

'And I think you have let it slip your mind that an officer and a gentleman doesn't treat a lady that way,' Kevin said quietly. By now the cottage was empty of all save Mary, who looked on in dismay, and Katy, who slept curled in a cot in the corner, blissfully unaware of what was taking place.

'And you're an expert in the field of romance, are you? You think now you've married your strumpet you're the rooster on the dunghill they call love and are entitled to hand out advice concerning affairs of the heart, eh?' Quinn sneered as he turned to watch Mary.

'Get out,' Kevin growled, his fists clenched, chest out-thrust.

'Or what? You'll call the constabulary?' He turned away from Kevin to down the rest of the rum.

'I'll give you one more chance.'

'Well, let me make your decision a little easier.' Quinn laughed and lunged at Kevin with a bread knife that sat on the bench. But his aim was no better that his judgement, and when he turned again to run at Kevin, the smaller man brought up his fist against Quinn's jaw. Quinn struggled backward, his balance betrayed by rum, before he fell back against the floor where, Kevin was glad to see, he appeared inclined to stay.

*

Emma turned behind her to see Phoebe's soldier at the door.

'Bit of bother here I see,' was Rory Ferguson's smiling statement.

'He drank too much and danced too fast,' Kevin said.

The young man read between the lines and shook his head at the sound of Gideon, who snored on the earthen floor.

'He can't stay here tonight,' Kevin told him in no uncertain terms. 'After all, it's our wedding night, and with the noise he's making, we won't get a wink of sleep.'

'Say no more, but consider it done,' he said, then returned shortly with another soldier. Gideon was deposited outside. 'At a fair distance from the cottage,' Rory said.

'Let him sleep it off until roll call,' Emma heard the other soldier say as they walked away and into the night. She supposed she ought to have felt concerned for Gideon's safety, yet it was relief she felt as she saw his body hefted between the two redcoats.

'Heaviest baby they've ever carried, I'd warrant,' Kevin chuckled along with Mary. The couple shared an embrace, and Emma realised that it was time to leave. Kevin walked her to the door.

'Thank you, Kevin, for trying to protect me.'

'Toby would've been disappointed if I'd turned a blind eye,

miss, feeling for you the way that he does. The last thing he wanted to do was leave, and he would sleep easy tonight knowing that you were safe.'

'Until the twenty-sixth of January,' Emma whispered, and they both knew what she meant.

'I'll watch from the door until I see you reach the surgeon's cottage, miss,' Kevin assured her.

'I want you to call me by my Christian name, Kevin, for we are friends, are we not?'

'We are, that's for sure.' She saw him smile as she walked away.

TWENTY

Emma watched as the children sat on small chairs before the parson. Kevin sat among them. It was just as well that his growth had been stunted during what was likely a lean childhood in London, she thought, because he would not have been able to perch on the stool otherwise. As it was, it was a perfect roost for him. Emma smiled to see him among the children, his face lit up every bit as much as theirs, and it did her heart good to see conviction settle over his features.

They all pondered the day's text.

'Do not drink wine or intoxicating drink, you, nor your sons with you, when you go into the tabernacle of meeting, lest you die,' the parson read.

'My da' is doomed then, is he parson?' Jimmy asked as he scrubbed his thatch of red hair with a grubby set of fingers. They wove in and out of his head as he searched for lice, and Emma realised that she would have to bring the spirits to douse him again.

'Not at all, Jimmy, but we should all exercise restraint when it comes to strong drink,' the parson said, 'for we are told in Proverbs twenty that wine is a mocker and strong drink is a brawler, and he whoever is led astray by it is not wise.'

'That's perhaps why Ma tells me da' that he's a brainless nowt with nothing between his ears.'

Jimmy was serious, but he appeared comforted by the parson's chuckle. Emma overheard Jimmy whisper loudly to the child next to him that the thought of his da' getting dumber and dumber with every drink that came his way was nothing to smile about. Still, Parson knew best, he supposed. Emma held back her own laugh when he sighed long and hard and set upon his head again in search of crawlers.

'It was good to see you learning more about the Bible, Kevin,' Emma said as the children filed out of the building. He grinned at the encouragement.

'It was me mate Toby that got me started on it.'

Emma's brows rose. 'Really?' She watched as he spread out the tattered piece of paper he had tried give her the night of his wedding.

'Gave this to me the day he left for Wallis Plains. I can recite every one now.' He seemed pleased with his accomplishment. 'Took that little Bible with him to keep him company and said I was to learn these when he was gone, and I've done just that. If he ever comes back, I'm going to tell him I know them all. Better still, when you go to Wallis Plains, miss, maybe you can let him know?' Kevin sounded hopeful.

'I will be sure to,' Emma told him earnestly.

'First Toby, and now you. It will be a different place without you, miss. Still, I've got a family now,'—he swaggered proudly— 'and on that note, I'm going home to my treacle tart.'

Emma cocked her head quizzically.

'Sweetheart,' Kevin supplied with a chuckle, and they walked down Prospect Hill together.

The day left Emma breathless; the harbour glimmered like a blue jewel. She knew Hunter's River was in the distance and meandered sleepily through Wallis Plains. Emma imagined Gideon on the open boat heading up river, nursing a bruised jaw, and wondered if he remembered the night before, or even if he had managed to get on the barge himself, let alone manoeuvre the craft.

*

Gideon got up stiffly in the dawn, his head heavy and painful. He wondered what had induced him to sleep beneath the hedge. He gingerly touched his jaw, dimly recollected the evening before, and thought that perhaps it had something to do with comely Mary, because the grubby little Cockney had knocked him down. After that he had no recollection at all. He would deal with him later. As it was, he didn't have enough strength to bruise a grape. Besides, he needed to check that the house was ready and that Emma's convict lover had been sent packing from the place.

Perhaps I should get rid of the kegs at the house, he thought as he got in his boat and pushed into the river. He didn't want Emma to find them in their bedroom. He knew he told her that the rum was a going away gift from the commandant and the other officers, and one keg would seem believable, not three. He would be better off if he sold the stuff to the comfort inns along the river and got the handsome profit, as he had done with the other kegs. It had been the easiest money he had ever made.

He could do without rum for a little while yet. Vaguely, it occurred to him that it had become as important to him as bread and meat of late, and he didn't think he would be able to stomach much of that either. Yet he managed to eat bread and drink a mug of sweet water, and decided at the last moment to slip a flask of rum between his shirt and his jacket.

'Hair of the dog that bit me,' he laughed to himself. Besides, he deserved to celebrate. He would be a gentleman farmer, no longer in the king's service, and he might as well enjoy it to the full. There would be time aplenty for sobriety. Not only that, he would have a young wife who would more than keep his interest in the near future, and spirits and sport did not make good bedfellows. He chuckled to himself again as the boat glided smoothly upstream in the early morning.

The sun shone through the mangrove trees that lapped the water's edge. The tidal flow tongued the tree roots and made a sucking sound as he passed. He closed his eyes and dozed in the warm sunshine. It was still too early yet to make him sweat, and he was glad that he had pushed himself to embark early, though he had longed to stay awhile beneath the scrubby banksias and sleep off the night before.

He wondered how on earth ants hadn't bitten him as he lay there. The country was overrun with them. They busied themselves over hard ground and under eucalyptus leaves that crackled dryly underfoot. Everyone knew sitting down for any period of time was chancy.

He scratched his back and belched once or twice, and before he drifted off to sleep considered what ought to be done with Tobias Freeman. Yes, he could have him sent back with the rest of the felons to the Coal River. He could even find some excuse to have him sent to Lime-burners' Creek for another stint and hope that he was lucky enough to hear of his demise; but knowing that the Irishman was as hard as a blacksmith's hammer, Gideon thought he might be better served in getting rid of him once and for all. Then it would be certain that Emma would never meet up with him again.

He yawned and his eyes fully closed as he smiled. Yes, that was what he would do, and before he did away with the inconvenience of the Irishman's presence, he would have him dig his own grave, for heaven only knew how hot it could get at this time of year, not just during the day, but also at night. He didn't want to get done in as he fashioned the felon's grave for him. He would have to hold him at gunpoint to get him to do as he was ordered, he supposed, but he would get some satisfaction as he watched the convict sweat and plead for mercy. He had none, of course, no mercy at all where the convicts were concerned, and he wondered that he hated the dregs of society so much.

His mind drifted to a memory of his mother. His mother, in the cheap finery of a street woman. He had loved and despised her at the same time. Never, he had told himself, would he live as he had in those early years as a youth, when he turned a blind eye and wished he had enough pounds to do with as he pleased and not have to scrape the gutter for a crust.

That was when he had met Adelaide, or Violet as she had been called then, a young girl with dreams not unlike his own, someone who also wanted a life without want and days spent without feeling society's scorn. This they had had in common.

She was one of the reasons his climb up the social ladder had been laborious for a time, because she had been like a thirst he could not quench, that and the liquor, but this too, in the end, he had tamed; until now. Yet he had conquered this before, and he could certainly relinquish it again. Emma would help in that, he was sure. But now he had time to enjoy life's luxuries. And as he floated downstream and dozed as the sun rose, he was in little hurry.

*

Emma was loath to see the upcoming days. She was in no hurry to walk down the aisle with Gideon, even though that would mean an end to the drawn-out suspense. The time she had waited for the twenty-sixth of January to dawn had seemed like an age, yet she knew it had been a short while since Gideon had set the important date.

'*We can have just as long a courtship as you wish, Emma dear.*'

He had said that, but it hadn't happened that way. Gideon had been impatient after all, and it wouldn't have helped Emma become accustomed to the idea had she stewed on it for a month of Sundays.

The Lord had brought Tobias to her attention, though what his purpose for the meeting was she still did not know. She felt as though she sailed in the darkness without a compass, yet she knew that trust was all she needed.

'*He has broken the sixth commandment*'

Why had Tobias made so sure that she found out? Did he want her to know so it would make marrying Gideon easier? So that she would not look back and yearn for him, now that she knew he had succumbed to murder? She hardly knew. Regardless of the blood on his hands she loved him, but she would marry Gideon because it was right, and because he was blameless in this. She could not condone murder, and she could wed no man who had committed it.

Tears squeezed between her lashes as she curled on her side in the trundle bed and looked out at the sea.

'Release me, Tobias,' she whispered. 'I can love you no more.' Emma turned on her side and sobbed silently into the feathers of the pillow.

*

Later that morning, Emma stood with Phoebe as they surveyed a peddler's goods outside her uncle's cottage. The peddler's tiny wife smiled and nodded at everything her husband said, yet barely opened her mouth. As Phoebe and Emma poured over his wares, he shared the day's news. He spit into the dust at his feet, and then slicked back the grey hairs on his head as he leaned against the dray, as though he had all the time in the world to chat.

'Heading out to Wallis Plains tomorrow.' He yawned and scratched his belly with thoughtful fingers.

'Have you been there before?' Phoebe asked. 'I must say that I, for one, am curious about the place, and my cousin Emma here is to go there any day now and set up her home.'

'Is that a fact?'

Emma told him that it was.

'And where might you be living?'

Emma suspected he hoped he could gain another steady customer. 'I cannot tell you what it looks like. I have never seen the place. It has just been built.'

'But it's your home you say?' The peddler scratched his head as he thought.

'Just so. I have not had the opportunity to see the house yet.'

'Head down river with the missus and me,' he said. 'There'll be enough room for our wares and us besides.' He looked to his little lady, who craned a little farther forward on her seat and nodded her head in approval.

'Yes, yes,' she agreed vigorously as she looked first to Emma and then back at her husband. She seemed to think it a splendid notion.

'She lost a babe a few months back,' the peddler indicated with a swing of his head in the dainty woman's direction. 'Do anything for some company, I'd reckon, wouldn't you, Dolly?'

Her smile dimmed a little but she nodded again. 'Yes, indeed.'

'Terrible heartbreaking for a woman,' he said as he spit into the gutter again, his eyes cast at the ground for just a moment. Although his tone was dismissive, Emma saw that it was not only the little woman who had been heartbroken.

'Still, where there's life there's hope, eh, Dolly me girl?' His voice still sounded strident as though he haggled a sale, but he patted his wife on the knee and it made her smile.

Emma felt their shared pain.

'So what do you say, me dear? Fancy a ride down river?'

'Do you think you should go?' Phoebe asked worriedly. Emma bit her lip and considered the idea. She felt for the woman called Dolly; more than that, she longed for a glance of Tobias, who worked even now on her house in the heat of the sun.

'You will not go, will you Emma?'

'I believe I shall,' Emma nodded. The little woman joined her and smiled to beat the band.

'Well,' Phoebe said, 'you shall not leave without me.'

Emma regarded Phoebe, who gave her a look which dared Emma to refuse her. The notion of such an adventure was a ludicrous one, but Emma's temerity overcame her usual temperate nature, and she would go with these country companions to Wallis Plains, with consent or without.

'Will your mother let you go?' Emma said. Phoebe shrugged while the peddler and his jolly wife looked first at one and then the other of the two girls.

'I don't suppose so,' she confessed with a crestfallen look.

'Then I won't see you in trouble because of me,' Emma said firmly, 'and I shall go alone.' She lifted her chin almost defiantly. Phoebe looked rather surprised at this side of Emma.

'When and where shall I meet you tomorrow?' Emma asked the peddler.

'Down at Mr Tucker's store, if you like,' the peddler said. 'You'll need to look sharp, though. Gets too hot to set off much after breakfast.'

The next morning both Aunt Adelaide and Phoebe accompanied Emma. They stood at the harbour to see her off. Adelaide wanted to verify that Emma's companions were suitable, not the cutthroats she envisaged, and she looked them over for any apparent want of morals but could find none. Still, she threatened them with ladylike decorum and looked down on them from the wharf as they bobbed below her in the open boat.

'I expect to see my niece returned presently in the peak of health,' she said. 'She is to be wed in less than a week's time, you know.'

Emma smiled and thought that if they intended any harm they would hardly worry that she got back in time for the wedding.

'We must not tarry, Phoebe. I need to get back to the hospital to see to your father. He will be out and about in a few days' time, so be sure you have returned by then, Emma my girl, or your Uncle George will be furious with me.'

So Uncle George hadn't been asked if she could go. Emma looked at her aunt and guessed rightly that the woman was a little ashamed at herself. It was certainly irregular for an unmarried girl to visit her beau, but Emma supposed her aunt thought she would be with the peddler and his wife. Emma flushed at her own temerity, and wondered at herself. She even admitted that she was a little scared. One thing she did know, and it was this: if Aunt Adelaide had any inkling of who Emma really went to see, she never would have been granted permission to see the house.

'Bushrangers lurk where you least expect,' she said. 'Yes, you may well laugh, but they are at large, you may be certain, dear, so be on your guard!'

*

'She's right, you know, that aunt of yours,' the peddler told Emma while his wife rummaged for the newspaper she wanted to give to her.

The man watched his wife with eyes that twinkled. 'Neither of us can read. The gazette was given to me, but you may as well keep it for all the good it'll do her and I, eh Dolly, me girl?'

Dolly bobbed her head, but apparently couldn't find the newspaper. 'I was told there was a piece in there about a group of convicts gone bush, and another column about some bushranger or another around these parts. Reward of twenty-five pounds and a ticket of pardon besides to any convict willing to give him up. There's many a place they can hide on these shores.'

'It's a vast country.' Emma nodded.

'I've served time,' the peddler said. 'Done some stupid stuff and paid the penalty. Got back on me feet and tied the knot with

Doll here,'—he gestured to the diminutive Dolly, who flushed and smiled—'but some of 'em can't stick the restrictions. They skip roll muster and head bush.

'Most of these outlaws are good men at heart who took a gamble, but like all gambles, miss, the dice doesn't always land square. They take the good with the bad and hope for better luck next time, I suppose. For anyone willing to work, they could live off the fat of the land.'

Emma recognised the truth in it. She gazed to the left at the mangroves that rimmed the riverbank, their thick leaves glossy in the sun; at the stretches of silver grass beyond; and as far as the eye was able to reach, the purple-blue mountains in the distance.

Emma realised anew that she had a fortunate life indeed. Soon she would begin to live a quiet life on Wallis Plains without so much as a whip crack to mark the passing of a long and sultry day.

TWENTY-ONE

The Wheatsheaf Arms didn't boast luxuries, Gideon noted, but there was conversation, a bed, food and refreshment. It didn't matter that the earthen floor was greasier than a dripping pot or that the salt mutton was badly cured and poorly cooked, because the tea was strong and sweet and the rum warmed the heart.

At a signal from Gideon's hand the publican poured him another mug. Gideon nodded his thanks.

'At this rate you will be buying back most of what you sold me.'

The publican's quip was good-natured but Gideon blinked, his eyes growing cool and his temper hot.

'Did you hear that when Admiral Nelson died on ship he was shoved in a keg of rum and transported back to the mother country for burial?'

'No,' said the publican, 'can't say I ever heard tell that was so.'

Gideon leaned in closer and saw he lit a flame of fear in the innards of the man. 'Be careful they do not find you in your cellar in a like manner.'

When Gideon left the inn the next day the proprietor took no payment from him. He thought that perhaps the publican considered the red wool twill and buff breeches of His Majesty's soldiers cut a fine figure. He had always thought so himself. Why, the man even had the stable boy shine his boots.

'I'll be sure to come again,' Gideon assured him, all congeniality. But as he strode from the public house to the riverbank, he thought the publican looked less than thrilled at the prospect of his return.

*

Emma gazed along the riverbank as she and her companions journeyed, fascinated by the scenery, until her eye caught sight of an inn along the riverbank. There, at a rough-hewn table outside the doors of the pub, apparently at breakfast, sat Gideon. With a quick intake of breath, Emma glanced away in the other direction. She prayed that he would not look up, that he would not catch her glance; for even at that distance, she knew it was him and he would realise the same of her.

As she and the peddler and his wife continued downstream, Emma's heart pounded at the close call she had had, and she was ashamed of herself then, because the man was her espoused and she had hidden from him as though he were a fiend. After all, when he arrived, she would have to suffer his company then, and was only glad that there would be others around to cool his ardour. Again her hasty decision gave her pause for thought. Still, there was no going back.

She spent the remainder of the journey in silence. Her time as an unmarried girl was about to end, her life as a married woman was about to begin, and she would be valiant in her effort to love the man with whom she would, for the rest of her days, share her marriage bed.

Help me, Father, to live my life as a woman of grace, in all that I think and say and do, she prayed.

When she came to her destination and stepped from the boat, Emma turned to the peddler and his wife. 'In case Officer Quinn is not able to find me suitable transport for my return, please ask for me as you pass through tomorrow and we will return to the colony together.'

'You may be certain of it, miss,' the man said, as his wife passed Emma the rolled-up gazette that she had finally found.

'Farewell, dear,' the little woman said with a smile. Emma smiled in return. She took a deep breath and hoped that when Gideon arrived he would not be displeased to find her at their home. She knew she had acted impulsively. At the thought of Gideon's displeasure, Emma almost panicked. Still, she reminded herself, Gideon had seemed disappointed that she would not see their home until after they wed, and on this she banked.

*

When Tobias heard a rustling sound from the rushes at the river's edge, he started, afraid he'd heard a snake, though he had never seen one. Yet when he looked up and saw Emma stood before him.

She will think me stupid, he thought, because he stood and stared, mouth agape, while his hands hung slack at his sides as though he had never seen a woman before.

She was a vision in white. The sun sparkled behind her and wreathed her body in an aura of light. His eyes went from her wide-set grey eyes to her beautiful mouth and down the length of her body. The woman that he dreamed about, that he had prayed would come to him with every passing day, had done so. No matter the reason for her presence, she was there.

Tobias felt his blood sing through every part of him. He dropped the shovel at his feet and grasped her hard with the strength of his emotions, then wrapped his arms around her for all and any to see. He claimed her lips, his mouth against hers, and Emma did not pull away.

*

He smelled of the sun and soil and honest work, his toil pronounced in the roughness of his calloused hands. He rocked her in his embrace. 'It is so good to see you, Emma darling,' he said, and she

241

heard a smile in his voice as he leaned in to kiss her hair.

She pulled away from him then as his words awakened her from her trance, because she had to, because it was only proper that she should. She was his darling, and he was hers, but she would not tell him because she was a woman betrothed to be wed. But oh, how hard it was to release him.

'Will you show me the house?'

His smile faltered and fell with his hands as he let her go, but he grinned good-naturedly. 'Aye, I will.'

*

The overseer nodded at their request, though he seemed peeved that he had not been given the opportunity to guide her. He wondered aloud, almost under his breath, if Quinn was aware that his affianced was at the house, and whether they had planned to meet.

It was not lost on Tobias what an honour it was to show Emma the place in which she would spend her days, the home that he had helped labour over, for her He watched her smile in wonder at all she saw.

'It is more than I dreamed,' she said. 'He has considered it all.'

'Emma, I love you.'

'You cannot, we cannot,' she shook her head.

'Only tell me,' he pleaded, 'tell me that you love me.'

*

Emma shook her head and turned away. Tears filled her eyes as she looked out the window and wondered when Gideon would arrive.

'Then why did you come?' he asked her roughly. 'Why, if there is no hope for us? Why travel down Hunter's River and seek me out, even allow me to embrace you, when you want none of it … none of me?'

'Because coming here to look at this house was such a good

excuse to see you, when a glance is all I can have. I am human, Tobias, and I sin even as I try to do right. Because I took a boat on an impulse and my heart's whim when I should have remained in the colony until I was wed so I would not be tempted anymore.'

'And marrying one man when you have feelings for another, Emma, doesn't this seem a sin to you?'

'I signed a binding troth in the church, and it amounts to a bill of sale.'

'You talk as though you are Quinn's purchase, Emma, but I know you belong with me.'

Tobias stood behind her and clasped her around the shoulders, then buried his face into her neck, into the tendrils of hair that had come loose. She felt his uneven breath against her nape and knew that he was perhaps as close to tears as she was. She was aware that, though this man had travelled miles in the rotting hulk of a ship, had known fear and dread and toil, that it was this, this relinquishing of the love of her that undid him more than anything had, and it humbled her deeply. Emma dipped her head and let her tears drop onto the dull sheen of the tallow wood floorboards.

In frustration he spun away, his hands tight fisted.

'You broke the sixth commandment, Tobias,' Emma reminded him. 'How can I forget that?'

Tobias jerked round to face her. 'What?'

'You think I can gloss over the fact? I can't.'

'Not me! Not me, Emma! It was Quinn.' He clutched her with desperate hands as he gave the confession. 'I witnessed as he shovelled a man to the earth. But worse than that, I dug and buried that man in his grave. I did it out of necessity, out of fear; fear that he would name me as the murderer. All to take me further from you.' His voice broke. She reached a hand to touch his cheek, the pain he felt showing in his eyes. Emma enfolded him in tender arms, comforting him.

'I should be getting back to my work,' he told her. 'I have to leave you all too soon. I want you in my arms forever.' He shrugged, his voice raw. 'Perhaps I am selfish, aye, but I would not be a man if I didn't fight for the right to have and to hold you. I'd fight to my last breath if that's what it took to keep you with me, Emma.'

Emma swallowed hard, smiling sadly through her tears as she listened, intent on every word that came from his mouth.

'Miss Colchester,' came the overseer's voice from below stairs. 'Are you alright?'

'I am perfectly well. I will be downstairs directly.'

'Right you are, miss. Oh, and by the way, Officer Quinn's boat has been spotted coming down river. I expect he'll be here within no time.'

'Thank you for letting me know; I'll come and greet him.'

Emma turned to Tobias and put her head in her hands. She tried not to cry and failed miserably. Then Tobias kissed her for what she knew had to be the last time. She clung to him for dear life, as she had done once before. It now seemed such a long time ago.

'Kick like fury, else we're lost.'

She didn't want to let him go. She was drowning in despair, and could hardly bear to leave his side.

'You go first, in case he sees you with me. He'll wonder at my tear-stained face, but at least if we don't walk out of the house together, he won't blame you for it'

Tobias nodded, his face a mask, but Emma knew that it veiled emotions every bit as heart wrenching as those that tore at her. She watched him stalk away, hurt and angry and just as close to tears. The man she loved, who she was letting walk out of the house and her future and her life.

She wiped her face and took a deep breath. There was no time for tears. Tobias's safety depended on her duplicity. Emma bit her lip and shook her head at her subterfuge. But then, she told herself, many a woman would do it for the man she loved; she was no different.

'Emma!' Gideon was pleasantly surprised, stepping onto the bank to see her there waiting for him.

'Good day, Gideon,' Emma tried to smile, and found it as greater task as any she had ever had to muster.

'Why, how came you here?' he was quite simply flabbergasted, but not at all displeased, and for this, she was grateful.

'A peddler and his wife on their way to Wallis Plains offered to bring me en route to their rounds about the houses nearby. They set me down here, and promised to take me back.'

'Nonsense, dear, that duty shall be mine,' he promised, kissing both hands. 'But we can talk about it later. How long have you been here?'

'Not long before you came.'

'Then I will give you a tour of your home, my dear, and you may see how you like it.' Emma worried her lip as she allowed him to take her arm and lead her on. 'You will see that I have spared nothing for your comfort. But here is the overseer, my dear, let me show you off a little, if I may be so bold.' He turned to smile at her, but it was more precise to say that he leered. Emma slowed her walk, looking up at him worriedly.

'Is there any need to introduce me?'

Gideon stamped his foot in mock affront, and said, 'Why how can you ask such a thing?' His breath was foul with the stench of stale spirits, and when he spun to face her, he almost overbalanced.

'I mean, what I'm trying to say is...'

'My darling girl, I know that you are not one to flaunt her charms, but as the man who will shortly be your husband, well, I would like all and sundry to see the kind of woman who is going to become my wife.' With that he took her arm again, embarrassing her with his foolishness. 'Where are they, the lazy sods? I know I pared the labour down to just a few, but it would be nice if the scoundrels met their master when he returned,' he complained, casting his gaze around.

'Doubtless they are working,' Emma began. He sent her a

sardonic look, and then, 'Oh, here's one of the reprobates now,' he cried, hailing Tobias from one of the outbuildings. They waited for Tobias to walk over to them. Emma swallowed uncomfortably, vaguely registering the sound of the moored boat as it lapped the water hollowly. To hide her discomfort, she glanced round to look at the small craft in the reeds. She noticed that Gideon had neglected to tie it to the post. Side-tracked upon seeing her, she suspected.

'Hoi! Felon!' Gideon greeted Tobias in mock joviality. He belched, and she was almost overcome. It was the hottest day Emma had every experienced, and she was nearly giddy with the heat and foreboding.

'Sir,' Tobias doffed his cap. This made Gideon smile. He turned to Emma and said, 'There's something about being called 'Sir' by one of my inferiors that never fails to make my day.' Tobias had no qualms in giving Gideon his mind.

'I've heard tell that all men are created equal.' Gideon turned to Emma as though wide-eyed with astonishment. 'Well, I never! You learn something new every day. Here I was thinking that there is the upper class, the middle class, and the dregs. You, of course, falling into the latter category.'

'The way I see it, it's not what lines a man's pocket, but how high he holds his head.'

Gideon laughed raucously at this. 'Indeed, and that would explain why you tried to throw your cap at Miss Colchester.'

Before Tobias made to reply, something caught Gideon's eye. Emma looked up too, and from one of the windows she saw a figure. The face registered surprise, and then disappeared from sight.

'Who is sneaking about in my house?' Gideon asked.

'Perhaps it's one of the men working on finishing touches,' Emma said.

'Inside is complete. Nothing needs to be "touched".' Gideon bit, removing his pistol from the holster and stalking up to the patio.

'Well, don't just stand there like sour milk,' he told Tobias.

'Stay there,' Tobias cautioned Emma.

Emma saw Gideon signal Tobias to walk around to the other side of the house. He disappeared around the corner and was hidden from view.

In the next moment, the intruder burst through the door and out and off the porch, followed by Gideon. Gideon stumbled, gun in his flailing hand as he drunkenly righted himself. He ran after the thief, whose vest was stuffed with objects. They fell out around him as he ran.

She saw Gideon try to aim his pistol in motion, and she moved to the side, just in case he foolishly thought to aim. The thief spied the boat made to jump into it, but Gideon dived at him and they struggled in the hull. It rocked like a cradle in the rushes as the two men grappled. Then Emma heard the pistol discharge and the men tumbled into the river. After an instant, the thief emerged on the bank, running with water. The next thing Emma knew, the man had clasped her to him, and Tobias was running towards them from the house.

'Easy, easy, girl, and you won't get harmed.' She heard the voice at her ear, felt the cool damp of the river against her skin, and her legs quaked.

'What do you want?' Emma pleaded. He squeezed Emma a little tighter as he pulled her closer against him.

'I want to get out of here, nothing more,' the intruder informed her. 'I'm going to take you with me.'

'What do you want to take me for?' Emma cried.

'The scrub is a lonely place, sweetheart.' He dipped his head slightly to breathe in the scent of Emma's hair. She felt the cool point of a blade against her throat. He ran it down to her collarbone. She understood the threat, and his foul intent.

'Leave the lady alone!' Tobias told him.

'Just as soon as I'm free of here,' the bushranger returned. 'I can't leave empty handed, now can I, sweeting?'

'You'll have a better chance at escape if you do' Tobias reasoned, his eye catching the flash of the blade.

'Let's find out, shall we?' He took her with him to the stable, casting a sly glance around before he lifted her to the horse's back, and jumped on behind her, all the while eyeing Tobias through the open stable doors.

'Go about your work,' the felon told him. 'The lady isn't your concern.' Tobias eyed the reins as though he thought of grabbing them.

'If I slit her throat, there'll be no glory in it for you, so think hard.'

The bushranger pressed the knife a little closer against her neck and she winced. Tobias took a step back. Then the felon dug the toes of his boots into the animal and it moved into a canter. As the reins came down upon the mare's neck, Emma felt the pressure of the bushranger's chest against her back as he leant forward a spurred the mount to a gallop.

TWENTY-TWO

Emma was sure she would fall. She didn't know what was worse, fear of the man behind her, or fear of the horse and the very real threat of falling from its back.

'Bushrangers lurk where you least expect.'

How right her aunt Adelaide had been. They tore up clods of earth as they galloped through the dense scrub. Emma felt the steadying arms of the felon on either side of her, and it was more than once that he righted her during the flight. It seemed a horribly long distance before the bushranger allowed the animal to slow the pace, but when he slowed the horse to a walk Emma found herself in the stillness of the hushed forest, thick with sheoak, cedar and spotted gum.

As they wove their way through the dense timber he began to hum. She wondered if he warbled tunelessly to try to lull her, or whether he was merely content to have made clean his escape. But when he stopped the horse and dismounted, he dragged her off the horse after him, dank with sweat and ale, and she understood all too well.

'A pretty flower for the picking,' he crooned.

'What are you about, sir?' Emma demanded, though she knew all too well and began to struggle in his filthy hands. 'Let go of me.'

'Come, sweeting,' he cajoled, his grip tight.

Then he pushed her onto the ground and held her there, as he grunted and arched his tongue inside his open mouth with the effort to take down her undergarments.

'Please, please, let me go!' The raucous squawk of the rainbow lorikeets, shrill in the branches above, drowned Emma's voice.

'Peccadilloes are sweet. Like kisses stolen behind the midden.' The lust in his eye grew with every pull on the string of her bloomers.

'Sins are never sweet!' Emma cried. 'They are foul like the filth you hide behind!'

When he at last freed her of her drawstrings. Emma clawed, scratched, and fought him, as she pleaded and cried.

'There be thorns on the rose bush,' he chuckled then he loosened his breeches. 'I will nip them in the bud.'

Emma realised that she wasn't thinking with any logic, for she thought she heard the rumble of thunder and looked up through the canopy of the trees into the cloudless blue of the sky. It was then she understood that the noise was at their back. It came closer, and drew near. Emma twisted to see Tobias come upon them, the din of his horse's hooves a frantic drumming that threw up the earth.

*

'Get off her!' Tobias cried as he drew up beside Emma and her captor and threw himself off the horse. The renegade prepared to run, his breeches unbuttoned, slipping to reveal the white moon of his backside.

'You can have her!'

'I'm going to take you down!' Tobias said. 'You won't go unpunished. I'll see to that!' He grabbed the bushranger by the neck as the man's knife nicked Tobias's hand.

Tobias felt his ire rise, and pounced on the felon. He was struck again, and the bushranger laughed.

'Aye, laugh while you may!' Tobias said. Taking advantage of the outlaw's lapse in concentration, he brought him down to the earth.

then yanked his hands as he twisted them up behind his back.

But the outlaw bucked and roared and writhed in his grip. The man swung a punch and Tobias tasted blood on his lip. His hair fell over his eyes as he levelled a blow at the bushranger. It knocked him senseless.

Tobias undid the rope that held up his breeches, and then looked up as he panted, and saw Emma.

'My pants will probably fall down,' he said but he would not risk the man waking before he could reach anything else that would hold him. He moved aside to turn the bushranger over and bound his wrists behind his back.

That job done, he took the rope reins from the horse, and cinched his pants with it. Then he walked to where she stood and took her gently in his arms.

'Are you alright?' He asked, looking down into her eyes.

'He didn't harm me,' she assured him shakily.

'Aye, but he was close,' he whispered, and pulled her to him again.

*

The overseer stood in the courtyard, open-mouthed at the spectacle coming towards him. Tobias Freeman was on his beautiful black mare with Officer Quinn's lady in front of him, and following reluctantly at the rear, a bushranger. Doubtless he was the one who had thieved implements and filched one of the lambs.

Here he had been thinking that the Irishman had done a runner, riding off on his own horse, when all the while he'd been occupied in some act of bravery. He'd missed the whole show whilst he had been out in the field with the others. He glanced at the bushranger and shook his head with newfound respect for the black haired convict.

'Are you hurt, Miss Colchester?' the overseer said. 'You look a little peaky.'

'I am just a little shaken.'

The bushranger stood, sharp-eyed. He clearly hoped for an opportunity to escape. Tobias Freeman glanced at him and then back at the overseer.

'What are you going to do with him?' the overseer asked presently, scratching his head.

'I'd hoped you'd trust me to take him back to the colony to meet the commandant.'

The overseer considered this, nodded, and turned to go. 'I suppose if it's alright with the master, you can leave just as soon as you're ready. Just don't spoil it for yourself and skip muster.'

'What, and miss your company and the good food?'

'I'll mark you off the roll.' The overseer turned back and frowned on an afterthought. 'Where is Officer Quinn?'

Tobias Freeman shrugged.

'He's probably laying injured in the reeds,' the young miss said, as though she had only just remembered his absence.

'Injured? Whereabouts?' He looked towards the river and as the Irishman made sure the bushranger was secure, miss Colchester walked with him, pointing to where the scuffle had taken place. 'We'll find him, miss,' he sought to comfort her with his words. 'Never fear.'

But when dusk arrived, the overseer scanned the river and still Quinn had not been found. The convicts had retrieved the capsized boat, and one man had dived down to the riverbed repeatedly to see if the master was still below, but had come up shaking his head and wiping the water from his eyes.

*

Tobias let his glance wander over the river, then settle upon the bound rebel sitting cross-legged on the floor of the boat.

The man had pleaded until the overseer quieted him with a gag, and Tobias made a mental note to be on his guard. Desperate men did desperate things.,

Emma walked down to the water's edge. He didn't want to leave her alone, yet how could he explain his reticence to the overseer?

'Journey safely,' she said. He nodded absently. Her safety was most on his mind.

'I would take you with me,' he said, then hesitated, 'but it is dangerous. You are better off waiting here.' It wasn't safe, it certainly wasn't seemly, and both of them knew it.

'The peddler and his wife will be back soon, have no doubt,' Emma assured him. 'There are not so many customers on the plains that will keep them away from the colony for long.'

'What about Quinn? What if he doesn't return before it's time for you to leave? What if he doesn't come back? If they can't find him, what will you do?' Tobias tried for nonchalance and failed. 'Will you return to England if you have been set free?' He wasn't sure he wanted to hear the answer.

Emma looked at him, considered. 'I will pray for guidance as to the course I should chart.'

Tobias knew he had to leave but was afraid he would not see her again. Emma was not his. Society held them oceans apart, for she was a lady and he was a convict. 'Farewell, Emma Colchester.'

'God bless you, Tobias,' she said as he untied the boat and pushed away from the shore. From that distance he couldn't see if there were tears in her eyes, but he had never wanted anything as much at that moment than to hold her in his arms.

'He already has,' he assured her with a smile, for Emma held his heart.

*

The overseer looked up as Emma rounded the yard. 'I'm afraid we leave you stranded, Miss Colchester,' he said. He looked both concerned for her comfort and uncomfortable that he was left responsible for her safety.

'Please don't concern yourself over my welfare. I shall read this gazette in lazy solitude, and when night falls I will doubtless be able to fashion myself a corner in one of the bedrooms with a spare blanket.'

It was not acceptable to cry over a rough Irish convict. Still, perhaps the overseer thought she pined for the lost love of Gideon Quinn, for he softened his voice accordingly and looked away in respect when he heard the quaver in her voice.

'We will have supper shortly, miss, and I will be sure to bring it to you personally.'

She knew he wasn't about to let one of the convicts have the privilege— you never know what they might be inclined to do—

It was strange sitting down at the large cedar table alone in the darkened room. A single candle, as lonely as she, burned a slowly forming puddle in the sconce. A tear rolled down her cheek as she thought of her farewell to Tobias, even as she waited for Gideon to return.

Emma looked out through the French windows into the blackness of night. She was anxious in the solitude, frightened and alone, and she dreaded Gideon coming in through the door, sopping wet at any moment of the loudly ticking clock.

A knock sounded and Emma started at the noise. 'Sorry to startle you, miss,' the overseer told her, acting butler as he came in with supper.

Emma held back an unseemly giggle; she could not remember being served by a butler in the whole of her life. At the long gleaming table she thanked him as he put the simple but plentiful meal in front of her.

'I hope it's cooked to your satisfaction, miss,' he nodded.

'I'm sure it will be,' Emma was quick to assure him.

'I've made a billy of tea too miss. There's no fancy cup, but the tea's been laced with plenty of sugar.' Emma smiled gratefully at his kindness.

'That's just how I like it.' The overseer bobbed his head again, and she saw that he was pleased at her thanks.

She didn't think she would be hungry, but she was, and realised that she had eaten nothing all day. She finished everything that was put before her, and relished the tea as though it were nectar. All the while she listened for a voice, a footfall, and then Gideon's face to appear at the door, and she waited out the hours with quiet dread.

When Emma woke, she sat upright in the chair, taking in the guttering candle and the empty table. The overseer had been in the remove her plate, and she was surprised to realise that she hadn't even woken at the sound.

She couldn't sit at the table all night, she told herself, and taking the light of the candle, ventured upstairs to the room she and Gideon would soon share. Even in the gloom she could see that things that been disrupted, and covers lifted and thrown back by the bushranger looking to see what he could take.

Emma took a large oiled canvas that was still partially draped over some furniture, and laying down upon the unmade bed, covered herself with it for comfort, even though the evening was very balmy. Emptiness surrounded her. Her heart was heavy. She wondered how far away Tobias was and whether his thoughts lay with her.

Emma felt the tears roll from her cheeks onto the pillow that cradled her head. Then, curling up like a lonesome child, she released the sorrow of her farewell of Tobias with every sob. In the daylight, Gideon would have doubtless returned, and the future would be another day closer than the one before.

'Heavenly Father, hear me. Let me know I am not alone.'

'I will fear no evil: for thou art with me; thy rod and thy staff they comfort me.'

Morning came but it didn't bring Gideon with it, and nor did it bring the peddler and his little wife. The hours dragged, and with little to do, Emma sat out on the porch at watched the current of the river moving on through Wallis Plains. Again that night the overseer served her, and the one after that, and Emma worried how on earth she would find her way back to Newcastle if they didn't return. She wondered what had happened to keep them so long. They had promised to return the next day, and Emma hoped that they had not stumbled upon misadventure.

When a man travelling by horseback left message with her that the peddler and Dolly were delayed and wouldn't make it for perhaps some days to come, Emma could do nothing but wait it out.

'The boat was damaged,' the man told her. 'The boat builder has been laid up and hasn't been able to get to fixing it.'

'But they will return for me?' Emma prompted.

'Indeed they will, miss. The peddler's wife was adamant that you should be told. I was coming through this way, so I told her I'd bring the news to you.'

'And where do you go now?'

'Newcastle, miss.'

'I would be so grateful if you could take news to my aunt that I am unhappily delayed, but will make my way back with the peddler and his wife just as soon as I am able?'

'Of course I can. It's no trouble whatsoever.'

She hesitated, wondering whether she should ask him to deliver the commandant news about Gideon. She bit her lip, undecided. But there was no definitive news to take with him, and so Emma chose to stay silent until she knew the outcome for certain. Who knew, Gideon might yet return, and were she to propose that a party of the constabulary venture to Wallis Plains to begin a search, he might well return in the interim, and then she would feel ridiculous indeed.

The traveller's horse grazed while the man talked, and hardly wanted to be dragged from the rich pasture. Yet Emma was relieved to wave goodbye a short time later, knowing that her aunt would know directly that Emma was well and would return as soon as circumstances permitted.

As the days stretched long and airless, Emma had to be content to busy herself about the large, lofty house of sandstone by the river. She swept, she dusted the few pieces of furniture that Gideon had had made with thoughts of their future together, and she waited.

Emma took down new linen and made up the bed that she would continue to sleep in until Dolly and the peddler docked in front of the house, and as the days lengthened, Emma sat out on the wide porch and contemplated the river and her future .

TWENTY-THREE

It was two weeks before Gideon's body surfaced in the reeds. The convicts had laid him in the long grass that framed the bank.

As the song of hammer on nail rang out, a hastily made coffin was finished off. Emma stepped off the porch, taking a deep steadying breath.

'You can't look at the body, miss,' the overseer warned.

'I was to wed the man. I was to share my days with him. The least I can do is fare him well.'

'He's not fit to look upon,' the overseer swallowed.

'Even so, I must do this,' and she stepped past the man and walked over to the body in the cushion of long grass. He was in his coat, bright red and sharp as a cut.

Emma looked down at the body and reeled away. She inhaled shallowly, hands over nose and mouth. The Hunter River could not wash away the smell of death. Emma steeled herself and turned back around to face what remained. She felt pity and guilt; guilt that she had not loved him, and guilt that she was relieved of her fear of telling Gideon that she would not wed him. Not after Tobias's confession about what Quinn had done.

She was repulsed by what she saw. She could not will herself to kiss his forehead, even though it was the only flesh on his face untouched. Doubtless he had been food for fish, for it was all too apparent, the lipless mouth a grinning parody in the light of day.

They buried him deep in the black earth beside the house in a spot that overlooked the river with the flask they had found bobbing by the bank days before. Yet although she said a prayer for his soul, Emma could no more love the man when he was dead than when he had been alive. She realised then that the death of the young Scottish convict, Alan Campbell had in some way been righted. The finger would never point in Tobias's direction, for the guilty had paid the price.

Still, she mourned for his passing, and joined her prayer with the overseer's.

'I hope your friends arrive soon, for your sake, miss,' the man told her.

'My uncle and his family will be worried, she agreed. But still, I'm sure I shan't be here for too much longer. Someone will come for me,' she smiled a little, but she was very close to tears. She missed Tobias terribly, and wished he was there if only to offer the comfort of his presence.

That night she dreamt that Gideon stood beside her bed in the darkness, chill as river mist. He watched her with a smile, and she thought she heard him laugh. 'You won't want me now, will you, Emma dear?'

Emma woke on a frightened intake of breath, to find that it was morning, and Gideon was not there.

Gideon lay beneath the black sod. For who else could be resting in the coffin but him, Emma asked herself. It had to be him, she knew, and yet a finger of doubt touched the hairs on the back of her neck. She pushed away niggling questions as she was haunted by the recollection of the body, and shook her head at her own foolish fancies.

She knew that the body could well have belonged to anyone, so changed was his appearance. Yet she knew it was the altered features alone that made Emma fear it might not be him. Fear that he would come back. Fear that he would expect his due. Foolish, yes, but understandable, she knew.

Still haunted by nightmares, she stumbled groggily from the canvas cover and dragged open the windows to let in the morning air and sunlight, glad beyond words that no shroud of mist lay visible on the grass below. Emma noticed the barrels in the corner that had been covered with the canvas and when she bent to look at the writing emblazoned on the sides, read the words, 'God save the king'.

A knot tightened in her stomach. These barrels were, without doubt, the contraband stolen from the corps' store. Gideon had lied; he had stolen, and had done deeds darker besides.

*

'Hello!' Emma heard, and she spun around to see a small craft as it made its way upriver with two passengers on board. It was the peddler and Dolly. They had arrived there at last.

'We came upon a spot of trouble,' the peddler began. Dolly nodded vigourously. 'When we were docked at the wharf, we got wedged in between the dock and another vessel. I've got to tell you it was a sight bigger than this. Well, the pressure cracked the old girl here from prow to stern, and we couldn't set off again until the boat builder had a chance to tar her up again, and goodness knows what else. It's almost a new boat. I think we were done a favour. All except for the price; no favours there,' the peddler chortled.

'I'm so very glad to see you.' Emma could say it with the utmost sincerity.

'Doll here was worried you'd think we'd got lost,' the peddler said.

'Indeed, dear, indeed,' the woman agreed, nodding her head.

When they pushed off from the bank a short time later, Emma waved a thankful farewell to the overseer, relieved to go back to

Newcastle, to her uncle's cottage, to cousin Phoebe, but most of all, to Tobias.

Emma set her sights on the distance, on the colony of Newcastle, on home. At that moment she understood that it was exactly that, and she took comfort in that fact as they made their way back.

'There are whispers of a convict gone bush,' the peddler began. 'Turned to bush-ranging they reckon.' Emma looked up from her perusal of the gazette to shiver at the remembrance. Emma told them her tale with few words.

She glanced down at the paper and smoothed it with her hands as the breeze caught the pages.

'A reward of twenty-five dollars and an unconditional pardon, that's what I heard he's worth,' the peddler said. 'Like I said before, me and Dolly can't read, but there's been plenty of talk about it hereabouts. And here you were having an adventure behind the horse of the very man himself!' Emma smiled and knew that the 'adventure' would have the peddler's customers enthralled for some time to come.

She looked down at the column about the wanted bushranger again. Now her heart fluttered with hope as the gazette tried to take wings with the wind. The unease of Gideon's untimely demise was forgotten for a time as Emma considered a new prospect altogether.

*

Tobias looked out towards the harbour at the bustle of the boats for the face he wished he could see. He turned back to the commandant.

'Do you know whom it was when you brought him in?' the man asked.

Tobias shrugged. 'A kidnapper of women?'

'It was none other than Max Metcalfe.'

Tobias waited, none the wiser.

The commandant explained. 'Max Metcalfe is dangerous. He

is without scruple, and he has evaded the law for a very long time. You brought him to justice, and that was no mean feat.'

Tobias smiled. It had been a long time since he had been given any sort of compliment from a man. He glanced out at the dock and squinted.

'Emma?' He spoke to no one in particular. Commandant Morisset looked at Tobias quizzically, then after a moment, knowingly.

They both looked across to see her step from a boat.

'Your ship has come in,' he said.

Tobias didn't heed the commandant's words, but he heard them. He hadn't dared hope to see her again. The commandant was not talking of the boat or even another vessel, and he knew it.

'What do you think she will do now that Quinn does not hold her?' the commandant asked. It was a question for which Tobias could not find an easy answer.

The commandant's mouth quirked in wry humour. 'You know, there is recompense for what you have managed to do. You will be given twenty-five pounds and an unconditional pardon.'

Tobias spun to face the commandant. 'What are you trying to say?' A mixture of frustration and joy caused him to raise his voice, so much that he saw Emma stop short.

'What are you saying, man?'

'That you are a very lucky man,' the commandant told him quietly.

Tobias stood open mouthed in disbelief.

'I never learned your name,' the Commandant Morisset said as he held out his hand and met his eye, almost in the fashion of an equal.

'Tobias Freeman.'

'And a *free* man you shall be.'

The commandant patted him on the back and chuckled at his pun as he turned towards Prospect Hill.

Tobias turned once more to see Emma, *his* Emma, a gazette

262

tucked under her arm. He smiled for the entire world to see.

'I've come home, Tobias.' Emma smiled.

'And what of old England?' A wave of unease washed over him at the possibility.

'In my memories.Ten thousand miles away.'

Tobias dared to take her hand and held it tight.

Emma held his gaze. 'My future is for you.' Emma opened the gazette and pointed out what she had read. Tobias cast a laugh heavenward, then turned to take Emma in his arms.

'So would you would take a man convicted for a life of censure? The distrust of the settlers of the colony?'

'No,' she said, shaking her head, 'I would take a man redeemed, for a lifetime of love.'

They made plans as they walked towards her uncle's cottage: plans for their wedding, their future, their family. When her time of mourning was over, Emma and Tobias would be ready, and Tobias understood that the term of his natural life would be nothing short of freedom.